Ann Oakley

is a sociologist and writer. She directs a London University research unit which carries out educational and health research.

Her previous books include *The Sociology of Housework*, which helped to establish housework as a legitimate area of academic study; *From Here to Maternity*, which charts women's experience of first-time motherhood; *The Captured Womb*, a history of medical care for pregnant women; *Taking It Like A Woman*, an autobiography; and her bestselling first novel, *The Men's Room*.

Ann Oakley lives in London.

D1584742

For Laura
(who made an angel)

Contents

1
The Cornfords' Conception

Willow Cornford leaves a sample of her hair to be analysed at the reception desk in Roman Hall clinic. There are three desks, but one has the sign 'preconception screening service' hanging over it. A red box underneath the sign is labelled 'Specimens: please leave here'.

Willow feels a little worried, leaving her hair in the box to the unkind fate of being (presumably) dissected, immersed in chemicals and otherwise scrutinized. But it is what the doctor here recommended. She'd tried to bring a sample of her husband, Anthony's, hair as well, but Anthony had said he didn't have enough to part with any. She has the feeling he doesn't take this preconception health check-up very seriously.

In bed that night Willow tells Anthony they can't have unprotected intercourse until the hair analysis results are back. 'What if I'm deficient in zinc?' she asks rhetorically. 'Or cadmium? I could have too much lead, Anthony.'

'Then what would you do, my love?'

'Do?'

'To set it right.'

'The clinic makes its own herbal vitamin and mineral pills. I'd take those, Ant, until the lab says my levels are right.'

Anthony finds Willow's enthusiasms engaging but not overriding. 'I'm sure you're in perfect health, Willow, my love. Good enough for me, anyhow. Let's make a baby. We've been talking about it for long enough.'

'Well, Ant . . .' Willow thinks about the cost of her hair analysis, but also knows from her temperature chart (the keeping of which on specially printed graph paper is recommended by Roman Hall) that she ovulated that morning. Intercourse on the day of ovulation is recommended for the conception of a male child. To this end Willow's also been careful to follow the high sodium and potassium diet (a lot of bananas) advised by Roman Hall.

Anthony's breath is slightly furred by Beaujolais nouveau – he's a wine merchant. Willow is too conscious of that little egg in her ovary waiting to have its zona pellucida penetrated by one of Anthony's sperm to relax and enjoy the prospect of conception. She imagines the sperm like the tip of one of the many corkscrews lying about Anthony's shop. Her egg, on the other hand, has its golden yolk exposed, ready and waiting. After Anthony has ejaculated, expostulated ('God that was good, Willow, it feels like a long time since we did that') and lies sleeping peaceably beside her, Willow stays awake and imagines the hidden historical drama taking place inside her. Half of Anthony's sperm have gone the wrong way for a start. She feels sorry for them, for their fruitless journey and existence. Of the other half, most will die, exsanguinated on the way, impaled on some bit of her blooming pulsatile reproductive interior. But one, the longest corkscrew of all, will make it.

Eleven weeks later, the Cornfords are able to discuss over breakfast in their kitchen where the infant should be born. What kind of place should be his – naturally a test's already proved the child's sex – first experience of life on earth, parted from his present succulent and rosy intrauterine anchor?

'A home birth,' declares Willow resolutely. 'Our son must be born at home, upstairs, in our bedroom, with the light of the moon nudging through the branches of the apple tree. A child has the right to be born in its own home, don't you think, Anthony?' She tosses her long yellow hair over her shoulder and leans her miniature frame back against the wall, putting the palm of her hand lightly on her stomach in anticipation of a pleasant maternity. Anthony looks at his wife lovingly but with some irritation. Willow is American, and has some dangerously romantic ideas. It's on such occasions that he's made uncomfortably aware of them.

'You know what I think. Home birth is a thing of the past. It isn't safe, particularly not at your age.' Anthony's remarks are made in the same tone he uses for telling his clients about the best years for a Château Margaux. Willow starts to protest – she's thirty-six. Anthony realizes he's said the wrong thing. 'You don't understand, my darling, how concerned I am about you and the baby. You're both so precious to me. If anything happened . . .'

'Come on, Ant, why should anything happen?' Willow gets up and starts banging some plates around in the sink. Against the sound of running water, and the metallic shaking of the pipes in the four-hundred-year-old cottage set in a shallow dip in the western Chiltern hills, Anthony hears Willow elaborate the philosophy of childbirth she's recently acquired from perusing the world literature on the subject. (In the same way, before the conception she reckoned she knew everything there is to know about how to get pregnant.) 'Ninety-seven per cent of pregnancies and births are normal,' expounds Willow. Anthony wonders where she's got the percentage from, but doesn't dare ask. 'It's important to *assume* normality, otherwise the doctors intervene all the time. It's a self-fulfilling prophecy, you see' (he doesn't). 'And as for this thing about age,' she swings round to face him, her white teeth glinting in the pale morning light, 'there really isn't much more of a chance of complications having a first baby at thirty-six instead of twenty-six. The whole thing has to do with nutrition in childhood, that sort of thing' (what other sort of thing? Anthony wonders). 'Healthy women in their thirties or forties aren't at higher risk,' she concludes. 'The obstetricians just want to make it *seem* more difficult.'

She's convinced herself, Anthony can see that. 'Have our second baby at home,' he pleads, assuming there will be one.

'I'm not going into any damn National Health Service hospital,' she responds, 'whatever you say.' She bites her lip and stamps her foot on the old pine boards, reminding Anthony of the thoroughbred horses on the farm in Minnesota, whence he'd removed her to the superior breeding of the English countryside. Anthony is aware of his wife's prejudices against the NHS – indeed, that was one of the reasons she'd chosen to go in for all this preconception stuff at the private clinic one of her health freak friends had told her about. After the pregnancy had been confirmed, Anthony had been amused when the hair results had come back declaring his wife severely deficient in nickel. But although he doesn't share Willow's prejudices against the NHS, the cutback in resources and recent militant action of the midwives do worry him. He has visions of his infant son arriving into the world on a bed without sheets or birth attendants of any kind, in an environment notably lacking in the prerequisites of health – nappies, warmth, Ovaltine, that sort of thing.

His wife's voice interrupts these miserable thoughts: 'Listen, Ant, you know that clinic where I had my preconception check-up, where I went for the c.v. test? Well, it does birth as well. It's actually an Alternative Birth Centre – I mean that's the main thing it does. It's run by a doctor called Steven van den Biot; he believes in natural

3

childbirth.' She opens a drawer in the oak dresser, and pushes around inside it looking for something. 'Here.' She pulls out a white brochure adorned with flowers not dissimilar to those on the Beaujolais nouveau bottles Anthony had been tasting on the day of the conception.

He takes the brochure. The front cover shows a white-painted Georgian mansion assertive against a copse of dark-green trees. On the gravel drive in front of the house a cream Porsche is parked. A man wearing a rainbow-coloured jersey holds the Porsche's rear door open for a smiling upright young mother who grasps a bundle of white cloth firmly in her arms.

2
Claudia
Comes to Dinner

Steven van den Biot pours himself a whisky and settles back in his Charles Eames black leather chair with a view of emerald lawns angled down to the trout stream. He closes his eyes, sips the whisky and imagines the currents of rich brown water passing through his property, affording the fish temporary haven from marauding humans. Blood flows similarly through the veins of his sturdy, athletic body, causing the temples beneath his silver-grey hairline to throb with a comfortable staccato rhythm. After a while, he sets the glass tumbler down on a nearby table. The abrasive sound of glass meeting wood, and resonating through the thickly carpeted room, pleases him. He leans over and flicks a switch on the Quad system to his left, so that Jessye Norman's rendering of Schubert's *Schwestergruss* fills the space a moment ago occupied by the encounter of material substances.

Steven's waiting for Claudia to come to dinner. It isn't necessary to check the evening's arrangements, as he's a highly organized and efficient man. Mrs Lemon, his 'daily', has prepared the pink and green vegetable terrine ready for serving, also the raspberry sauce for the nougat ice cream. For the main course there's a light cheese tart, mangetout, and a radicchio salad: the tart's on a timer in the oven, and Steven will cook the mangetout at the last minute. Claudia is a vegetarian; Steven himself is whatever the occasion demands. Two bottles of peach champagne stand coldly in the fridge, and pine nuts nestle all round Steven and Jessye Norman in the drawing room in little blue marble dishes, like eggs waiting to hatch.

The house is in the grounds of Steven's birth clinic, Roman Hall. The clinic building itself is original to the estate, and cost a good deal of money to restore and adapt to its current commercial reproductive purposes. Steven lived at first in a suite of rooms at the top of Roman Hall, but found this too stressful, as he seemed perpetually to be within earshot of the cries of labouring women. Although he is deeply drawn to the dramas and mysteries of childbirth, their penetration into his sleep had produced in him an irritability that had interfered not only with his work but – for reasons that weren't entirely clear to him – with his underlying peace of mind. Enough money had already been spent on soundproofing, and it's against his philosophy to recommend efficient analgesia, so he'd had a new modestly sized house built on the other side of the stream – in local Cotswold stone, of course. The physical arrangement works very well. Steven is on hand whenever needed – it takes him a mere five minutes to reach any one of the four labour rooms in the clinic. His assistant, Paul Monkton, took over the Roman Hall suite, and now does a lot of the routine administrative work as well.

Alternative birth is big business these days. From being a minority fad in the eighties, it flourished with the privatization of the NHS in the nineties, shored up by the policies of the health insurance companies who find it cheaper to support natural methods of child-birth than the interventionist strategies that still reign in the large city hospitals. There are plenty of women who can afford the £4000 upwards it costs to have a baby at Roman Hall. Steven van den Biot's discovered what many male obstetricians in the past have traded on: namely, that one satisfied customer attracts her own weight in gold, by spreading the message to other women anxious to buy their fetuses an expensive welcome. The preconception and prenatal screening services the clinic runs as a sideline help, by introducing women gently (albeit technologically) to the possibility of experiencing natural birth.

Lady Claudia Foxman is one of Roman Hall's satisfied customers, and one of its richest clients. Her father turned his aristocratic background to commercial use by making a lot of money out of the new craze for organic farming (specializing in frozen organic vegetables). Claudia's husband is a backbench Tory MP, more ambitious than intelligent, but with the right connections to make this unimportant. The Foxmans' baby boy, John Dominic, had slithered out on to the floor of number one labour room at Roman Hall one warm August night, seeming to smile as he hit the embroidered red cushions. Before the birth Claudia had been seized with anxiety, some of which Steven attributed to her NHS consultant threatening her with a Caesarean, but most of the rest of which he considered due to her impending separation from John Dominic's father. In fact the birth had been scarcely any trouble at all, but Claudia herself believed that

Steven van den Biot's skill was responsible. He himself had said nothing to dissuade her from this opinion.

When Claudia arrives, they open the first bottle of peach champagne. Steven inquires after the welfare of John Dominic.

'Oh, he's gorgeous,' enthuses Claudia, 'quite amazing. Do you know, he lifts his head right up now, and he smiles at absolutely everything!' Claudia herself smiles as she says this, maternal joy radiating like a child's sun from her rich grey eyes. 'I really believe, Steven,' she goes on – she's taken to calling him Steven, and again he hasn't objected – 'that the personality of these children is affected by the calm and natural way they're born.'

Steven nods. He too would like to believe this.

'I want to talk to you seriously tonight, Steven.' She levels her eyes, now with their radiance suitably reduced, at him. He sees the ivory skin of her face redden slightly like a sunset.

'Of course. What about?'

'I want to give you some money.'

'All contributions gratefully received,' he parries.

'I'd like to support a programme of research into the development of Roman Hall babies. I want you to show the world what the long-term benefits *really* are.'

Steven van den Biot had been trained in medical science some years previously, and the memory of his training, lodged in some mental fibre or other, might have impelled him to say no to Claudia Foxman's offer. In any case, he doesn't believe the benefits of Roman Hall could, or should, be proved.

'What a splendid idea, Claudia,' he says, 'let's talk to Paul tomorrow about how to set the arrangement up.'

He is aware, as always, of his necessary talent in preventing other people from seeing into his head. 'The Claudia Foxman Research Programme.' He sees the writing inscribed on a door, on a letterhead; even, despite his antiestablishment scruples, affixed to an article in the *Lancet*: 'Developmental evaluation of infants delivered in an Alternative Birth Centre (on red cushions)'.

'No,' says Claudia. 'I'd like to call it after Abelard.'

'Abelard?'

'My first baby.'

It takes a while for Steven to recall the traumatic abortion buried in her case-notes. 'I didn't know it – he – had a name.'

'Oh yes. I always thought of him as Abelard. His existence was castrated, you see, by a culture hostile to life. This is only a child-orientated society on the surface. If they get in the way, we have to get rid of them.' A bitterness seeps out of her like a curly lettuce refusing to be held back by its light layer of dressing.

Steven's radiopager bleeps at his elbow. He picks up the phone, presses a button: 'Van den Biot.' He emphasizes the 't', but gives the word a crisp French lift. Paul wants to tell him that the midwife, Mary Elliott, is worried about the progress of a woman who's been in labour three days. What does Steven suggest?

'Has she had some celandine tea?' Roman Hall is famous for its use of herbal placebos.

'Pints of it.'

'Move her to the blue room, then put her in the bath.' Paul isn't entirely happy about this; his resisting voice is like the water gurgling down the plughole.

'Trouble?' asks Claudia. She finds Steven's work fascinating. His nearness to both the squalor of human existence and women's sexual groundplan appals and delights her.

Steven laughs somewhat morosely. 'Not really. I forget, were you in the bath for John Dominic's birth?'

'For a while. But I didn't like the idea of him drowning.'

'They don't, of course,' he says absently. 'That's not the problem.'

'What is, then?'

'Oh, other things,' he says, not wanting to be drawn on the subject.

Over the cheese tart they discuss the size of the grant Claudia envisages making to Roman Hall (£500,000) and the state of her relationship with John Dominic's father. Tears enter her eyes: 'He was screwing Nanny, you know. I caught them at it.'

'Nanny?'

'Nanny Pilkington. She was recommended by the Dorsets. They had her for Jessica for ten years, but Cheryl couldn't have any more children, you know she had a terrible infection with the coil, it was all Raymond's fault, he insisted on it, and Jessica's at Letchworth now. So Nanny came to us. She'd settled in nicely, or so I thought. There *were* one or two odd things. But then I found him in Nanny's room with his trousers down.'

'Oh dear.'

'She's forty-four,' says Claudia crossly.

'There's nothing wrong with age, my dear,' he says, 'I'm a few years older than that myself.'

She looks embarrassed. 'But it's not the same for men, is it?'

'Haven't you looked me up in the Medical Directory? I thought that's what all you ladies did. What did Nanny Pilkington say?'

'It was odd,' muses Claudia, 'she said, "They're all the same. Every single one of them", and then she packed her suitcase and walked out. I didn't know she was like that. I had no idea. I told Cheryl. She had no idea, either.'

He looks sympathetic.

'Do you have any advice about schools?' asks Claudia suddenly.

'For whom?'

'For John Dominic, of course.'

'I don't know anything about education. I only know about birth. That's enough, I think, isn't it?'

'No, Steven. I think you should start a school as well. An alternative school. Then you could have an alternative nursery and a whole alternative Roman Hall product!'

But he has enough ambitions of his own without taking other people's on board. 'No,' he asserts firmly. 'I intend to stick to what I know about.'

She watches him with admiration across the bowl of mauve vegetation catching the light at its edges. His bleeper goes again.

'It isn't working, she's still only four centimetres. And the water's going cold.' They bought the cheap version of the birth pool, which has to be filled and emptied with hoses.

'How's the fetal heart?'

'She won't let me listen. She's getting quite upset.'

'All right, I'll be over in a few minutes.' He looks at his ivory-skinned guest. 'I'm sorry, Claudia, I'll have to go and take a look. I shan't be long. Have some more dessert. We'll have coffee when I get back.'

The bridge over the trout stream squeaks under Steven's weight as he crosses it, and the moon, gliding between oedematous clouds, fastens its light on the vanilla building across the grass. The blinds are down in labour room number two, and so is Mrs Daniels, the wife of a computer software firm's managing director. She's sprawled in the pool groaning and crying, while Mr Daniels sits in a chair reading *The Financial Times*. He looks up as Steven comes in. 'Ah, Dr van den Biot,' (he pronounces it Buy-it) 'I hope you can do something for Diana, isn't seventy-two hours enough of nature? She's really had as much as she can take. How about a Caesarean? You *can* do them here, I take it?'

Diana groans again.

'Where's the midwife?' asks Steven.

'Gone for a pee, I think.' Mr Daniels continues to study the stock market closing prices.

Steven goes outside and looks for Mary Elliott. 'Have you examined Mrs Daniels recently?'

'Four centimetres, didn't Paul tell you?'

'When was that?'

'Half an hour ago.'

'You'd better get in the bath and find the heart.'

'I can't,' says Mary, 'I've got a diabolical period.'

Steven looks at Mary but says nothing.

'Blame it on Mother Nature,' she suggests.

'Mrs Daniels,' he shouts over the water's edge, 'Diana, would you mind coming out of there for a moment, we want to Listen to Baby's Heart.' They help her out, lay her down, and he slides a stethoscope over her wet abdomen. The baby's heart thuds regularly somewhere inside her compulsively contracting uterus.

'How do you feel?'

'Fucking fed up,' she hisses.

'Would you like some help?'

'You can do what you fucking well want as far as I'm concerned,' she says remarkably clearly, 'and I can tell you one thing, I'm never doing this again. Peter! Peter!' Mr Daniels puts his face over the top of *The Financial Times*. 'It's all your bloody fault, I never wanted a baby anyway. I was quite happy as I was.'

Peter Daniels looks sheepish. 'I suppose you often get this sort of thing, Dr van den Buy-it, don't you?'

After doing Mrs Daniels' Caesarean, Steven leaves Mary Elliott to clear up, and takes the path back across the trout steam. Claudia Foxman is nowhere to be seen. She must have given up and gone home. He's not totally dismayed. Women, even those not currently giving birth, are, like happiness – with which they are too often equated – better in small doses. He makes himself a cup of Typhoo tea and climbs the stairs to bed. The navy paisley sheets are welcoming, and the African violets, of which he's acutely fond, bloom enthusiastically on the low shelves encircling the room, their centre point a thin silk scarf, red, purple, green and blue, pinned to the wall directly opposite the bed. Steven gets into bed with relief and a book of Peter Levi's poetry, *The Gravel Ponds*.

3
Matilda
Makes It

The office of the Council for Consumer Affairs is in Holland Park, in an area that some would describe as Ladbroke Grove. Other houses jostle round it, painted pink, dark blue, green, all sprouting organized window boxes. Number 88 Juliana Crescent itself is white, with a brass plate which, Matilda Cressey observes on her way into the house that morning, clearly needs cleaning.

Matilda's office, on the top floor, offers an expansive view of rooftops to which the November sun is being ridiculously kind. Its lemon light turns the roofs into layered jewels, and the purple pigeons dotted across them might have been made of marble. The CCA's secretary, Margaret Watteau, is ready with the coffee; Matilda takes a mug that says 'World Cup 1982' on the side. She scrutinizes Margaret, whom she's met only once before, on the day of her interview for the job. Margaret looks about seventeen. She's wearing a blue print dress, a white cardigan and black boots. A thin but appealing face is hidden by ill-fitting glasses. The coffee is instant. 'We must start as we mean to go on, mustn't we, Margaret?' says Matilda firmly. 'I don't like instant coffee. Isn't there a coffee machine?'

'No, Miss Cressey, there isn't.'

'Well, we'd better get one then, hadn't we?'

'Had we? I mean yes, Miss Cressey.'

'Perhaps you could go out and buy one at lunch time?'

'Oh, I don't think the petty cash would stretch to that, Miss Cressey.'

Matilda sighs and sits down. On her desk is a white envelope marked 'To the New President'. She opens it and sees a stream of bunnies throwing bluebells at a large white rabbit. The card is signed 'From your new staff, Margaret Watteau, Matthew Ansden, Rita Ploughman, Jeffrey Rowley, Mrs Trancer'.

'Who's Mrs Trancer, Margaret?'

'She's our cleaning lady, Miss Cressey.'

'How much does she cost?' asks Matilda sharply.

'I don't know, Miss Cressey. You'd have to ask Matthew, he deals with that sort of thing.'

Matilda makes a list: (1) Interview all staff. (2) Make list of reorganization priorities. (3) Operationalize. (4) Have staff meeting, decide research/action priorities. (5) Buy coffee machine. Matilda is good at making lists, it's one of the skills that got her this job in the first place. She *is* pleased to be here, as after fifteen years in journalism it dawned on her that she was unlikely to get a major editorial job. The tide has turned against women in such highly competitive fields. People don't like Matilda because they say she'll get married and have children, just as they used to say that about all single women under forty in the bad old days. The excuses are nineteenth-century ones, but then the nineteenth century is in fashion again.

The job of President of the CCA is an odd one. The organization itself was set up in the early days of Thatcherism, when there was still some need to seduce left-wing opinion. It remains crossbred and somewhat nebulous. Until now it's been run by a Dame Ferguson-FitzGerald, who wasn't much interested in it, and finally retired to live in Cannes. Matilda's appointment – the appointment of someone who might *do* something with the job – was the result of active political pressure from a mixed party group of younger MPs, alarmed for different reasons about the untrammelled growth of private enterprise, particularly in the welfare, education and health fields. The privatization of water had been the last straw, forcing even some unrepentant Tories to feel things had gone a bit far.

Matilda works steadily through her first morning at the CCA, then summons Matthew Ansden, the administrator, who certainly wasn't used to surveillance from the retired Dame Ferguson-FitzGerald. Matthew has a lock of white hair amid a more ordinary brown. For some reason he reminds Matilda of a horse. Every question Matilda asks about money receives a long answer in which she gets lost. For example:

Matilda: Our annual budget from the Home Office is how much?

Matthew: The Home Office make us an annual grant which relates to the projected costs we put in each year for the following year. These are based both on commissioned work and on noncommissioned work – that is, work not commissioned directly by the government.

Matilda: But how much is it?

Matthew: I could show you the accounts for the past few years, but I don't think these will help you greatly, as there isn't a lot of continuity from one year to the next.

Matilda asks to see Rita Ploughman next, but she's out completing the final steps of a survey of small businesses in high crime areas. Jeffrey Rowley runs the shop on the ground floor of 88 Juliana Crescent, sending out all the CCA publications and reports. He's very fastidious in appearance and personality, though he too has a cilial curiosity: a closely shaven chin and neck disappear into a tight light pink collar over which poke fronds of unconfinable dark chest hair. Jeffrey is anxious to please. He'd like to employ more staff, though, as the mail order side of things has built up recently. When he leans towards her to make this request, Matilda feels she's being asked for a Christmas present, but she isn't sure she feels like putting anything in Jeffrey's stocking.

At four o'clock the office cat walks in, a very large marmalade edition called, unenterprisingly, Sunny. He marches straight across Matilda's room to the radiator under the window and arranges himself next to it, blinking hard in the direction of the door. Margaret comes in with a saucer of milk. 'He always has his milk in here,' she says.

'He always *used* to have his milk in here,' corrects Matilda, answering the phone, which rings at the same time. It's William, her lover, wanting to know if they'll meet tonight. She tells him yes, but not until later, as she wants to stay and meet Mrs Trancer, the cleaning lady.

Mrs Trancer comes at six and installs herself in the downstairs kitchen with the *Evening Standard* and a cup of (instant) coffee. Matilda looks in and introduces herself. 'Oh, you're the new boss, pleased to meet you,' says Mrs Trancer, continuing to read the *Evening Standard*. She looks incredibly old. Blast-off 1950s glasses obscure her eyes, and her hair resembles a plate of congealed spaghetti. Matilda explains that she's stayed specially late to meet Mrs Trancer today but she might, when she's got into the job properly, stay late quite regularly. 'That's okay, duckie,' says Mrs Trancer in a relaxed fashion, 'I always leave the top till last, anyway.' Matilda tells her about the grime on the brass plate. 'I'll see when I can fit it in,' promises Mrs Trancer. 'You do know my times, don't you, duckie? Monday six till eight. Wednesday and Friday I come in the mornings, eight till ten. That's to fit in with my other jobs. Dame Fitzy and I, we used to have quite a chat in the mornings, and it's handy because I can do the washing-up, you see.'

Matilda feels most discomforted on her way home by this last interview. Mrs Trancer's attitude is a continuation of the cat, Sunny's, claiming his milk by the radiator without so much as a by-your-leave.

William wants to take Matilda out to celebrate, but Matilda wants to have an omelette and go to bed early. William is the son of a well-known Conservative MP. Instead of following in his father's footsteps, he runs a garage. Not an ordinary garage, but one stocked with 1930s convertibles. Much of Matilda and William's relationship is taken up with negotiation concerning whose flat they meet in how often, whether they eat omelettes, and whose feelings have been most injured by giving in. On this occasion, William has made up his mind to be generous – it *is* Matilda's first day in her new job, after all. But when, in the middle of making love, she starts talking about the office cleaning lady, William gets terribly cross and tells her he wants more from the relationship than this. Her face looks startled against the cornflower-dotted pillow. She holds him tightly, but he knows her mind is still a long way away.

In a place where, fourteen years ago, Matilda Cressey came face to face with Matilda Cressey: in a Chinese park early in the morning, as the sun rose over Shanghai harbour.

At twenty-two, Matilda Cressey had been all the things young women are supposed to be: vulnerable, naive, trusting, thin, pretty, dependent, decorative, wilful, inconsistent, self-centred, filial, passionate, unassertive, curious, angry, daring, eager, afraid, drawn to babies and chocolate, and enormously keen to find a permanent solution to everything. After university (Manchester, English), she fell in love with a forty-year-old writer of travel books who regularly left his wife for other women with whom he travelled emotionally, sexually, and geographically but not, unfortunately for Matilda, permanently.

Matilda and Derek went to China together. Matilda enjoyed being Derek's travelling companion – sitting with him, cuddled up close, on trains with plastic seats journeying through waterlogged country-side; looking into the faces of brightly wrapped Chinese children on bicycles; seeing the clash between political and domestic ideologies;

eating sea slugs boiled in vegetable water; using truly earth closet toilets; noting the huge sweeps of the Great Wall dividing the land like the seam on a newborn baby boy's testicles. On the Great Wall, the wind blew in their faces and Matilda was unbelievably happy; but Derek later proved to have been thinking about the jade necklace he would buy his wife. Derek and Matilda finally came to rest at their journey's end in the Friendship Hotel in Shanghai and had a herculean row, at the conclusion of which Derek waited till Matilda, exhausted, slept and then left the hotel – and her. The note he left, poised against a reproduction Longchuan urn, simply said: 'Dearest Tilly, thanks for a good time. Sorry it's over. Ticket (and money) in suitcase. Will pay hotel bill. Love, Derek.'

Matilda had the feeling of this being a routine event in Derek's life: the termination of a contract, as it were, with material ends being neatly tied up. But what about the others? At 4 a.m., which is when she'd woken to see the Longchuan urn's message, she piled on her clothes and rushed out into the street, to escape the enclosure of agony in which Derek had placed her. The whole of the six weeks they'd been in China, she'd never gone out on her own, without Derek. Now, amongst the crowds of blue-overalled Chinese – though early, it was the hour at which people travelled to work – she didn't know whether to feel safe or afraid. Were she to be accosted, or have any other trouble, there would be no one to call to her defence – no one, indeed, would know anything of her whereabouts, or fate. On the other hand, there was something so reassuring about the way the busy Chinese thronged past her, intent on their own lives, treating her as a mere technical obstacle in their way, or as a foreign object of passing interest only.

She came to the harbour: little avenues of trees, a low wall, and a misty parade of boats. There were many people under the trees, arranging themselves in odd postures, doing t'ai chi. A shrivelled old man placed one foot high on a tree trunk and looked through Matilda, even her tear-ridden face, as she passed him. And then suddenly, out of various hidden loudspeakers in the trees came weird tinny music, and the people lined up and moved together like some rural keep fit class, except that they were leaderless, powered only by the canned music that fell from the tree tops. In the middle of this Matilda stood still and felt very alone. Without Derek, without anyone. Except the entire world of other human beings going about their business. She had the oddest feeling that it always would be like this. She would always be alone, whatever else happened to her. And then the sun, coming up over the surface of the water and turning everything a pinky-gold, confirmed this by seeming to reward her with warmth and colour and radiance for having got something right at last, for having at least had a thought with some helpful permanence to it.

Matilda recalls Shanghai less frequently these days, but as an *aide-mémoire* it still serves. In the years since, she's built a successful career as a journalist and had many affairs. Her friends and her parents look on and bemoan this latter fact, but she herself isn't much bothered. She does wonder from time to time whether her lack of lasting attachment is still a consequence of her thwarted passion for Derek, of her determination never again to be so vulnerable. But in so far as this explanation makes sense, Matilda feels it's a good thing, not a bad one. Not surprisingly, men tend to take a different view, reacting petulantly to Matilda's inability to pursue a relationship into normal dusty corners. She wants a light at the end of the tunnel that beckons her, and men who make demands pull a blind over the light. She had thought William wouldn't do that, being so unattached to responsibility himself. But if he turns out to run true to the male form, Matilda knows she will be sad but not inconsolable; particularly now she has the CCA to think about.

Over the next month Matilda reorganizes affairs at 88 Juliana Crescent. She rings up Norman Newfield at the Home Office, and gets him to have a meeting with her and Matthew Ansden, which requires Matthew to come clean about the budget. The result of this is a certain amount of internal glaring. Rita Ploughman is located and seems affable; even a kindred spirit with respect to some of the issues Matilda thinks the CCA might investigate. She makes a list: the impact on families of the privatization of essential household resources; access to private medical insurance; computer shopping facilities. Rita asks sensible questions about which kinds of projects they can realistically hope to pursue, whether they'll be politically acceptable, how they could be made so. Matilda asks Rita's advice about Margaret Watteau's wan appearance. Rita takes Margaret to lunch one day and sorts her out. Jeffrey Rowley is allowed to hire an assistant, but the two remaining problems, Sunny and Mrs Trancer, prove more obdurate. Sunny's milk is placed in the lavatory, where he ignores it, stalking at his customary time every day across the carpet in Matilda's office; and it takes Mrs Trancer three weeks to buy some Duraglit. The coffee machine doesn't turn up until Matilda buys it herself, but even then there's a problem with the plug, because there isn't a screwdriver in the office.

In early December Willow Cornford rings Matilda and suggests lunch. Willow and Matilda met when Matilda did an MA in journalism in Minnesota in 1976. Willow proposes a Japanese restaurant; she needs to be careful about her diet, she says, as her doctor has told her that the key to a natural childbirth is a healthy pregnancy, and the right food is the foundation of this.

Matilda thinks Willow looks well. Her skin glows, her six-month pregnancy forms a neat orb beneath the surface of her jade cashmere dress. Willow, tangling with tiny portions of sushi, tells Matilda about Roman Hall and the charismatic Steven van den Biot.

'He's such a *gentle* man,' she enthuses, 'he behaves quite differently from the usual way doctors behave. Do you know, Tilly, he actually asks women what they want and then he tries to give it to them! Imagine!' Apparently Willow's (and Anthony's) predilection for a male child has been confirmed by the technique of chorion villus biopsy, which was pioneered in the mid eighties and is now routinely available in almost all centres.

'So they do use some standard medical techniques, Willow!'

'Choice, Tilly. That's what it's all about. I wanted the test: not just to confirm that it's a boy, but to rule out any abnormality – I am thirty-six, after all!' Willow bites her lip, remembering how in a different context she wouldn't let Anthony cite age as a reproductive risk. 'I think it's sensible, Tilly. To use technology to rule out fetal abnormality. After that, I mean so far as prenatal care is concerned, Roman Hall doesn't go in for much in the way of tests or routine monitoring.'

'So what does it do?'

'Singing, yoga, acupuncture. One of the midwives *will* examine you if you want her to. Also, every month we all go with our husbands, they put a monitor on everyone and turn them all up so the whole room is filled with the sound of babies' hearts!'

'Do you all have husbands?'

Willow considers. 'Yes, I think so.'

'Well, you certainly all must have money. I suppose that's where the husbands come in.'

'You're too cynical, Tilly.'

'Realistic.'

'You disapprove, don't you?'

'I don't disapprove of natural childbirth,' says Matilda. 'At least, I don't think I do. It's not the kind of thing you can disapprove of, is it? But I do disapprove of private medicine. As you know.'

'I wonder what *you'd* do if you were having a baby.'

'I'm not having any babies, there are quite enough other women doing that.'

'Don't you want to at all?' Willow is incredulous.

'No.' Matilda eats her last piece of bright pink fish. 'And how's Anthony?'

'He's fine. How's William?'

'He's fine too.'

'That's all right, then.'

The next day Matilda reads about Steven van den Biot in the *Guardian*. There's a half-page interview with him, including a photograph. He has luminous dark eyes and silver hair like flat Christmas tinsel. The theme of the article is van den Biot's new book, *Herbal Childbirth*, which argues that modern-day obstetrics would do well to use some of the empirical remedies of the preindustrial midwives, including vervain, feverfew, greater celandine and meadowsweet. There's a small insert photo of van den Biot with his arms round a newly delivered woman nursing a mucky infant. He's described as the high priest of the natural childbirth movement. Although trained as a doctor, he'd apparently not made it through an obstetrics and gynaecology internship, quickly becoming too disgusted with conventional approaches to managing pregnant women. When asked how he sees himself, he's reported to have answered, 'as a facilitator. I believe that's what all professionals ought to be.'

Matilda shows the *Guardian* piece to William, who has stayed the night with her and is cross again, because she's said she doesn't intend to spend Christmas with him. 'Sounds like a real quack,' observes William, childishly sticking the edge of the *Guardian* in the marmalade.

'I'm not sure,' says Matilda thoughtfully.

It's Matilda's idea that the CCA should hold a press conference in early December. The budget disclosures consequent on her and Ansden's meeting with the Home Office have revealed an unspent £2000 under the 'entertainment' heading. Matilda agonized about what to do, and in the end decided to hire a room for an evening in the Royal Institute of British Architects in Portland Place, and lay on a white-wine-and-interesting-bits event. They'll make up some display boards of the CCA's activities and Jeffrey can bring his stall and his new assistant, who's called Jason, along and get rid of some literature.

Matilda plans to make a speech. She writes and rewrites it very carefully, then rings up all the journalists she knows and tells them to come. The Friday before the event, she slips out to buy a dress. She's already decided on bright blue, a colour which suits her, although it really shouldn't, as she doesn't have blue eyes and her hair is dark. The dress is satin, with a high neck. She'll wear a pearl necklace with it. The afternoon of the press conference, Matilda locks herself in her office and practises reading her speech; although she's become good at a lot of things over the past fifteen years, she's done very little public speaking. Hearing her muttered, clipped tones behind the shut door of his dairy, the cat, Sunny, walks away in disgust and rampages through a few back gardens until he has a fat sparrow to deal with instead. But Matilda's practice is worth it, for the journalists are impressed. The newspapers carry reports of her, and her speech, and the *Guardian* arranges an interview with her to fill exactly the same slot as Steven van den Biot occupied the previous week.

William doesn't like to admit quite how switched on he is by this new persona of Matilda's. But he wisely absents himself from her big night, going out to dinner with his father instead. Father and son find each other just as irritating as they usually do, and William's father makes things worse by asking when he and Matilda are going to get married.

4
Away
in a Manger

Steven van den Biot always looks forward to Christmas. Unlike most people with such expectations, he usually enjoys it as well, chiefly because he spends it on his own. This gives him the opportunity to bury any pangs of nostalgia he might feel for earlier more sociable celebrations in a firm grasp on the pleasure of his own company – limited but predictable, enclosing but therefore safe. Since starting Roman Hall, it has been his custom to purchase a goose or a duck from the Foxmans' organic farm, which he takes the trouble to stuff and cook properly. Before eating his Christmas lunch in the mid afternoon, he always takes a long walk across the hills. When people ask Steven about his family, which they always do at Christmas, he just says he doesn't have any, which isn't quite true. No one believes him. They all invite him to their homes on Christmas Eve or Christmas Day or Boxing Day, and he always refuses. This year Claudia Foxman tries particularly hard, but he doesn't give in, except in consenting to have a drink with her and the precociously calm John Dominic on Christmas Eve.

The clinic is quiet. Only three women are due Christmas week: a Frenchwoman, whose husband, a helicopter pilot, is poised waiting on their Normandy lawn; a woman from London, booked into a local hotel in readiness; and Willow Cornford, an American with a husband in the wine business. It's already crossed Steven's mind to wonder whether the Cornfords might pay some of their bill in kind, as he's currently gathering together quite an ambitious cellar. It pleases him to think of the bottles collecting there – ruby red, fetal pink, a nice unsedimented urinary white; all the fluids properly segregated, contained and labelled with a terminology so differently evocative from the labels on the clinic bottles across the trout stream.

On December the 23rd he takes a few bottles of Domaine de Diusse up to the clinic for a Christmas drink with his staff. Mary Elliott has put a bowl of holly and mistletoe – the estate's full of both – in the small first-floor staff room. Lena and Ransen, the twin Danish daughters of the second midwife, Karin Druin, have licked pink and green paper chains together and strung them round the picture rail; their mother's put white Scandinavian candles in glass bowls of water high up on the shelves, so that a clear white light flickers questioningly on the ceiling.

A baby was born at five-thirty. Paul and Mary were present for the birth, an awkward posterior presentation. The mother was very tired and got through a whole pot of Cotswold honey, Roman Hall's alternative to the glucose drip. The baby weighed only five pounds, but seemed cheerful. Dad was more than usually overcome, as all this had been preceded by fifteen years of infertility. But it was the same with every successful delivery: the staff, exhilarated, found themselves looking almost coyly at each new mother-and-child pair – mother gazing at baby with wild animal wonder, baby screwing up its little face and fists, testing freshly pink limbs against air instead of water for the first time. How strange it must feel! And the smell of the newborn – raw, immaculate, secret. Each time the same mystery, and each time something different. Steven, too, is affected. He's especially infused with the great admiration he has for women at these times; it surges messianically through his body like warm electricity. Not sexual, exactly: though in the creases and folds and apertures exposed to the fullness and illumination of birth there is an element of flesh enjoyed, or rather of flesh known in other guises re-presenting itself, excitingly, anew. The bodies of women who've had children are always more than they seem. Entire histories can be detected in them, the geography of the skin, stretched, torn, reassembled, serving merely as a surface guide. Steven is aware of the child as well as the man in him on these occasions – though he never thinks of his own mother's body giving birth to him, only that this must once have happened. He himself must once have been intimately joined to another in the unholy mess of childbirth, to which he now daily acts as witness, delivering women deftly of their destinies as someone, probably somewhat less deftly, once delivered him.

Upstairs, in the staff room, Mary Elliott says to Paul Monkton, 'That baby gave me a nasty turn, I can tell you!'

'Yes, it was rather blue,' Paul agrees. 'But then they often are at first, after such a complicated struggle.'

'In the old days people used to turn posterior presentations, didn't they?'

'Not with much success,' says Steven, overhearing. 'Of course, the Chinese still do it. They use moxibustion. Do you know about moxibustion? It's a traditional method of Chinese medicine, as old as acupuncture, but used for chronic rather than acute conditions. A herb, moxa – mugwort to us – is burnt at the acupuncture points of the body. For correcting difficult presentations they use the indirect method, burning the dry moxa leaves at the mother's feet.'

'Had you thought of introducing it here?' asks Paul.

'I had,' says Steven, 'but I don't know how to do it. We'd need to find someone.'

'Jung would know,' offers Karin. 'She might even be able to do it herself.' Jung is the clinic acupuncturist. She comes from Korea.

Paul and Steven continue to discuss moxibustion: whether it would require a special room, how much they could/should charge for it. Karin and Mary sit in the corner earnestly discussing something else. Steven looks at them from time to time out of the corner of his eye. Karin's full Danish face is flushed with the Christmas punch, her camomile hair streaked with flickers of the waxy light. Mary Elliott, short and practical, wears a dress tonight – Steven can't ever remember seeing her in a dress before. Both midwives usually wear loose cotton trousers, T-shirts and clogs. He wonders what they're talking about. Midwives fascinate him. He always says you can tell a midwife by her hands, by the way she waves her hands around when talking about something: that's how a midwife expresses her spirit, her personality. Yet they're also the most capable of people, combining a sharp intuition with practical skills, and the more experienced among them have a confidence both in themselves and in women that Steven has learnt to trust. He likes to watch them at work, regarding himself as the observer, standing on the sidelines: the midwife and the mother are at the centre of the stage. The father's at the side as well. Steven thinks the way men behave at birth reflects very poorly on men as a class. Some of them hover, wittering around like nervous old women. Some are here on sufferance, and make it plain. Some sleep while their labouring women make excuses for them: 'Poor George, he's had a very tiring time at work recently'/'Don't mind Raleigh, he's only just come back from the New York office.' There *are* a few men whose rapport with and support of their partners is a joy to watch; then Steven wants to put his arms around all three of them – mother, father and child – and sometimes does.

Paul is saying something to him.

'I'm sorry?'

'I think we ought to start keeping proper statistics, Steven. People are criticizing us, you know, for not doing that. If we believe in our work, we need to be able to prove it's good to the outside world. I think we should write up our cases – we must be nearing a thousand by now.'

'We could write articles in the *Lancet* till the cows come home,' answers Steven. 'But you're younger than me, Paul. I don't want to sound patronizing, but you've still got things to learn. Only our friends will ever believe in us. People who work in an alternative paradigm – in whatever field – are never believed in their lifetime. And what are statistics? How can you put love and happiness and peace in a statistic? Those are my views, Paul. I'm not about to change them now.'

Paul is silent. He's recently come to feel that Steven van den Biot's opposition to conventional medicine is too extreme. As a matter of fact, Paul has been collecting Roman Hall statistics privately for some time. He started when he saw Steven on television claiming that their perinatal mortality was zero. It isn't. In their first year, there were two stillbirths – admittedly probably unpreventable, but still they'd happened. And so Paul started to write everything down – not only for the cases he supervises but for Steven's and the two midwives' as well. Most of the time, of course, Steven *is* right: childbirth *is* a natural process and nothing does go wrong. He agrees with Steven that it's important to believe in nature, in normality, but it's also important to be interested in the few times when things don't go right. At the beginning, he had a lot of respect for Steven van den Biot's point of view. When they first met at a rally to protest about working hours organized by the Junior Hospital Doctors' Association in 1988, Steven's views were directly responsible for Paul's decision to leave the health service and the North Staffordshire Maternity Hospital to its own divided, short-staffed, over-technological fate. But Paul's initial enthusiasm for what Steven calls 'the alternative paradigm' has worn off. The old caution has reasserted itself – together, it must be said, with an image of himself as an alternative head of Roman Hall, running the place on visibly cost-effective lines. This will naturally mean the keeping of large amounts of data in a readily inspectable form. 'Performance indicators' they're called. Part of Paul's interest in these is a concern with indicators of his own performance. He hadn't liked being a junior doctor in Stoke-on-Trent, and he sees private maternity care as a way to climb the ladder quickly. He wouldn't like to admit it about Steven van den Biot's lifestyle, but he wouldn't mind sitting on an Charles Eames chair contemplating trout, either.

Paul knows that the midwife, Karin, agrees with him, and that's what she's talking to Mary Elliott about. But both of them feel a little guilty about creating division at Roman Hall, and assure each other that their concern for science in no way represents a basic loss of faith in the van den Biot philosophy.

The grounds of Roman Hall are stiff and sparkling with frost on Christmas Eve morning. A cold mist hangs over the trees and the hills, and the trout move slowly, chilled in their brown waters. Behind the mist, the sun and the moon share the sky, two toneless orbs staring at each other accusingly above a still landscape.

Karin Druin and Paul Monkton reach for each other in Paul's bed on the top floor of Roman Hall. They slip their hands over and around one another, feeling pleasing curves and hollows and protrusions. 'Have we got time?' Paul asks Karin. 'It'll be the last one before Christmas.'

'No, Paul, I'm on duty in five minutes!' She laughs at him, quietly, childishly, in the pillow. But he bends down and kisses her white breast anyway.

Downstairs Mary Elliott sits with Clare Paynter, an economist expecting her first child. Clare came to Roman Hall early that morning from the nearby hotel in which she and Ralph Scull, the baby's father, were staying. She sits tensely on a chair in the green labour room, which Mary had chosen for her. Just now Mary's holding her wrist lightly to feel her pulse; and then she puts her hand on Clare's grey maternity dress. She's concerned because Clare seems already quite distressed by the pain, but ought only to be in early labour. Mary suggests a bath, with a comforting dash of orange and almond oil. Clare agrees, allowing herself to be led to the bathroom and undressed and helped into the warm redolent water. It's amazing, thinks Mary as she often does, how dependent some women become during labour, almost childlike and anxious not to cause offence.

In his little house by the wood, Steven van den Biot puts on his jogging clothes and pushes the back gate open so he can sprint off through the wood, round the lower fields, and then back round the half-curve to the front of the estate, cutting through the side gardens, laid with herbs, down the sloping lawn over the trout stream and back up the other side. Steven runs every morning when he can.

Sometimes he pauses by the stream and lets his eyes survey its muddy waters; he's recently purchased a new batch of entirely sexless fish, which are said to grow bigger and live longer than any other kind. His early-morning run is the best moment of the day, not only allowing him a view of his whole territory, the clinic and its provisions and surroundings, but stretching his lungs with the fine cold air and shifting the blood round his body in great warm gushes. His bleeper's always hooked on to the waistband of his jogging trousers ready to remind him of his duties, though sometimes when it does he thinks it's a bird calling from a tree, or from even higher up in the atmosphere.

Willow Cornford wakes at six to a stillness everywhere but inside herself, where everything seems to be happening. Her abdomen rises to a point with an iron hardness and then falls away to its usual smoothness, waits as if to gather breath, and then does the same thing again. A fierce ache across her lower back and front encircles the baby's head – or so she imagines, having been told that's where it is.

She kicks Anthony, who's instantly awake and leaps out of bed. Like Karin Druin, she's amused by such impulsive, unthinking male energy. 'There's no hurry, Ant, darling,' says Willow in her Minnesota drawl. 'I guess it'll be a long while yet.'

He looks at her in the faint light that frames the window blind. 'How can you be sure? You've never had a baby before!'

She laughs at him again. 'Neither have you, Ant! Relax. Get me a cup of tea. Raspberry leaf tea. It's on the shelf above the kettle in a packet labelled "Roman Hall". And maybe you should call the clinic, just to warn them we'll be on our way later.'

He's impressed by her confidence, but doesn't feel it himself. However, the woman who answers the Roman Hall phone sounds just like Willow, telling him to take his time bringing her in. 'And mind the roads,' she warns, 'there's a lot of ice about today.'

So this is the day his son will be born! Or tomorrow – Christmas Day. The child isn't actually due till 30 December, but Willow's fragile undersized frame has always seemed to both of them unlikely to bear the weight of a full-term pregnancy. Anthony can't wait to hold this child, Maximilian Anthony Charles Cornford, in his arms. They'd had him named the day the c.v. result came through, and had laughed at the representation in the two first names of the two chromosomes X and Y. As Willow lies drinking her tea, intended not only to soothe but to tone up her uterus, Anthony steps into the next-door room, which is to be Max's. A small light-blue room under the eaves, warm from the hot-water tank in the cupboard, above the big old kitchen, so that the child will be soothed in his early years by a cacophony of domestic noises. Kettles whistling, lids bubbling off saucepans, spoons rolling on to the floor; a symphony of plates and conversations. Anthony stands in the middle of the room on the ice-blue carpet, with the Inca rug portraying capering sheep and goats to his left, in front of the wicker cradle hung with old-fashioned pale-blue muslin – a present from Anthony's mother. In the chest of drawers layers of white and blue clothes rest sweet-smelling, waiting; and on the top a tray holding Johnson's talcum powder, baby cream, gripe water – the best of everything for Max, his son.

At ten they're in the car, not because Willow thinks they should be, but because Anthony can't stand it any longer. 'Have we got everything?' he interrogates her. 'Evian water? The Mozart tapes? Massage oil? Moisturizing cream? The camera? Max's teddy bear? Socks? The cushion?'

'Yes, yes.'

'I'm not entirely sure about Mozart,' muses Anthony. 'I've brought Bruckner's fourth just in case.'

'Hurry up,' says Willow, 'I want to piss. Or something.'

Roman Hall is busy. Mary Elliott is still with Clare Paynter, who's still in the bath. Steven, showered and suited, is on the telephone to the Semeries in Normandy advising instant takeoff as Rose Semerie's waters have broken. Paul's checking the resuscitation equipment that's cleverly hidden behind a different Magritte painting in each of the four labour rooms. Karin's unwrapping some new synthetic washable lambswool fleeces for the babies. Then she goes to prepare the purple labour room for Willow Cornford, who she knows is on her way. Karin has a faint feeling of unease about Mrs Cornford – is something unexpected going to happen? She's learnt to trust these feelings of hers, but nothing rational can be attached to them in this case. Willow's pregnancy has been straightforward. The baby – Karin checked it herself last week – is in a good position. Nothing augurs badly.

As Karin goes into the hall she looks out of one of the tall windows and sees a grey squirrel cross the gravel drive, like a large piece of fluff. The Cornfords' car, propelled at considerable speed by Anthony's nervous anticipation, has alarmed it. Steven comes out into the hall, having finished talking to the Semeries. 'Mrs Cornford is here,' says Karin. 'I think you should take a look at her, Steven. Something's worrying me, I don't know what it is.'

'When's she due?'

'A few days. It's not that.'

Steven shakes Anthony's hand. 'May I ask you something, Dr van den Biot?' says Anthony almost immediately. He pronounces the name with excessive care, making it sound as authentically French as some of the best wines on his list.

'Of course, Mr Cornford.'

Anthony takes Steven on one side while Karin bears the contracting Willow off to the purple labour room.

'What do you think of Bruckner?'

'I beg your pardon?'

'Anton Bruckner. You see, Dr van den Biot, we went to a concert at the Barbican the night Willow first felt Maximilian move. They played Bruckner's fourth. It's one of my favourites. But I'm not sure if it's the right music for childbirth. You do have a stereo cassette player in the labour room, don't you?'

'Oh yes.'

'With Dolby?'

'Oh yes.'

'Dolby C?'

'Naturally.'

'Well, what do you think?'

'I think you should wait and see what you both feel like, Mr Cornford. By the way, who's Maximilian?'

'The baby.' Anthony nods. 'Yes. That's right. That's what we ought to do.'

Two o'clock in the afternoon of Christmas Eve. Willow Cornford sweats and sleeps a little between contractions. She lies on the purple mattress, propped up with cushions, including her own, supplied by Anthony – who is standing by the stereo machine twiddling with the black plastic knobs; a jumpy bit of Mozart's piano concerto number seventeen comes out of it. His other hand holds the can of Evian water, which he's just shot all over his wife's face. Through the window of the purple labour room, which looks out on to the back lawn of Roman Hall, he sees a helicopter land. He rubs his eyes, but it's still there when he takes his hand away. The blades have scarcely stopped whirring when the door opens and a pregnant woman in a black fur coat manoeuvres herself out; and Dr Steven van den Biot goes across the lawn to help her. The woman is having difficulty walking. Anthony looks at Willow, wanting to tell her what he's seen, but Willow has her eyes closed. Anthony looks at his watch; no one's been in since one o'clock. He thinks about all the money he's paying for this and feels anxious, so he opens the door and peers out: 'Nurse!'

Karin Druin looks up from the front hall desk, where she's doing some paperwork. 'Yes, Mr Cornford? Did you want something?'

'Don't you think you ought to check my wife?'

'If you like. Has she asked for me?'

'No, but . . .'

Karin follows Anthony into the room, disliking him for his use of the term 'nurse'. It has always amazed her how many people in England don't understand the difference between nurses and midwives. She resolves to suggest to Steven that they rewrite the Roman Hall brochure making the distinction quite clear.

Willow's contractions are three minutes apart. Karin thinks it might be time for an internal examination – they try not to do too many at Roman Hall because of the risk of infection.

Willow is six centimetres dilated. 'You're doing very well, Mrs Cornford.'

'Am I?' Willow opens her eyes. 'Please tell my husband I want the music off.' Her silky lemon hair is wet at the roots with the effort she's making to stay in control.

Karin smiles to herself and relays the message, suggesting also that Anthony might like to go for a short walk or have a cup of coffee. 'But Willow . . .'

'It's quite all right, Mr Cornford, I shall stay with your wife.' Karin sits down on the purple mattress beside Willow. 'Perhaps you would like some back massage, Mrs Cornford?' She lifts the back of Willow's nightdress a little, spreads coconut oil over the small of her back, and rubs with light methodical strokes; Willow groans with appreciation.

On his way to find coffee, Anthony passes the door of the red labour room and hears screams. He feels agitated and opens the front door. Outside a man is standing, smoking. He offers Anthony a cigarette. Anthony takes one, though he hasn't smoked for years. The two men pace up and down, making scrunching sounds on the gravel, blowing smoke circles as they go, frightening all the squirrels in the vicinity. After a while the other man says, 'I'm Ralph – Ralph Scull.'

'Anthony Cornford. Pleased to meet you. Is your wife . . . ?'

'Not my wife, but yes, she is. Is yours?'

'She is.'

'How long have you been here?'

'Too long.'

'Me too.'

'Willow's six centimetres dilated,' confides Anthony, mournfully.

'I don't want to think about it.' Ralph Scull blows out an enormous quantity of smoke and coughs violently.

'Yes,' agrees Anthony. 'I know what you mean.'

In the hallway Mary Elliott, walking quickly from the green labour room to the office looking for Steven, sees the two men out there blowing smoke rings in the gravel, and feels sorry for them.

Steven is with the Semeries in the red labour room. They're causing him some consternation, as Rose Semerie is bleeding and Claude Semerie is worried about his helicopter.

'Is everything all right?' Rose, sweating from the pain of the examination Steven's just given her, looks anxiously into his eyes.

'You're bleeding a little, I'm not sure why. Did you have an ultrasound recently?'

'At the clinic in Calais at thirty-seven weeks. They found nothing abnormal.' Steven presses his ear to the wooden trumpet they use for listening to fetal hearts at Roman Hall, in preference to the modern technical kind. Its fluted end makes a white circle on Rose's stomach, but successfully picks up the regular beat of a baby's heart.

'Is the baby all right?'

'Fine.' Steven straightens up and looks down at Rose. 'Try to relax. I think we should wait a while and see what happens. But if you feel any more bleeding . . . I'll send my assistant in to sit with you.'

Rose nods. 'Could you come with me a moment, please, Mr Semerie?' says Steven firmly to Claude, who's still wearing his pilot's uniform.

'I zink I should move et,' said Claude, 'if ze vether freezes tonight, et might be deefficult.'

'You can put it lower down, over there,' Steven waves, 'where the ground's less likely to freeze.'

Claude hurries off to move his machine. Steven hurries off to find Paul and meets Mary, who wants him to examine Clare Paynter.

Clare, in the green room, still refuses to lie down. She's now wearing a flowered flannelette nightie and sitting on a chair. Her face is white, like the flannelette, with pink spots of pain on it. 'I don't understand her,' whispers Mary to Steven, 'I have this strange feeling she doesn't want this baby to be born.'

'Have you tried the celandine tea?' asks Steven.

'Of course.'

'What about the skullcap?'

'She refuses to have any more. I think she didn't like the name of it much.'

'Oh.' Steven's puzzled by Clare's behaviour. 'Mrs Paynter?'

'I'm not a Mrs,' objects Clare, gritting her teeth.

'Clare?'

'Yes.'

'Her bloke's called Scull,' explains Mary softly.

Steven's more worried by Clare's behaviour than by the names of teas and men. 'I think you might be more comfortable lying down.' Without waiting for an answer, he takes her by the hand and leads her to the bed under the window. She lies down on her side, gasping.

'Remember your exercises,' chides Mary Elliott gently. 'Breathe with me . . . that's better.' Mary and Steven exchange a look in which Steven says: leave this one to me.

He takes his coat off and lies down beside Clare. It is part of the Roman Hall philosophy that childbirth helpers help best by showing women directly – by example – how to relax. So Steven lies on his back, folds his hands on his shirt, and breathes along with Clare. Taking her cue from Steven, Mary lies down on Clare's other side.

It's peaceful in the room and outside it, except for the whirring of the blades of Claude Semerie's helicopter on the lawn as he moves it to an ice-free zone. After twenty minutes or so, the door opens suddenly and Ralph Scull comes in. He's quite taken aback by the sight of the doctor and the midwife – but especially the doctor – lying on the bed next to Clare. 'What the hell do you think you're doing?' Steven opens his eyes and knows trouble when he sees it. At the same time, Clare lets out a yell: 'I want to shit!' It's the first thing she's said for ages.

'What does it feel like, Clare?' inquires the midwife.

'Don't be daft, woman!' says Ralph Scull. 'If she says she wants to shit, she wants to shit!'

'Mr Scull,' says Mary impatiently, 'the feeling of the baby moving down the vagina is very like the feeling of wanting to open your bowels. Some women find it difficult to tell the difference . . . What does it feel like, dear?' She repeats the question.

'It's not the baby, I *do* want to shit.'

Mary fetches a bedpan. Ralph Scull and Steven leave the room.

An hour later, all's quiet again. Clare Paynter is more relaxed, and Ralph Scull is reading a Tom Sharpe novel. A half-empty bottle of brandy stands on the table beside him. In the labour room next door,

Claude Semerie is drinking raspberry leaf tea with his wife, who can feel a trickle of blood leaving her body but doesn't want to say so. In the third room, Anthony Cornford's got the headphones on and is listening to Bruckner. Willow has now reached eight centimetres.

Karin Druin slips upstairs to check a mother and baby she delivered the previous day. Both sleep in the same narrow bed; outside, the sweep of earth and sky are flaked with white as it starts to snow. 'Christmas!' thinks Karin warmly to herself; she thinks of her young daughters in the village with friends; and of Paul's dark muscular body. She meets him on her way down to the labour floor. He's hung mistletoe above the main door; he traps Karin there, and they embrace. The spirit of Christmas and of nature around them removes their inhibitions, and Paul, fixated on a memory of Karin's breast, is pushing her T-shirt up to reach it just as Ralph Scull comes staggering out of the green room.

Seeing doctor and midwife thus together, Ralph rightly or wrongly decides that Roman Hall is a corrupt unsafe place, full of people doing things they shouldn't. Clare must be removed from it as soon as possible. He lumbers back into the green room. 'No!' she cries as he goes for her recumbent body, trying to get her up and through the door, out into the indomitably falling snow. 'Stop it, Ralph! You're drunk! Leave me alone.'

Ralph Scull, who *is* drunk, swears back at her: 'Listen, Clare, this place is full of orgies. I've just seen one in the hall back there. God knows what'll happen if you stay here. It's not a clinic at all, my love, my darling stupid little lady, it's some sort of massage parlour. I'm going to report it to the Department of Health as soon as I've got you home.'

As Ralph Scull struggles with Clare, Rose Semerie haemorrhages in the red room, and in the process pushes a little boy out on to the bed. Claude Semerie presses the bell and shouts loudly in French for the midwife. Rose sits up, sees the sea of blood with the little baby floating in it, and faints. Fresh from his exploits under the mistletoe, Paul comes in and grabs the baby, who responds by making a mewling noise; and Karin, close behind him, leans heavily on Rose Semerie's partially collapsed stomach. 'Give me the baby!' she cries to Paul, who does, and Karin shoves the poor little baby on to his unconscious mother's breast, hoping that his fierce sucking will stop the bleeding.

Outside in the corridor, Steven overpowers Ralph Scull and drags Clare back into the green room. He uses the internal phone to summon one of the two postnatal midwives from upstairs. 'Please take Mr Scull to the first-floor sitting room and give him some strong coffee.' He lowers his voice. 'And a large dose of diazepam.'

Clare, crying, can't remember what she is doing here or why; how did she ever get herself into this position? Tears run down her face. She puts her arms round Steven's neck and appeals to him: 'Please, Dr van den Biot, help me! He's a bastard, that Ralph Scull. Keep him away from me!' Steven, always moved by women's distress, tells her to be quiet, his job is to get the baby born safely and well, and he promises her that he, Dr van den Biot, will do everything necessary to achieve this. He sits next to the mattress this time rather than lying on it, and he too, sitting there as Clare Paynter quietens and her cervix finally starts to open, sees the curtain of snow coming down across the trees as it fast becomes the night before Christmas Day.

Willow Cornford labours through all these commotions, remembering her childhood in Minnesota, and especially her mother, who died when Willow was fifteen, a stalwart no-nonsense woman who loved Willow and her brother intensely but without ever saying so. Willow feels a strange need for her mother now; she even finds the word 'mother' on her lips as each contraction grips her, and every time the midwife, Mary, comes close to her, she smells the smell of her mother's apron at high summer in the horse stable with the flies buzzing around. Willow's mind, racing everywhere, thinks about the time she took Matilda Cressey to the farm to meet her brother Randy, her little brother, who now runs the place and has a wife and four fair-haired little girls springing long-legged all over the place as Willow herself once did. Matilda had taken photographs, and they'd had steak and sweet potatoes for dinner, with the blood from the steak running pink through the potatoes and streaking the white of the marshmallow like an airplane sunset.

Steven remembers the drink he's supposed to have with Claudia Foxman. He telephones her: 'I'm sorry, Claudia, I won't be able to make it after all, we have two women in labour, I daren't leave. I'm sure you understand.'

Claudia doesn't want to. 'But I'm only five minutes away, Steven,' she pleads, 'you can be back in a jiffy.' When he won't retract, she becomes angry and slams the phone down: 'But it's Christmas!'

The next thing Steven remembers is the grant Claudia Foxman has promised Roman Hall. He puts his coat on, tucking his bleeper into the pocket.

* * *

32

In Micklesham village, the church is full of carol singers. As Steven drives past the gate they begin to process out between the rows of broken grey headstones and frostbitten chrysanthemums, some of them hesitantly breaking the air with a mixture of 'While Shepherds Watched' and 'Hark, the Herald Angels Sing'.

In Claudia Foxman's house, John Dominic is sitting in his baby chair in the lounge. Claudia's sister is in the kitchen; her boyfriend is upstairs having a bath. Claudia's own husband is in Africa, though not with Nanny Pilkington. Claudia is finishing the tree; and John Dominic, splendid in his blue velour Babygro, laughs, as his mother intends him to, at the way the candles make the tinsel dance and the silver balls sway and have pictures on them.

Claudia gives Steven a pewter mug containing something hot and spicy. For a moment, Steven feels like giving in and enjoying himself. He bends down and tickles John Dominic's tummy: the child stares hard at him for a moment, then his face crumples and a large bellow hits the air. 'Oh God, I'm sorry, Claudia – I didn't mean to upset him!'

'Don't worry, it's just the stage he's at.' Claudia takes her son out of the chair and balances him on her hip, whence he glares balefully at Steven, unable to remember that it was Steven's hands that first enclosed his head and helped him out of his mother's vagina. 'I forget,' says Claudia, anxious to make allowances after her outburst on the phone, 'you must be so used to newborn babies, but not to older children. You haven't had much to do with them, have you?'

'I did a locum paediatrics job once,' offers Steven. 'But other than that, no.'

'You never had any children yourself?'

It's a curious question, Claudia realizes: as though she's suggesting that Steven might have casually had some children along the way and abandoned them. On the other hand, that's exactly what her own husband did with John Dominic.

'I never had the time.' He smiles.

Claudia thinks: a screw; a screw with Nanny Pilkington, it doesn't take long, surely. But she says, 'Do you regret it?'

'Sometimes.' Steven likes John Dominic now, gurgling on his mother's lap, his fat pink baby hands grabbing for her hair, his tiny velour feet pushing against her to stand up, little noises of delight bubbling out of him; but he didn't like him a moment ago when his mouth went into a square black hole and shouted reprovingly at him. Maybe the baby seemed too much an incarnation of Steven's own childish demands – made but not met; almost, but not quite, forgotten.

They talk next of the grant. Steven wants to persuade Claudia that the research should not be aimed at proving scientifically the superiority of Roman Hall babies, but rather at describing and exploring the clinic's use of herbal remedies. Claudia promises to think about it. Her sister and boyfriend join them, and Steven is conscious of being shown off: here's the wonderful doctor who knows all sorts of intimate secrets about women, about me and my baby. The carol singers come from the church and sing 'Good King Wenceslas', and are given punch and cocoa, mince pies and a discreet cheque for the church fabric fund. Steven's bleeper goes off as the choirmaster – so called, actually an antique dealer – raises his hand for 'Away in a Manger' – a reference, presumably, to John Dominic. Steven goes upstairs to Claudia's bedroom to phone the clinic.

'Mrs Paynter's in the second stage,' Mary tells him. 'But she's still resisting a hell of a lot.'

'Is she standing up?'

'No, she was.'

He sighs. 'I'm on my way.' He can never understand why the midwives don't keep the women upright and moving, it's much the best thing.

'Where's Mr Scull?' Steven asks when he gets back.

'Asleep. We've put him in one of the postnatal rooms. Deirdre's keeping an eye on him.' Deirdre from the village is a matronly ex-psychiatric nurse, who does three nights a week at Roman Hall looking after the postnatals to get away from her own insufficiently postnatal family.

Clare is now lying on her back, her thighs apart, but there's no vestige of a head to be seen. With each contraction she heaves and sighs but nothing seems to happen. 'She's really tired,' says Mary.

Steven asks Clare to stand, or move on to all fours, but she refuses. The only thing she says is, 'I want to go to sleep.'

'The spirit seems to have gone out of her since Mr Scull's outburst,' observes Mary quietly to Steven.

He takes off his coat and rolls up his shirt sleeves. He stands and looks at Clare, then touches her head lightly. 'Mrs Paynter – Clare – I think it's time you had your baby now. Don't you want to see it? You must want to see it. Have you chosen a name? What's the baby called, Clare?'

She looks at him through half-closed, heavy-lidded eyes. 'I don't care. But I do want this to be over.' She closes her eyes, then opens them fully for an instant and stares at Steven. 'Beatrice,' she says. 'After Dante's, you know. A little girl.' Tears form on her dark eyelashes like baubles on a tree.

Steven lifts his hand off the bed and straightens up, alerted suddenly by something. But, 'That's a beautiful name,' is all he says. The strange look in his eyes is quickly gone. 'Get some gloves, I'll do an examination.' He can feel the head, jammed against the cervix. 'Listen to the heart,' he commands.

Mary does. 'It's taking a while to recover,' she says.

Clare speaks: 'Can't you *do* something? I want to go to sleep.'

'Relax, it won't be long now.' Steven decides to use suction. He and Mary spend a while manoeuvring and affixing to the head inside Clare a machine that, acting like an obstetric hoover, will suck the baby out. Half a hour later there's another person in the room, with a head that looks as if it's got a beetroot growing on it. But the baby, a girl, cries, and Steven and Mary both say to Clare quickly, 'The swelling will go down soon, don't worry about it.' Clare takes the child and cries also, but with relief and thinking of her unhappy liaison with Ralph Scull.

The snow settles. Willow Cornford labours on. Anthony has listened to Bruckner's fourth three times and is restless. 'Willow darling,' – she scarcely hears him – 'would you mind if I went for a quick walk?' He goes round the back of the clinic to where the lawn slopes and Claude Semerie's helicopter huddles near the bridge over the trout stream. The sky is full of snow; what a night for a child to be born! Anthony, who's feeling most light-headed, wouldn't really be surprised to see camels walk across the meadows and a star appear in the sky over Roman Hall, for Maximilian his son.

He hears cars across the drive behind him: visiting time. Men with Christmas presents. Women don't stay very long at Roman Hall after the birth – it costs too much. A day or two is usually enough. Anyway, the proof of the pudding is in the eating: a successful natural birth produces a mother who can get up the next day and leap about performing her usual duties, thereby convincing her husband that it was worth spending all that money in the first place. Anthony reflects that Willow and Maximilian will spend Christmas here without him. What will he do? He turns to go inside and ask, but hears quarrelling voices coming from the ground-floor office. Dr van den Biot and a nurse: 'But why did you use the suction? Surely another half hour . . .'

'I'm tired, Karin. It was my judgement.'

'In that case, your judgement is affected,' she says.

'You don't *have* to work here.'

'The baby will have problems.'

'No, it looks bad but it isn't.'

Anthony is seized with panic for the unborn Maximilian, and rushes back to find Willow stirring, throwing herself around on the purple mattress. He kneels and takes her hand. 'Get me some ice, Anthony, I'm so thirsty.'

He fetches it from a purple plastic bucket, toned to match the room, and drops it on the bed.

'Oh, for God's sake, Anthony, can't you do *anything* right!' Anthony remembers how in the book about childbirth Willow gave him to read, it says that when women complain a lot they're probably in transition between the first and second stages of labour. So this is it! He retrieves the ice, puts it in his pocket and takes some more for Willow, slipping a cube neatly in her mouth this time.

The midwife comes in: 'How are we doing, Mrs Cornford?'

'What time is it?'

'Ten o'clock.'

'How long have I been in labour?'

'When did it start?'

'Six o'clock in the morning,' says Anthony.

Karin says: 'Sixteen hours. But it's not a bad thing. Didn't we tell you when you came to the birth preparation classes that a natural labour is often long? Provided the baby's all right there's no harm in it.' She takes the wooden trumpet from her pocket and pushes Willow's robe up, revealing the mountainous abdomen with its pigmented zigzag line. She's very attentive for a few minutes, shifting the trumpet around to find the right place.

'Is he all right?' Anthony is hovering behind Karin.

'He, or she?'

'It's a he, Willow had the test,' says Anthony proudly. His attention is drawn suddenly to a stream of water coming from his trouser leg.

'I see.' Karin replaces the trumpet, looking briefly at him, her eyes also noting the pool of water on the floor by his feet.

'Ice,' he says. 'I put it in my pocket.'

Karin, used to strange male behaviour in labour rooms, ignores Anthony's liquidity. 'Do you feel any urge to bear down yet, Mrs Cornford?'

'Yes!' Willow sits up, excitedly. 'Get me some more pillows!'

Anthony goes out again to the lavatory and to dry his trousers. Then he comes back and fixes up his video camera. There's a problem with the lights. Births at Roman Hall are always by candlelight, or in the dark by natural light only. Occasionally the moon is full and on a cloudless night the blinds are left up – *those* babies, Steven thinks, are particularly good ones. So Karin doesn't allow Anthony to put the main light on. 'Either you will see it on your film or you won't, we must have everything best for the baby' – her English lapses at times like this.

Willow wants Steven van den Biot there for the birth of her son. 'We're paying for him, Ant,' she says, very American-like, 'I want him here. Go get him. And I want to go in the pool now.'

'Willow!' Anthony has never liked this particular idea. 'Willow, please, we said . . .'

'*I'm* having this baby, Anthony,' she commands, Queen-Victoria-like. After a pause needed to deal with the next contraction, she says, 'You wouldn't let me have it at home, so this is what I'm going to do instead. Our son will be born underwater, and Dr van den Biot will be there!'

'But I'll have to move the camera,' protests Anthony.

Willow is rendered speechless by the next contraction. After vast organizational upheavals, the party repair to the blue room, which has the swimming pool in it. Willow flings her nightdress off and with Anthony's help climbs naked up the steps into the pool. She sits on the ledge which runs around the edge, hands on her knees, concentrating hard. 'Something's happening,' she reports after a few minutes, 'the baby's moving down. Where *is* Dr van den Biot?' Steven puts his head over the top of the pool. 'Well, you aren't much use there,' says Willow crossly. 'You'll have to get in here with me.'

Anthony fusses with the camera, trying to arrange it so he can take pictures inside the pool. 'I want the doctor!' screams Willow. Steven sighs, takes his shirt and his shoes and socks off, and rolls his trousers up to his knees. Pulling a standard stethoscope up after him (the wooden ones don't do well in the water), he climbs into the pool. Willow is too distracted to be amused by his appearance. She gets hold of him, pushes him down in the pool so she has her hands on his shoulders and he becomes thoroughly drenched, and leans heavily against him. Steven tells her to get off the ledge. Karin takes her clothes off and comes round the other side. She has very pretty breasts, notices Anthony guiltily. He's left his Bruckner in the other room and is just about to go and get it when Steven says, 'Okay, it's coming now,' and Anthony stands on a chair to see better and Willow says, 'Where's Anthony? Why isn't he here?' and Anthony doesn't know what to do and Karin tells Willow to push and something shoots out on to the bottom of the pool, and the midwife and the doctor are rooting around in the water, the one with his trousers flapping wetly, the other with her white breasts floating, looking for something – his son! Anthony can't see properly, realizes he has his reading glasses on, but if he takes them off he won't be able to see the dials on the camera clearly.

Steven van den Biot finds the baby and holds it like a half-drowned kitten above the water. Willow's crying and holding out her arms: 'Welcome, Maximilian!' Anthony takes his glasses off. Something is wrong. The baby is a girl.

5
William's
Chicken Kiev

While all this is happening in Roman Hall to her friend Willow Cornford, Matilda Cressey is attempting to have a civilized Christmas. The office Christmas party is a little spoilt by Rita Ploughman going overboard with the punch, and by Jeffrey Rowley's amorous attentions to Jason, which result in Margaret Watteau falling over the cat and breaking her glasses. She wails in a peculiarly desperate and unattractive way. 'At least this can only happen once a year,' sighs Matilda. Mrs Trancer, sitting in the doorway drinking tea in her best maroon and olive print, looks quite meaningfully at her.

William is waiting for Matilda when she gets home from the party. He's cooking dinner tonight. This normally means he goes to Marks and Spencer's and buys one of their ready-made meals; only this time he didn't, as Marks and Spencer's was as full as the proverbial Christmas stocking. He went to a shop called Snowland instead.

William says they're having Chicken Kiev. Matilda runs a bath and puts the radio on. William brings her a gin and tonic. She begins to relax. But he comes into the bathroom and lodges himself on the side of the bath and begins a sentence with the words, 'About tomorrow . . .'

Matilda and William met a year ago at a dinner party in Battersea. She was attracted by his childish openness and total lack of ambition, and he fancied her elegance and air of impending success. Out of bed, they'd subsequently proved there was nothing remotely compatible about their coupling, but because of this – the absence of that conventional contorted striving for intimacy – the relationship had been a remarkably easy and happy one. They are fond of one another. Matilda knows exactly what she wants William for – sex, humour, a cinema companion and an occasional repair man. As this is still very much the era of AIDS, she also appreciates being able to have reasonable trust in the fact that William won't give her anything she *doesn't* want to have. For his part, William lacks Matilda's thorough understanding of the politics of heterosexuality, but likes her, finds her interesting, imaginative in bed; and – a great plus, at least at the beginning – she seems to be different from all the other women he knows, because she isn't looking for a husband or for a baby-maker. Something, however, has happened recently inside William. He's become aware that while Matilda isn't out to trap him, she isn't willing to give him very much either. Six of one, half a dozen of the other. She sees herself as a free spirit, and William as some sort of attendant sparrow. Matilda is the big bird in the sky and William the little one. The dreaded lifestyle is gradually taking on a different aspect. William finds himself dreaming about houses in the suburbs and wedding rings. What has always been pressure has re-formed itself as fantasy.

'What *about* tomorrow?' Matilda slides down into the bubbles of Fenjal – her Christmas present to herself.

'I want to spend it with you.'

'You know that's impossible, William. We've been through it a hundred times.'

'Why is it impossible?'

'William, do we really have to go through it all again?'

'Yes.' His eyes glare redly at her in the steaming bathroom.

'I always spend Christmas with my parents. It means a lot to them, that it's just the three of us. It's a family *tradition*. I thought we'd agreed that I'd spend Christmas with my parents and you'd spend it with your father.'

'I don't want to spend Christmas with my father,' objects William petulantly. 'I'm not in love with my father, I'm in love with you. I don't care a fish's tit about family tradition. You don't care about me.'

'But William, we've already *discussed* this!'

'You discussed it with yourself. It's always what *you* want to do, isn't it? When have you ever done anything for me?' He joins the rest of his gin and tonic to her Fenjal and slams the door on her.

'Oh, for God's sake!' Matilda, feeling enormously tired after the office party and the drink, drags herself up out of the bath, puts on a robe, and follows William into the kitchen, where he's pretending to read the instructions on the Snowland packet.

'Okay. If it's that important to you,' she concedes.

'Okay what?' William keeps his eyes strictly on the packet.

'I'll phone my parents and tell them to expect you as well.'

He hears her on the phone meeting some resistance and feels a pang of – what? Guilt? Suspicion? Are there things Matilda hasn't told him?

He serves the dinner. 'Come and eat, Matilda the Great.' He often calls her that since she got the CCA job. It doesn't sound funny tonight. Matilda, dressed and clearly resentful, sits down opposite him. She pokes at her chicken. 'What's this?'

'You know what it is, it's Chicken Kiev.'

'But it's minced!'

'Is it?'

Matilda gets up and takes the packet out of the kitchen bin. '. . . chicken pieces *shaped* and *filled*,' she reads, 'ingredients: chicken – *minimum* 45 per cent, breadcrumbs, butter, vegetable oil, water . . . sodium polyphosphate . . . Oh, William, how could you! It's disgusting! Can't you do *anything* right?'

He gets up and with a very pink face says, 'That's it. I can't take any more of this, Matilda. You are simply *impossible*.'

'If you like,' she says, resigned.

'It's *Christmas*, can't you make *any* sort of effort?'

'Fuck Christmas,' she says.

John and Christine Cressey, Matilda's parents, live in Kensington, where John Cressey works as a GP. Matilda is the Cresseys' only child and in their eyes can do no wrong. So when she tells her mother, first of all that William is coming to Christmas dinner, and then that he isn't, owing to the fact that they've had a row about reconstituted chicken, Christine Cressey just pats her daughter's hand and says, 'That's all right, darling. Are you sure William's *worthy* of you? You need someone who can *stand up* to you. In any case, it'll be much nicer just being family today, won't it!'

Matilda gives her father a book about Limoges porcelain, and he gives her a halogen lamp. She gives her mother a red Liberty wool shawl, and her mother gives her a peach silk nightdress. After lunch they listen to a new CD version of Honegger's Christmas Cantata – another family tradition – and play Monopoly. Then they have turkey sandwiches and celery, her father falls asleep in his chair, and Matilda says she'll go home, and her mother tries to persuade her not to.

When she gets home, Matilda makes some phone calls to her friends. First Janet Hoskins, with whom she was at school; then

Henry, a university friend who makes a small living as a poet in Dorset; then Willow Cornford.

Anthony answers the phone. 'She's had it,' he says. 'Willow had the baby last night.' His voice sounds odd.

'How is he – the baby? And Willow?'

'Willow's fine. She'd like to see you, as a matter of fact. The baby's fine, too. Only it's the wrong sex.'

'What do you mean, the wrong sex?'

'Well, they told us after the c.v. test it was a boy. But it isn't. It's a girl.'

'Good God.'

'They got the test wrong. Now we've got to think of a new name. And we're going to have to repaint the nursery,' says Anthony gloomily.

'Did you sleep last night, Anthony?'

'Not a lot.'

'You're probably feeling rather overwrought,' suggests Matilda.

'Am I? It was a weird experience. Of course the baby's beautiful, but it is a bit of a shock, and Roman Hall's an awfully strange place.'

Matilda decides to go and visit Willow. A drive into the country will be just the way to spend Boxing Day.

6
An
Unofficial Visit

Matilda sets off early. Once out of London, by the roundabout before
the M40, she begins to see fields of light snow. She listens to a
Leonard Cohen tape: a purple sixties voice, making soulful promises
to an archetypal unnamed woman; promises born of radical pain,
promises that won't be kept. The throaty voice fills the warm car and
overflows through the slightly open window in waves on to the
bleached countryside. Matilda feels sad, but also hopeful. Relation-
ships change. Some feelings endure, others enter history. As she
speeds out to the open countryside, she senses William slipping into
the past. She will miss him (and he her?) but someone will take his
place, for love *isn't* curable; both passions spent and the need to spend
passions persist as the nuts and bolts of the human soul.

Roman Hall is marked from the A414 by an AA sign. There's more
snow down here, evidence of a heavy fall in the night. Snow ploughs
are out, and on the hills farms are welded to the land, like white
ornaments on the icing of a rich dark cake.

Willow has her own room on the first floor. The lamp's on by the
bed, but she appears to be sleeping, her golden hair spread out on the
pillow, liquid in the light. In a Perspex cradle, the baby lies absolutely
still, its tiny fists clumped together above its head. Willow sits up,
startled: 'Tilly!'

'Did I wake you?'

'Not really. I was just dozing.'

Matilda goes over to the bed and kisses Willow, who looks pale and
almost as tiny as the baby. 'Well, how was it?'

'Oh, Tilly, I can't tell you how awful it was! Everything went
wrong!'

Matilda takes her coat off and sits down. Willow rings the bell and
asks for coffee, which is dandelion, with a glass of freshly squeezed

orange juice and some yoghurt and honey for Willow. 'Everyone gets this the day after,' she explains.

'But the baby,' says Matilda, wanting to begin at the end, 'how's the baby?'

'Oh, she's fine,' says Willow, casting a sideways glance at the cot. 'No problems. A good weight, seven pounds six. They say she's tired, she had an exhausting journey.'

'What are you going to call her?'

'Maximilian,' says Willow wryly, swallowing her yoghurt and honey. 'I suppose Ant let off at you about that. He's completely furious. How could they get the result wrong? As soon as I get out of here I'm going to find out what happened. I guess we could sue them, even! It's really out of order, Tilly. You spend the whole pregnancy thinking it's a boy, and then you . . . well, you do feel disappointed.'

The baby makes a little rustling sound like a piece of paper in the wind. Matilda stands by the cot and wonders how anyone could be disappointed with *that*. 'You'll get used to her, Willow,' she says after a bit.

'Oh, I know. Listen, Tilly, I want to tell you about this place. I've become quite suspicious.'

'What about?'

'Well, first of all I'm not sure they know what they're doing. I mean this Dr van den Biot,' Willow lowers her voice, looking at the door, 'the one I told you about; well, he's certainly a charming fellow, but *he* didn't really seem to know what he was doing yesterday. There was this awful fiasco with the pool . . .' In its retelling Willow finds herself turning the birth into a tragicomedy; she's even tempted to make Anthony fall in at the end. 'And then I met this really nice woman in the bathroom, she had a baby yesterday as well, and she said *her* husband – well, he's not really her husband – walked into some sort of orgy in the hall. When I told Ant that, he told *me* he heard a terrible argument between a midwife and a doctor about one of the babies – the midwife said the doctor had done something terribly wrong, that the baby would be damaged for life. Poor Clare – she's the woman in the bathroom – *her* baby looks like a beetroot, at least its head does. I hope that's not the one they were arguing about.' Willow, exhausted, reaches for her orange juice and lies back against the pillow.

Matilda thinks. 'How does Roman Hall describe itself? Is there a brochure?'

Willow nods. 'In my handbag. On the side over there. I think it calls itself an Alternative Birth Clinic. I suppose it might be licensed by the Ministry of something, it would have to be, wouldn't it?' Willow is obstinately vague about British officialdom.

'The Department of Health,' says Matilda absently.

'Don't you – doesn't the outfit you work for – investigate things like this?'

'Well, it hasn't,' says Matilda, 'so far. Of course we've done surveys of consumer satisfaction with maternity care, and we're doing some work at the moment on the costs of private health insurance.' She pauses.

Willow smiles. 'But you could, couldn't you?'

'I suppose so.' The baby wakes up, and Willow asks Matilda to wheel the cradle over. She picks her out of the cot a little uncertainly.

'But I would have to know what I was investigating,' says Matilda.

'The standard of care. The qualifications of the staff. Promises made and not lived up to. Value for money. Does it matter?'

'Yes, it does. And we can't take this sort of initiative on our own. There has to be a complaint.'

'I'm sure that won't be difficult. It'd better not be me, as I know you. But I guess from what she said Clare Paynter's man might do that for you. I'll have a word with her when we next meet in the bathroom.'

Just before Matilda leaves Roman Hall, Dr van den Biot comes to see Willow Cornford. 'My friend Matilda Cressey, Dr van den Biot' (Willow pronounces it 'Bi-oat'). Steven peers at Matilda, wondering where he's seen her face before, and then at the baby.

'Are you going to examine her?'

'Never wake a sleeping baby, that's my motto, Mrs Cornford.'

'She never does anything *but* sleep,' complains Willow.

'Give her a chance. She's only practising.'

'Dr van den Biot,' says Willow a little aggressively, 'you know the c.v. result was wrong, don't you?'

'So your husband said.'

'Can you explain why?'

'I didn't do it, did I?' says Steven. 'We don't do the cytogenetic work here in any case, we send to Oxford for that. I don't know what happened, Mrs Cornford. I'll have to make some inquiries. There's probably some simple explanation. But the baby's fine and healthy, that's the main thing, isn't it?' He moves back a pace or two towards the door, folding his arms. 'Girls are supposed to be less trouble in any case, you know.'

'Are they?' Willow doesn't look convinced.

'What about the birth?' continues Steven. 'How do you feel about that? Have you had your birth counselling yet? One of the midwives – ' Steven turns to Matilda, feeling somehow he ought to include her in the conversation, 'One of the midwives comes and goes through with the mother every detail of what happened during the birth. We find it helps with later adjustment.'

'No, I haven't,' says Willow.

'How are you feeling physically?'

'I don't know,' says Willow, 'I've never had a baby before. My bottom hurts. I think my stomach's the same size as it was before I had the baby. Do you think you might have left one in there? I haven't got any milk.'

'Well, you will have. I'll make sure one of the midwives comes to help you with that. Are you taking your meadowsweet two-hourly?'

'It's revolting,' says Willow, screwing up her face. 'You can't seriously expect me to go on eating *that*.'

Matilda and Willow laugh when Steven's gone. 'That's not all, Tilly, we're told to paint this mint tea' – Willow points to a bowl on the side – 'on our fannies. It's quite hard to remember what to put where.'

'You gave him a bad time,' observes Matilda. For some reason, the idea is growing on her of finding out about Steven van den Biot. Perhaps it's his way of standing in the doorway with folded arms, pronouncing authoritatively on women's mysteries? His posture recalls others from her own girlhood. The dark outline of contained knowledge against the light to which it leads. Figures medical and paternal, solid and undemonstrative, holding secrets that may ooze out or be fought for only against apparently hopeless odds. And the urge to fight being the flame that always burns – for whatever the knowledge gained, it's never enough to satisfy the longing to get in there and find out at first hand what it's all about.

'Do you know what this whole thing is costing, Tilly? Four thousand pounds. The good doctor should *have* to work hard for his living.'

Anthony comes then, laden with parcels like a Christmas tree, including a packet of cold turkey from his mother, half a bottle of Taittinger, a new nightie for Willow from his cousin – who knows all about babies, including having six of her own – and a bag of books, including Tolstoy's *The Kreutzer Sonata* ('Oh, Ant, how could you, why didn't you buy me some Jackie Collins?'), and a nasty minuscule pink rabbit ('I bought it at a service station, nothing else is open today, it's for Belinda.' 'Belinda! Anthony, you can't possibly . . .')

Matilda leaves them arguing and makes her way slowly out of Roman Hall, observing as much as she can on the way. But the first-floor landing's quiet, except for the sound of a lone baby crying, and downstairs Karin sits at her desk in the hall smiling Danishly at her. There are a couple of cars – a Volkswagen estate and a large red Fiat – parked in the drive. But there's certainly nothing remarkable to be seen.

7
In the
Herb Garden

Steven van den Biot walks between the graves of Micklesham church on the day after Christmas, kicking the frozen snow away with his shoes, scouring the lichen with his pigskin gloves and trying to read the inscriptions on the graves. He walks with the face of a ghost against the dark church and the dull grey sky. This place, this countryside, might be where he lives, but he's not entirely of it; such success isn't really enough to sustain anyone's soul.

In the corner of the churchyard, up against the wall in the shelter where snow hasn't fallen, is a clump of agrimony. Steven stops to examine it, peeling its pinched stems out from under a triangular stone. Because of the weather he decides not to uproot it now for the herb garden at Roman Hall. He'll fetch it later, in the springtime, when it'll be more likely to take root and grow.

The idea of new growth lifts his mood an inch or two and he walks quickly out of the churchyard, turning right outside the gate towards Claudia Foxman's house. She comes to the door in jeans and a pink silk shirt, with dribbles of John Dominic's milk on her. 'You know what we were saying the other evening,' he begins without more ado, 'about documenting the herbs we use at Roman Hall?' He pauses. She looks, he thinks, a little disappointed, but says yes. 'I wondered if you'd like to come with me one day soon, perhaps tomorrow, to the Chelsea Physic Garden, or maybe you already know it?' For a man so used to communicating with women, it's a curiously stilted invitation.

She agrees. Then she invites him in but he declines, as he's anxious to walk back across the fields to Roman Hall, where there is, as usual, a woman in labour. On the way back, he wonders why he called on Claudia without his usual planning and forethought. Of course he admires her – the way she coped with Lord Foxman's deviation and disappearance; as a mother, in her dealings with the velour-clad John Dominic; and she's an attractive woman, a classic English beauty –

hair like a racehorse's mane, skin like Devon cream, cheeks the colour of a healthy smiling cervix.

Steven has told Paul of Claudia's offer of money, but not the original purpose for which she offered it – to follow the development of Roman Hall babies. This would be dangerously close to Paul's own heart. He's told him about the herbs, though, so it's perfectly logical to tell him that he's planning to take the day off and show Lady Foxman the Chelsea Physic Garden to give her a better idea of how she'd be investing her money.

It's a bitter day, with a wind creasing the surface of the Thames into a badly cracked mirror; clouds run a marathon above the chimneys of Battersea Power Station. In the streets between the Embankment and the King's Road, the upper classes recover from Christmas and burglar alarms go off with regular vacation glee. Steven parks his car in Swan's Walk, opposite the gate to the Garden. Claudia studies the green board announcing its presence on this site since 1673. 'But Steven, it's closed, it's only open from April to October!'

'Except to Friends,' he says. 'I have a key.' Inside the garden, the red Chelsea brick peers down on them from all sides, making them feel they're being watched by a party of rudely healthy schoolgirls. The plants are laid in rectangular plots, on ground that slopes frostily but firmly towards the river; a statue of a gentleman with ringlets keeps internal guard over them.

Claudia takes Steven's arm. 'I realized when you asked me to come here with you the other day that you know an awful lot about *me*, Steven, but I know almost nothing about *your* background. Why are you so determined to keep it secret?'

'Ah, that's a secret.' He touches her arm abstractedly. 'There *are* reasons for it, of course. Let me tell you a bit about the garden, Claudia. It was founded by the Society of Apothecaries, to teach physicians how to recognize and use herbs. Now, if we go along here . . .'

'Tell me something,' she says eagerly, 'just one thing. Your name, for instance, where does that come from?'

'It's French,' he tells her. 'Well, a mixture of French and Dutch. Now, over this side . . .'

'So your family . . .'

'Was European.'

She giggles, wraps her grey fox fur more closely round her knees. 'It's hopeless. You won't give anything away, will you!'

Standing in front of the largest outside olive tree in Britain, with his foot by a nearly extinct potato plant, Steven van den Biot remembers a time when he had, twenty or twenty-five years ago, and nothing but bad had come of it. His head aches with the memory.

'Come, Claudia, let's go round to the south side. There's something I want you to see there. Look,' he guides her past the hyssop and the valerian, the squirting cucumber and the flowering salvia, to a bed labelled 'officinal plants'. 'These are some of the ones we now have at the clinic. Vervain, medicinal rhubarb, dandelion taraxacum and papaver somniferum – dried opium poppy to you. Liquorice, meadow saffron – good for muscular pains. And over here sea buckthorn – now the fruit of that's exceptionally high in vitamin C. And this,' he stops in front of a nondescript plant that looks, in this season, scarcely alive, 'monkshood – it's probably the most poisonous plant known to man. Or woman.' Claudia notes a strange gleam in his eye as he says this, and immediately glances past her to the cream metal arcades of Chelsea bridge.

Simultaneously, someone passes on the avenue between the herbs, across from them, someone with a familiar face. At first Steven can't place it, and then the figure says, 'Dr van den Biot!' (pronounced as he himself does) ' – Matilda Cressey, we met the other day at Roman Hall.'

'Ah yes, Mrs Cornford's friend.' He still thinks he's seen that face somewhere before, but can't recall where. They shake hands. 'Are you a Friend of the Garden, Miss Cressey?'

'No. You left the door open. I actually came for a walk in the Royal Hospital Gardens, but I knew this place was here; my father's a doctor, he's often mentioned it to me. I thought I'd come and take a look.'

Steven looks around to see if there's someone with Matilda, but there isn't. He introduces Claudia. Matilda examines Claudia's silver fox fur and Italian boots decorated with gold chains. 'We're looking at herbs,' says Steven lamely to Matilda, 'for Roman Hall, you know. We use a lot of them in our work there.'

'So you do. Willow told me about your book, it sounds fascinating.' Matilda turns back towards the lavender bushes. 'Nice to meet you again, Dr van den Biot.'

'And you.'

'Striking woman,' remarks Claudia when Matilda's gone.

'You think so?'

'I've seen her picture somewhere. It was the *Guardian*, I think.

Yes, that's right, she's the new President of the Council for Consumer Affairs.'

Steven realizes that's where he must have seen her face. 'So Mrs Cornford's friend is a powerful woman.' Steven's intrigued. 'She looks rather too young to hold such a position.'

'We don't all have to be fifty, my dear doctor.'

Steven, warming to Claudia, suggests a meal at a pub in Beaconsfield on the way home. Matilda, warming to the idea of investigating Roman Hall, gets back in her gold Renault 5 and goes home to Chiswick via a bookshop in Notting Hill where she buys *Herbal Childbirth* and *Plants for Life*, by Steven van den Biot. The blurb on the back of each describes him as a paediatrician who trained in England and the States, but came from a Mediterranean background which had taught him as a child to respect the curative capacity of Nature rather than of Man.

The jackets carry a sentimental photo of Roman Hall with the sunlight on it: 'Dr van den Biot's Alternative Birth Clinic'. Does this count as advertising, wonders Matilda?

Before she goes home, she calls in at her parents'. 'I want to ask you something, Daddy.' John Cressey stirs in his armchair. 'Have you heard of this man?'

He takes one of the books and scrutinizes the cover carefully. 'So this is he.'

'What do you mean, this is he?'

'Gordon and I had a lady last year who wanted a home birth. We wouldn't touch her with a bargepole. So she went off to this place and had it and it died. Most unfortunate case.'

'What was wrong with her? I mean, why didn't you want her to have the baby at home?'

'Red hair,' says John Cressey uncommunicatively.

'What?'

'Always spells trouble. They get hypertension. And they bleed. Babies are flat, like kippers. Nipple problems too. I remember . . .'

'Oh, John!' Matilda's mother has always been embarrassed by the way her husband speaks of women.

'Why?' John Cressey looks at his daughter keenly over his half-moon glasses. 'Why on earth are you interested in van den Biot and Roman Hall?'

'I'm thinking of doing an investigation of Alternative Birth Centres, Daddy.'

'Good idea.'

'Do you really think so?'

'Very much so.'

When Matilda gets home with her books, she puts the kettle on for a cup of tea, and decides to get into bed and read them. But she finds William already there, wearing nothing but an expression that says nothing has happened. 'Like a bad penny, Tilly,' he admits. 'You always said I was, didn't you? You're right. But I do need you, Tilly. I've had a sodding awful time. Come into bed and warm me up.'

When she does, Matilda realizes she's missed William too.

'It's nice to have you not tired, and not with a headache, and not having to get up early to go to the office,' he remarks.

'I can't help it if I'm a busier and more important person than you are,' she replies.

'Back to our old tricks, Tilly,' he says.

8
Steven
Under Surveillance

January in London: heaps of grimy snow decorate the edges of the pavements. Matilda's car has developed an almighty shudder, so she's taken it to the garage and the bus to work. And arrives complaining about her journey. Margaret Watteau doesn't understand why Matilda is complaining, as she takes the bus every day, and it's always late, or arrives with five others. She gives Matilda a cup of coffee from their new automatic Salton coffee machine.

Matilda goes through her in-tray with devastating speed, scribbling 'Yes', or 'No', on letters and handing these to Margaret, who is supposed to compose replies – a feat she was never expected to manage for Dame Ferguson-FitzGerald. Then Matilda demands to see Rita. Margaret listens while Matilda and Rita talk. 'We're going to get a letter about an Alternative Birth Clinic in Oxfordshire, Rita. Don't ask me how I know, but we are. So I want a list of all the Alternative Birth Centres in the country, with details: how long established, who runs them, how they're licensed, where they fit into the whole private medicine scene.'

Rita, who knows nothing about birth, wonders why Matilda is so interested in the subject. She takes a quick look at Matilda's stomach, but it's redeemingly flat behind her navy leather skirt. 'That shouldn't be too difficult,' says Rita. 'Give me a day or two. By the way, what are we going to do with this information when we've got it?'

'Go and visit them, of course. Well, you can go to the others, I'll take the one in Oxfordshire.' Margaret Watteau, listening, thinks about her sister, Lesley, who's just had a baby in Hammersmith Hospital, and lies in a thirty-six-bed ward with a sore bottom full of stitches. This will be something to tell Les, to cheer her up, though Les keeps telling her to be careful not to make her laugh. Miss Cressey's on the phone now. Margaret listens intently.

'But could you give me their number, Willow? . . . All right, his

. . . His name and address, then . . . Whereabouts is that, do you know? . . . Okay, there shouldn't be too many Sculls there. One other thing, Willow, how do I know about it?' Miss Cressey laughs then. 'Fine, sounds sensible. Yes, I'll get back to you.'

Margaret starts typing a letter. Matilda bursts out of her room: 'Telephone directories, Margaret?' Margaret points and goes on typing. Miss Cressey frowns. 'This is ridiculous. We must get the office computerized. Get Matthew up here in about half an hour, will you?'

Margaret feels panicky. Computerized? She doesn't know if she could handle that. Before Les had the baby, she'd worked in an office in Acton on an Amstrad with a green screen that hurt her eyes, so she had to get glasses. Margaret feels her own eyes prickle a bit round the edges.

There are two Sculls in the telephone directory with the initial R living in North London. The first is a woman. The second has an answering machine. Matilda leaves a message and both her work and home telephone numbers on it. But it isn't until the evening that Ralph Scull returns her call. Matilda is in bed with William, whose brief exit from her life seems to have rejuvenated him – them – sexually. William is screwing her from behind when the phone rings. After she picks it up, he continues to wiggle his penis inside her, thus making it difficult for her to concentrate on the conversation. However, she does gather that Ralph Scull is adamant that Roman Hall is a den of iniquity, and will write a letter to this effect – also that he never should have got involved with Clare Paynter in the first place. 'Can't trust economists, you know,' he keeps saying, 'they pick figures because they've got no feelings.'

'Who was that?' asks William.

Matilda explains. William is still, thinking. 'You don't fancy him, do you, Tilly?'

'I've never met the man.' Oh God, is William going to get into one of his jealous phases next? He turns her over, wishing to examine the veracity – or lack of it – in her eyes. She smiles peaceably at him. Comforted, he enters her again. Throughout their conjugation, she plots her investigation of Roman Hall.

There are three reasons for Matilda's interest in this project. The first is that whatever Matilda is doing, she always wishes to make a name for herself. When she worked as a journalist, she had a reputation for writing pieces that gave people a completely new angle on something. In 1980 she won the Bowler Prize for journalism – the youngest journalist ever to win it, and only the second woman. Now, in her new job as President of the CCA, she wants to impress upon the world that she, Matilda Cressey, is making something of the office that has not been made before (and will doubtless therefore eventually constitute a reason for the powers that be to close it down). There's a lot of interest these days in alternative medicine. Opposition to it comes mainly from the medical establishment. The lay public's attitude is wishy-washy and ill-informed. Because of her father, Matilda's always had an interest in medical matters and isn't quite as ill-informed as most people. She wants to be a moulder of public opinion, and sees an exposé of the alternative birth movement as a way to do it.

That's the first reason: an entirely serendipitous one. The second reason has something to do with maternalism. Matilda is against children for herself, but not for other people (though her glimpse of the Cornfords' unnamed baby produced a reaction in her which is not quite in line with this position). Thirdly, there is the man himself, the place itself. Matilda's visit to Roman Hall imprinted the place on her mind as the container of almost Gothic secrets; its monolithic vanilla edifice, framed in the evergreen copse, spelt out the fact that things fantastic, bizarre, savage, uncultured, might go on there. The long drive up to the house, the coffee gravel forecourt cluttered with smart cars, the wood, the estate, the fertile trout stream, the village of Micklesham, with its sixteenth-century church – such settings seemed the breeding and hunting ground for murder mysteries, people poisoned with myrrh, dark blood oozing across old stones, blank, mad faces, a medieval world in which spiders dash across the face of the moon, angels burst out of snowclouds, and foxes chew on little children while heartless parents, caught up in their own satanic rituals, watch silently.

Babies. Roman Hall is more than a birthplace for babies, Matilda feels sure of that. Indeed, this must be one of the things that draw people towards it, for what they hope it will do for them is deliver them safely not only of the unborn, but also of other less obvious burdens and constraints. Fetuses are not the most important things holding people back. The weight of the past, which cannot be written on a medical card, does that.

Matilda's imagination folds in on Steven van den Biot as well. Who and what is this man? Where has he come from? Is he satan or saviour? The whole of her patriarchal childhood tells her that men who believe in nature and garden plants instead of medicine and drugs can hardly be benefiting womankind. None the less, her matriarchal infancy, anti-reason, informs her that Steven van den Biot's philosophy antedates the contemporary scientific scene; it's a far older wisdom. But why should Steven van den Biot have anything to do with the knowledge possessed by old women in black, whose longevity draws on their faces lines like furrows in the earth? What is he trying to prove? Since Matilda herself is always trying to prove something, she naturally assumes other people are too.

The moment in the herb garden constantly comes back to her. Against the silver Chelsea sky, between the olive and the monkshood. The woman, in her fur, differing from the sky only in texture and expense. Haughty, with chained boots. Steven van den Biot, distinguished, overcoated, holding out to Matilda his warm hand, reeking of the lavender secreted in a cashmere pocket.

Rita's list has ten names on it. They're all in the south of England, except for one in Glasgow. All were set up in the mid eighties and, under the new system of licensing brought in by Thatcher to encourage private medicine, have been given a free run for five years at a time. Their licences spell out carefully the fact that they are not to meddle in abortion – the only sector of private medicine to contract rather than expand; Conservative MPs nowadays send their mistresses to Normandy instead, and working-class women, starved of the help of the pregnancy advisory charities, wait until later and later to have an NHS abortion, eventually resorting to old dangerous means, or facing another childbirth with less equanimity than other people always imagined they had.

'Well, I don't want to go to Glasgow,' says Matilda, 'I hate the place.'

Rita, thinking greedily of nights in five-star hotels, says, 'We must write a questionnaire.'

'Undoubtedly,' says Matilda, 'only would you know which questions to ask?'

'I know how to put the question and how to get the answer,' says Rita proudly. 'In general, that is. I'll need some help with the medical stuff. But I can easily go back to the contacts we used for the maternity services survey.' Matilda offers her father as well, and they do consult John Cressey about one or two things, but mostly Rita manages efficiently to get the questionnaire done on her own. She takes a train to a two-star hotel in Glasgow; Matilda can be as tightfisted as Dame Ferguson-FitzGerald when she wants. Matilda herself sends to Roman Hall a copy of the letter she and Rita have drafted, explaining to all directors of ABCs that, following a complaint from a client, the CCA is carrying out an investigation of them. An appointment is made for her to visit Roman Hall in early February. She will take Margaret Watteau with her, to keep a record of events. Margaret's very excited about this, as she never did that sort of thing for Dame Ferguson-FitzGerald, and her sister Les, with nothing to do except feed baby Damian all day, is herself feeding hungrily off the news from 88 Juliana Crescent.

Dressing on the morning of the day of Matilda Cressey and Margaret Watteau's visit, Steven van den Biot looks at himself in the eighteenth-century mirror on his bedroom wall. He can admit only to a faint note of unease about the visit. But instead of giving in to his anxieties, he plans the lunch menu – nothing too elaborate, in case suspicions of overcharging are aroused: a large mixed salad, a warm bean soup, partridge pâté, a gooseberry tart. On his way over to the clinic Steven fetches up three bottles of a 1982 Chardonnay, which make him remember Willow Cornford's unpaid bill.

Matilda Cressey arrives armed with a questionnaire and a twittering young assistant dressed in a damson suit of unbelievable awfulness. The assistant keeps looking around her with big eyes, as though she's never had anything to do with birth or medical institutions before (which she hasn't). Matilda herself retains the competent aura Steven discerned among the Chelsea lavender bushes. While she talks in crisp concealing tones from the other side of his desk about the purposes of her investigation, Steven watches the chill opal light falling on her face from the window on his right; he sees Matilda as a figure in a cool Dutch domestic interior, the soft blue of her dress merging with the greys and browns of the room, with the olive grass outside, whence the light comes, picking up some of its verdant colour on the way. Hers is a strong face, with a determined chin, but there are laughter lines around the eyes, even the suggestion of a dimple as she talks. Her straight brown shoulder-length hair is suggestive, in ways Steven finds it hard to define, of a comfortable domesticity. In short, and used as he is to looking at women, he can't recall seeing such a package as Matilda Cressey before. She seems to him in this illuminated moment to represent the unreachable arche-type: a woman of both the female and male worlds, swanning her way between the two with a rare verve and poise. In this he is conscious of reneging on his own background and class. For there are no

Matilda Cressey models lurking there, least of all in the persona of Steven's own dead mother, a woman for whom he feels a prodigious fondness, akin to the swelling and receding of salty tides which move volumes of soggy detritus across otherwise unmarked beaches.

But Matilda Cressey wants to know all sorts of things about Roman Hall: number of births per year, fees asked for and paid; staff on duty, their qualifications; methods practised – their scientific rationale; results, including intervention rates; types of clients, ways solicited; follow-up and/or readmissions; evidence of consumer satisfaction (or otherwise); links with other birth centres; technical facilities and back-up for emergencies; postnatal care – content and duration; profits – how many and to whom; Steven's own background, skills, consultancy work elsewhere? The list, read out from the hard white questionnaire on the soft blue lap, makes Steven's head ache. In the end he interrupts her and Margaret Watteau, surprised, drops her pen, which he then has to retrieve from beneath his desk; handing it to Margaret, he says to Matilda, 'Of course you realize, Miss Cressey, that Roman Hall doesn't operate within the same paradigm that has generated your list of questions? They are irrelevant to us. We do not believe in statistics. We do not handle the currency of such data. Childbirth is not an act amenable to such outcome measures. It is about the soul, the soul of the woman and the man who have made the baby, the baby's soul. Our job at Roman Hall is to reduce the material world, to confine its interruptions to the minimum, so that the birth of the soul may proceed unheeded. By material I include the medical, of course. The finest medicine is no medicine at all: *primo non nocere* – first do no harm, first and last.'

Matilda Cressey tilts that strong chin of hers, and waits a moment before replying. In the meantime, Margaret Watteau's mouth falls unattractively open – what she'll have to tell Les tonight!

'Yes, I thought you might say something of that kind,' responds Matilda at last, 'but all the same, as I'm sure you appreciate, we must have answers to our questions. Roman Hall may be an alternative paradigm, but I am from the nonalternative one. We live in a suspicious world, Dr van den Biot. My purpose in coming here is to be suspicious of you.'

'And I am sure you will do that excellently, Miss Cressey. But before we proceed any further with this dialogue, may I suggest that I show you and your assistant round the clinic? It might help you to gain an idea of what we do here.' He opens the door into the marble corridor for them, and Margaret goes out first, then Matilda, who feels a light touch on her shoulder as she leaves the room; but when she turns back, Dr van den Biot's face registers nothing. Proceeding down the corridor, he opens the doors one by one, doors into Aladdin's caves of colours – red, purple, green, blue – lit by candles, with incense burning and light music. The red and the green rooms are empty, but in the purple one, where Willow Cornford gave birth to little Unnamed One, a woman – a fine black woman with a bush of inky hair – lies on her side, and her partner, a man in a kind of embroidered Moroccan robe, is smoothing an aromatic almond oil over her back. To Margaret Watteau it looks just like her mum basting the turkey at Christmas, spreading melted butter carefully over its raw pink surface, while the Queen talks about her corgies on television. To Matilda Cressey, who also has never seen a labouring woman before but who has different experiences of animality from Margaret Watteau, it looks, simply, like lovemaking. 'We have her consent,' says Steven van den Biot in a low voice. 'She knows who you are and why you're here.' (Which is more than I do, he thinks to himself.)

In the purple room, the stereo that had been so occupied with Anthony Cornford's Bruckner is playing another kind of music now. With a start, Matilda realizes it's the same tape she has in her car, and was listening to the first time she came to Roman Hall: *I'm Your Man*, by Leonard Cohen. Her memory of the words – more of their message than their meaning – makes her dizzy, as does the seductive sonorousness of the voice, the scent of smoky musk, the scene of love, its peace and safety; so that she sways a little and instinctively turns towards Steven van den Biot, who catches and steadies her and closes the door firmly behind them, saying nothing about what might have induced Matilda to behave in such a fashion.

She looks around abruptly. 'Where's Margaret?'

'Margaret?'

'My assistant.'

They find her down the corridor, standing with her face to the wall. 'What's the matter, Margaret?'

'Oh Miss Cressey, I've never seen a thing like that before!'

'Neither have I,' says Matilda. 'But you must pull yourself together, Margaret.' Margaret bites her lip and picks up her notebook. They go to the blue room next, where a birth in the swimming pool is imminent. Margaret is totally overwhelmed by the size of the woman's pregnant abdomen; her mouth gapes again, and she's quite unable to write anything. The husband's in the pool as well, but with his swimming trunks on. As they watch, Karin, the midwife, gets in as well.

'Is this normal?' Matilda finds herself asking.

'Yes, it is normal. Does it disturb you?'

'What happens to the baby? I mean, when it's born in that – swimming pool.'

'It swims.' Steven smiles. 'I can show you a video later, if you like.'

'Well, I'm not sure,' begins Matilda, wanting to see it.

'Whether it's part of your brief? Yes, I do appreciate that.'

They have lunch. Steven introduces Paul Monkton as the man with the statistics. 'Despite what I said earlier, we *are*, as I'm sure you know, obliged to keep a minimal record of the births that happen here. Paul will be happy to show you anything we have this afternoon.'

Margaret gorges herself on the partridge pâté and takes considerable advantage of the Chardonnay as well. Matilda drinks Perrier and watches the oak trees on the lawn swaying in the winter wind, as she herself did some moments ago. She shivers.

'Are you cold, Miss Cressey?'

'No, no. Not at all.'

'Someone walked over your grave?'

She gathers her bag from under the table. 'Perhaps. I think we should get on now, if you don't mind.' The word 'grave' makes her feel she wants to get away from Roman Hall.

In Speedwell Avenue, Acton, Margaret Watteau tells her sister Lesley all about the visit to Roman Hall, with some embellishments to make the story go a little further. Les wants to know about the midwife in the swimming pool and Dr van den Biot. 'Are they having a thing, do you think, Margaret?'

'Well, there were two doctors – himself and another one. And more than one midwife.'

'It must be a peculiar man who wants to get his hands into women and babies,' reflects Lesley, carrying the memory on her body of the junior doctor at Hammersmith Hospital who'd practised needlework on her. 'I mean, what sort of man would that be?'

'I don't know,' admits Margaret, to whom all men are foreigners with funny ways. 'Have some more chips.' She pushes the paper full of chips towards Lesley, who eats them reflectively, nursing Damian on her other arm.

'Is he married, this Dr van den what?'

'Buy-it,' says Margaret authoritatively.

'Well, is he married?'

'I don't know,' says Margaret. 'He's about forty or fifty. Or sixty.'

'He must be married,' decides Lesley. 'Otherwise the women wouldn't trust him.'

'I don't know,' says Margaret again, 'they looked a rum lot to me.'

'Did he talk to you, Margaret?'

'To me? No, why should he? He talked to Miss Cressey.'

'And what did *she* think of him?'

'I don't know, Les, she wouldn't tell *me*, would she?' Margaret takes another chip. On the other hand, Miss Cressey isn't married herself, is she? She has a bloke who phones her up, but Margaret doesn't feel Miss Cressey takes him all that seriously.

Matilda tells William about Roman Hall. He's quite interested in her story; the more offbeat and spooky anything sounds, the more William's mental energy is aroused. As his father often laments, it's only in relation to the ordinary unexceptional but necessary things in life, like earning a living, that William's mental energy lacks the necessary spark.

'Tell you what, Tilly,' says William over cocoa in bed (he's better at cocoa than Chicken Kiev) 'let's go down there one night. I've got a Bull-Nosed Morris in the garage just now that needs a decent run. Let's take it down there after dark and see what we can see.'

'Don't be daft, William. I'm supposed to be carrying out a proper investigation of Roman Hall, not creeping around in the dark.'

'Well, you *are* carrying out a proper investigation. You would be. This is just a bit of extra, off-the-cuff evidence, sort of. Go on, Tilly.' He nudges her so she spills her cocoa on the sheet. 'Go on, it'd be *fun*!'

She moans at him for making her spill her cocoa, which reminds her obdurately of the chocolate body of the woman who'd been listening to Leonard Cohen while her lover stroked almond oil into her back. 'Make love to me, William,' instructs Matilda dreamily, 'it might just about make up for the mess you've made of my bed.'

The Morris whistles down the M40, and Matilda and William have an argument about which tape they should listen to on the way. William absolutely refuses Leonard Cohen. He wants Bach's unaccompanied cello suites instead, but by the time they've stopped jamming one and then the other in the cassette deck, the Bach tape has extruded itself in a worm's mound of unaccompanied plastic, and they're forced to put the radio on instead. Matilda retires into a silent 'I hate William' frenzy, seeing nothing good in him at all. Even his driving makes her feel sick. William despises Matilda for always wanting, and normally getting, her own way. He decides not to speak to her again until she speaks to him.

Which she doesn't do until they're approaching the Micklesham turn. She just says, 'Left here'. William brakes very abruptly, throwing Matilda forward to the dashboard, and smiles with the side of his face she can't see.

It's misty in the village. He puts on the foglights. Matilda, jolted out of her mood by the sudden turn and then by the sight of Roman Hall – visible now in the hollow beyond the marshy meadows, and lit to a pearly glow against the black lace trees – decides to forgive William temporarily, so they can make something of the evening. It is St Valentine's Day, after all.

They dim the lights as they take the approach road to Roman Hall, and park the car off the road well before the driveway starts. 'Just what are we looking for, William?'

'Don't ask me, Tilly. Anything. Come on, we'll have to walk through the wood to the side of the house.'

Is this sensible? Matilda asks herself. They're both wearing jeans and dark jackets; walking hand in hand through the wood, only the sound of denim surfaces brushing against each other counterpoints with the crack of the usual twigs. I mean, I'm a professional woman, goes on Matilda to herself, winner of the Bowler Prize, President of the CCA, daughter of a Kensington GP; who am I, allowing myself to be thus led by a mischievous, irresponsible young man? (William is a year younger than Matilda, and he knows what Matilda thinks about his maturity.)

A kitchen window is slightly open round the back of Roman Hall, and the smell of tandoori chicken creeps past the magnolia, giving it culture shock. Voices are raised above the whirring of domestic machinery, but not enough for William and Matilda to hear what's being said. They bend down and skirt the house. The blinds in what must be the four labour rooms are down. In the blue one the main light is on, and the blind hasn't been properly lowered. William peers through it first. 'Crikey!' (William's language can also be young at times.)

'What is it?'

'I think it's ladies' night,' he says.

Matilda looks next, and for some reason she thinks of mermaids. The pool is full of water, and four women are arranged in it, like fruit slices on a small French tart, hair outspread, feet all pointing to the middle. 'They must be midwives,' whispers Matilda.

'I don't see why. Anyway, what are they doing there?' William tries to get another look; he wants to inspect their lower regions. 'Perhaps they're having a staff meeting?' He giggles. Matilda stuffs a handful of Virginia creeper in his mouth.

She decides they're too close to the house, so they take the path back to the cover of the trees, being careful to avoid the gravel, which would have made an unconscionable noise.

'Come on, Tilly, let's walk round, so we've got a proper view of the back.' The trees shelter them, and are set a sufficient distance away for them to see into the rooms on the middle floor. Most are in darkness, but one on the right captures a moment clearly not intended for the public gaze. It's an examining room of some kind; it looks from this viewpoint much like any standard medical examining room. Steven van den Biot had told Matilda that all the specialist equipment was kept on the first floor, the ground floor where the labouring women and their partners enter being given over wholly to the assumption of normality. There are tubes and pipes and buttons on the wall of this room, and something that could be a locked drug cabinet. Against the wall, too, is an examination couch, high and white. On this lies a naked person, in itself perhaps to be expected, but on top of this naked person is another, of similar kind, who appears to be bouncing up and down on the first like a large white yo-yo.

'I think I've seen enough, William,' says Matilda faintly.

William's eyes would have stood out on stalks had he been able to make them. Then, as they continue to scan the back façade of the house, a door at the bottom opens and a small group of figures comes out of it: a woman in a red robe, steadied on the arm of a man, also in a robe; a second man, more conventionally dressed, holding something wrapped in a cloth in his arms; and, bringing up the rear, a woman in clogs and trousers holding a spade.

'Jesus Christ!'

'We mustn't let them see us.' Matilda moves behind the thick stem of an oak tree, pulling William with her. The procession passes within a few metres of them, and then Matilda is able to decipher the face of Steven van den Biot, but she doesn't recognize the others, and can't see what the other man is carrying. The figures move slowly over to where the lawn becomes earth, and a number of young trees are planted. The woman starts to dig methodically. At the same moment, a bright half-moon escapes from the clouds, and throws the four figures into relief against the garden and the rolling, ebony Cotswold hills. The company begins to chant something, but the words can't be made out – other noises come from the trees and the woods: owls, foxes, rabbits – and the man holding the cloth hands it to the berobed woman, who kisses it and lays it gently in the earth, and the woman with the spade tosses more earth on top of it, like a sandwich.

9
A Baby Called Eve, and Other Stories

The problem with illicitly gathered information is that nothing much can be done with it. But Matilda and William discuss the meaning of the scenes they witnessed at Roman Hall, and the shared secret does at least serve the useful purpose of making them feel one again. William wants to go back and take another look – perhaps the mermaids will still be having their staff meeting? Matilda says no, for a number of reasons. One is her realization that no further progress will be made without the means to make an interpretation of what they've seen.

The following day, she receives in the post the questionnaire she left with Paul Monkton. It's immaculately completed. The other questionnaires, distributed by Rita, are coming in as well, and Roman Hall doesn't seem out of line in any obvious way, except that the fees charged are higher. Matilda spends some hours staring out of the window at 88 Juliana Crescent, puzzling about what to do next. Margaret Watteau brings her many cups of coffee. The cat, Sunny, uses Matilda's introspection to reclaim his run of the place. William keeps phoning her with increasingly wild ideas about black masses and suchlike; he goes off to the House of Commons library – the librarian is an ex-mistress of his father's – to look it all up, which makes his father hope his son's phase of tinkering with cars might at last be over.

Willow Cornford rings and invites Matilda to dinner. 'Do you want to bring William?' she asks. 'I can't remember whether it's off or on at the moment.'

'Well, it's off but on, if you know what I mean. I'll ask him.' William regards dinner parties as anathema and doesn't behave well at them, but Matilda guesses he'll want to come to this one.

Since the village where the Cornfords live isn't far from Roman Hall, Matilda decides to go to the clinic in the afternoon, and then directly to the Cornfords' in her own car, meeting William there. She asks Margaret to telephone Roman Hall and say she'd like to come at two o'clock on the Friday afternoon to check a few details on the questionnaire. Margaret, who hates telephone calls, makes an even worse impression than usual, as it's *him* who answers the phone, and she's developed quite a few . . . well, fantasies . . . about him since her visit, aided by some of the conversations she and Les have been having about doctors and babies and women and so on. Lesley is of the opinion that Dr van den Biot is some sort of charlatan, maybe not even a doctor at all; that Roman Hall's an excuse for him to get his hands on women; that he is, in other words, some kind of sexual pervert. In Lesley's view the midwives are all part of it – they aren't midwives at all, but high-class prostitutes. Probably some of the husbands of the unfortunate women who have babies at Roman Hall use their services. This would explain why the fees there are higher, being as they have to cover both reproductive and sexual services. Lesley is entirely happy with her explanation, but privately Margaret thinks Lesley has a little too much time to fantasize, now she's alone with baby Damian all day. On the other hand, there *is* something odd about the place, and she's seen that look in Miss Cressey's eyes. Miss Cressey is clever, and knows when she's on to something.

A glowing young couple are leaving Roman Hall as Matilda arrives. They climb into a Porsche just like the picture on the brochure, and Karin, the midwife, hands the baby to the mother in the back seat. Matilda's vision of this scene is somewhat clouded with a memory of a half-moon, clogs and a spade.

Dr van den Biot's in his office. 'Good afternoon, Miss Cressey. I was just writing to the laboratory that does our prenatal tests. Your friend, Mrs Cornford – she had one, did she not, that proved to be wrong?'

Matilda nods. 'We've had a couple more since. It's really quite perplexing. And the parents seem so disturbed by it; they worry so much about what is pink and what is blue, and that sort of thing. I wonder how, on an unconscious level, the bonding between mother and child is affected?'

Matilda thinks of Willow, and the sleeping Unnamed One.

'In any case, we must follow it up. What can I do for you today?'

She explains: some details about client–staff ratios. After her initial analysis, Matilda had given all the completed ABC questionnaires to a man in the Department of Health for a medical opinion, and had been told that the perinatal mortality rate at Roman Hall looked as though it might be considerably higher than it ought to be. Babies were dying here.

'Of course,' says Dr van den Biot, when informed of this opinion. 'But Miss Cressey, what the Department of Health doesn't understand is that death is a part of life. Childbirth has always been about tragedy as well as victory. The challenge is to meet the tragedy in the same way as we greet the healthy living baby: with joy and understanding that what was meant to happen has come to pass, and must now be assimilated into the fabric of human experience.' Dr van den Biot, Matilda notices, curls his lips down slightly at the end of these promulgations, as if to indicate that what he's said should be regarded as being wrapped in invisible quotation marks.

'In any case,' he goes on, having not yet addressed the question she's asked him, 'there is an important reason why we may perhaps have more such cases than other places. You see, we believe – *I* believe – that it is *especially* where there are complications – a bad obstetric history, a previous Caesarean, a breech presentation, a very large or a very small baby, twins – it is *especially* in such cases that the mother must be left without interference, so that nature has the biggest chance of doing it right. I hope Dr Monkton gave you what information we do have about the obstetric histories and current pregnancy complications of the women who deliver here?'

Matilda can't remember whether he did or not. She slips her hand into her briefcase to find the form. As she does so, Dr van den Biot gets up from his desk and walks to the window so that his back is towards her, and light streams round the dense contours of his figure with a curious intensity. 'I have something to tell you, Miss Cressey.' He pauses. She waits. 'I wasn't sure whether to tell you or not, but I am not a man to hide things. You are investigating me in more ways than one. I don't know the nature of the complaint made against us, but I can guess. Ralph Scull is a most aggressive man. I do not like aggressive men, particularly not at a birth. Indeed, I am increasingly coming to believe that men have no role at a birth at all. And that includes me, you understand. But the point I am trying to get on to is a different one; it is that I am aware you were here one evening a week ago, and that you may have seen things you did not understand. I should like to help you understand them. However, I do not feel this is the right time and place for that. I should like you to have dinner in my home, where we will have more time and peace to discuss these things. I wonder, could you stay this evening, Miss

Cressey? My housekeeper tells me it's time I had a lady to dinner. Also, she has laid her hands on an excellent pheasant.'

When he swings round to face her, Matilda, desperate to see the expression on his face, finds it quite impervious. She doesn't even know what position his lips adopted during this speech. 'But how do you know', she inquires simply, 'that we – I – was here?'

'I was in Paul Monkton's rooms on the top floor. I saw a car coming from the village which never arrived. And I was puzzled. Cars which come down that road are coming to Roman Hall, and that one didn't. And then later, you walked across the path to the wood and again I was watching, though it was an accident, I was not trying to survey you, I promise. I recognized you by your hair. Not the man, naturally. I take it he's another of your assistants?'

Matilda splutters slightly. 'Yes, that's right, he's an assistant.' (Forgive me, William.)

'So what about tonight, Miss Cressey? Can you stay?'

'I'm afraid not. I have another engagement.'

'With Mr and Mrs Cornford? To see the baby, who must by now have a name, I hope?'

'I don't know. How do you know I'm going to the Cornfords'?'

'I don't know. But it is logical. They live not far away. You work in London. Why not combine the two? Tomorrow, then? Are you free tomorrow? The pheasant won't wait for ever.'

Matilda thinks quickly . . . but she'll have to accept, if only out of curiosity. Curiosity killed the cat. 'Thank you, that would be lovely.'

The baby has been called Eve. Willow appears reconciled, Anthony less so. He confesses he's had to ring a number of preparatory and public schools to remove the name of Maximilian Cornford from the list of putative entrants in the years 2000 and 2005 respectively. A decorator has repainted the nursery primrose yellow. Willow has cracked nipples. On the evening Matilda visits, baby Eve lies in her cradle looking at a mobile of ripe fruit and stars, while real starlight tries its best to twinkle through the window. Anthony has gone out to buy some Perrier water, as Willow refuses to drink anything alcoholic in case baby Eve sees more stars than she ought to.

Matilda tells Willow everything she's learnt about Roman Hall. 'I simply don't know what to think, Willow,' she ends.

'I think you need to find out more about Dr van den Biot.'

Matilda tells her about the invitation. 'But please don't say anything to William. I can't handle the complications. He doesn't own me, does he – I've got a right to my own life, haven't I?'

Willow agrees, thinking how little of her own life there is at the moment. 'I've invited a young midwife from the village and her husband as well tonight,' she tells Matilda, 'she's a great lass. I've got to know her quite well since Eve came, the aftercare at Roman Hall is simply awful. You may pay a fortune to get the baby born, but that's only a small part of the problem. You feel so *abandoned* afterwards.'

Anthony returns with the Perrier and with the midwife, Angela, and her husband, Simon, an engaging youth who runs a second-hand bookshop in the town. William doesn't arrive until after they've started dinner. 'It's not my place to apologize for him,' says Matilda, apologizing. 'He's old enough to do that for himself.' She contains her fury, but William knows he's sitting opposite a volcano. Unfortunately, during the dessert, Willow, whose exhaustion, due to Eve's nightly detours round her nipples, resembles alcoholism in its amnesia, lets slip the fact that Matilda will doubtless have the Truth About Roman Hall Revealed Tomorrow Night.

Matilda coughs.

'Oh, he's invited you to dinner, has he!' exclaims William. 'Will he be wearing his robe, I wonder? And what is underneath it? You'd better be careful the good Dr van den Biot doesn't bury you in the garden, Tilly!'

Angela, who's a sensitive soul, launches helpfully into a story about a local girl who delivered in a cowshed, owing not to her induction into methods of alternative birth but to her utter failure to recognize the signs of labour. 'I don't hold with it myself,' she offers.

'What Angela means,' translates Simon, 'is that she doesn't go much for alternative birth. Of course she believes childbirth is a natural process, but that's different.'

'It is indeed,' takes up Angela. 'I mean, what's normal about having a baby in a paddling pool? Poor wee mites. And placenta stew, now what could be more disgusting than that!'

'Placenta stew?' William's spoonful of chocolate mousse stops halfway to his mouth.

'You cook it with carrots and onions and bay leaves.'

'What's the point of that?'

'It's got hormones in it', explains Angela, 'that the mother needs.'

A thin wail from upstairs signals Eve's need for her mother. Willow gives her to Anthony while she goes to wash something off her nipples which she puts on them to make them less sore.

'Women in California put it in the freezer and slice it, like liver,' continues Angela. 'They eat a bit every day till it's all gone; it's supposed to help with postnatal depression.'

William gulps.

'I think that's enough, Angela,' says Simon protectively.

Eve has her feed and the others have some Calvados, except for Willow, who has a cup of jasmine tea. Angela, Willow and Anthony offer to help in any way they can with the Roman Hall investigation. Matilda is glad William and she came in two separate cars; as they stand in the black lane with the lights of the Cornfords' cottage making squares on the grass, she suggests, just before William is about to, that they'd better go their own ways tonight. 'And tomorrow night as well,' adds William, 'and all the other nights too, don't you think?' His childish fury roars into the distance while Matilda is still fumbling with her seat belt.

Steven van den Biot cancels dinner with Claudia Foxman in order to have it with Matilda Cressey. 'An obstructed labour,' explains the man who never hides anything. An obstetrician has a veritable jungle of excuses at his fingertips. On this occasion, however, Claudia is sympathetic, as John Dominic has been having a bout of colic and she's tired anyway.

At 3.05 Steven sees a little blonde baby into the cushions in the green room. The baby has a large birthmark on its cheek. Steven holds it; smoothes the dark red mark, in the shape of a fig leaf, with his finger, indicating to the parents that it's nothing to be ashamed of. It is to be accepted, along with the rest of the baby; the baby doesn't know it has a birthmark, it's the same as any other baby with the same need for love, warmth and nourishment. The parents cry and are grateful. The mother has a labial tear, and Steven tells her Mary Elliott will fix it, she's a far better seamstress than he is.

When he gets back to his house there's a call from his agent on the answering machine: the Japanese want to translate *Herbal Childbirth*. How bizarre, thinks Steven, don't the Japanese have their own traditional way of doing things? What could they possibly learn from a few recovered memories of the West? He rings Allan back and says yes, fine, go ahead. Then he puts on his tracksuit and does an evening tour of the estate to replace the morning one he missed. During it, he notes the returning swallows in the oak trees, the pale sun dropping in the sky.

At five o'clock he falls into a deep bath. His back aches. He's a little hot and bothered, not by the exercise only, but by Matilda Cressey's impending visit. When he gets out of the bath, he puts through a call to Jung, the clinic acupuncturist who also does massage. She's over in ten minutes. He lies down on his hard bed, and she gets to work with confident strokes of her small brown hands. They chat about this and that. Jung likes doing massages for Steven van den Biot; he has a good body, he looks after it, and she feels she's able to help him relax in places and ways that otherwise he wouldn't.

Afterwards, Steven sits in his Charles Eames chair and has his usual whisky. Tonight's an important occasion, he needs to get it right. His reputation, the reputation of Roman Hall, is at stake: and also something else, perhaps. But that's the very thing he's afraid of. Talking of love and nature and closeness all the time, he eschews these things for himself. Those who facilitate do not partake. Charisma depends on distance. But love is the beast that chains one up, roars in the night, pounces with its great black paws even when there's no warning sign on the gate; tears at souls like pieces of meat, scattering scarred coagulated flesh in gutters, along with the debris of smashed bottles and rancid orange peel and odd socks and stinking spermatic condoms and a child's broken clown, where a jagged spring takes the place of a painted face and the red china lips are long gone, chased by acidic rainwater far down into the city's sewers.

Matilda Cressey smells of the night. Her coat carries the fine February drizzle that lies all over the Cotswold hills at this time of year, and the fibres of her navy wool dress seem to have woodsmoke on them. Steven and Matilda smile awkwardly at one another. She admires his carefully built and well-tended house, especially the comfortable dining room, and the view down to the stream with the old bridge beyond leading off into the figuratively dreaming distance.

'I was afraid you would think, if I showed you my house,' he begins ingenuously, 'that I was making too much money out of the clinic.'

'Why shouldn't you make a decent living?' Matilda crosses her long slender legs. He sees she's wearing high-heeled shoes and, further up, a small camomile butterfly brooch. 'I don't exactly live in poverty myself.'

'Where *do* you live, Miss Cressey?'

'I know we are in a professional relationship,' she says, 'but I

should like you to call me Matilda. I will call you Steven, Steven.'
She laughs and puts her head on one side. 'I have a flat in Notting
Hill. What they call a garden flat, though God knows why, because
it's got no garden at all. It has a small patio. I keep geraniums and
tomatoes on it in the summer. It's a nice flat, one very big room with
a kitchen alcove, two other rooms – one I use as a study. Nothing like
this, of course. The only problem with it is you can hear everything
that goes on above. I'm used to that, though. There's an antique
dealer with regular habits up there. I even know when he goes to the
lavatory, I can hear him unzipping his flies!' She laughs again,
amused at her own brazenness.

'And you live alone, like me?'

'Yes,' she says, for the sake of simplicity.

'Why are you so interested in Roman Hall, Matilda?'

'It's my job.'

'Yes, but why?'

'I don't know,' she answers. 'I actually don't know. What *are* you
doing in it, Steven?'

'Helping women to have babies as nature intended.'

She makes a gesture of impatience. 'Yes, but what else?'

'What else do you want me to say?'

He leans forward and pours a little more of the dry martini cocktail
he's mixed into her glass. 'Roman Hall is like any other place where
people work and live and have their being, and get on with one
another – or don't. No, perhaps it isn't quite as ordinary as that. I
believe that birth, the awareness of birth, heightens these things. But
perhaps it would help me to answer you, Matilda, if you were to tell
me what you suspect *is* going on here.'

She hesitates. 'Some of your practices are unusual.'

'Certainly.'

'For instance, is it customary for the staff to have to . . .' she
searches for the word . . .

He waits.

'I've heard it said', she continues finally, 'that sex is recommended
in some places as an aid to childbirth.'

'Some of the women suggest that,' he agrees, 'but the men do not
like performing on demand. In my experience, that is.'

'And the staff?'

'I have never made love to a client,' he says stiffly.

'I wasn't suggesting . . .'

'Oh, I think you were.'

'What were you burying in the garden that night, Steven?' she asks.

'You thought it was a child, didn't you? A dead child. Some kind of sacrifice or whatever.'

'Was it?'

'Of course not. There's an old custom that the placenta is the twin of the newborn child, so if you want the child to do well, you must treat the placenta with respect. At Roman Hall we offer our garden for this purpose as a resting place, to those who want it. As you've probably noticed, we have a number of young trees. I had them planted when I came here. Placental tissue is an excellent fertilizer. I am even thinking of growing grapes. That's all it was, Matilda, I promise.'

Matilda feels relieved. She realizes she doesn't now want to believe ill of Steven van den Biot, though she had done.

'Shall we eat? I would like to talk to you some more about all of this.'

Over dinner, he tells her of his philosophy of health, of his vision of the union of body and spirit, of how emotional wellbeing, encouraged by caresses of every kind, can so inspire the immune system and the hormone-producing organs of the body that it functions harmoniously even, or especially, in the act of reproduction. He tells her of how allopathic medicine views the body as a machine without a soul (Matilda thinks of William's convertibles; she's sure he thinks of them as souls). The result of this mechanical view is the doctor as repair man, with toolkit and fluids in cans and a whole language of mystifying technical terms. 'I do not see myself as a mechanic,' pronounces Steven, 'but as a guide. I like to show people their way round their own bodies, which is, of course, even more necessary in the case of childbirth, as the woman's body isn't a broken-down car but a smoothly running one that will stay on the road provided nothing gets in its way. The aim of childbirth, we have to remember, is not the cure of symptoms, but the production of a person in a state of love, which is only another word for health.' Though his lips curl characteristically with these pronouncements, somehow this habit of his isn't in the least disturbing any more.

She stares at him. The candle in its turquoise glass holder flickers above the water round its base, showing the contours of the bubbles in its rough glass sides. Matilda traces the exterior smoothness of the glass with her fingers. She sees the midwives floating like mermaids, and she sees the two white figures in the upstairs room. 'And do *you* love, Steven?'

'My work,' he replies. 'I love my work. Naturally. I can think of no finer occupation. Which is why . . .' (he's leading her skilfully away from the question again) '. . . which is why I do not want this investigation of yours to result in discredit for Roman Hall. I do not expect approbation. Innovators – or recoverers – of tradition, which is what I am, never get that in their lifetime. I simply want to be left alone to get on with my work.'

Matilda remembers another of her objections. 'Why charge for your services? Why don't you work within the health service? Wouldn't that be better? Wouldn't you reach more people that way?'

'State medical systems have an inbuilt resistance to new ideas. The structure is anti-innovation. The objectives are always historical: we haven't done this before, why should we now? It shouldn't be like that, but it is. I should like to bring about a revolution in the NHS. Many people would. When I was a young doctor I was really committed to the health service. But I think, in order to change things within it, you have to change things outside it first. Are you persuaded yet, Matilda Cressey? I see you are beginning to be. Have some more salad. There are raspberries next. Or some cheese, if you prefer. I have a particularly nice Stilton.'

'Could we go for a walk, Steven? I feel like some air.' He looks at her shoes. 'I've got some boots in the car.'

They walk the route that's familiar to Steven: by the river, over the bridge, skirting the wood on the other side. A low crumbling wall divides one field from another, and a plant like holly, but with small smooth pointed leaves, grows out of the wall, its berries blood-red in the full light from the moon and the house, over the water.

'If I tried to prick my finger on those,' says Matilda, 'I couldn't; I could try and try, but the leaves would only bend and the winter sap would stain my finger. But the berries are menacing somehow. Or inviting. I don't know which.' She plays with them, moving them from side to side like toys.

'Cotoneaster,' says Steven. 'That's what they're called.' He looks past her into the night full of ravens and foxes and nightmares in cold bedrooms. 'And they're the same in French, did you know that?'

These two, Matilda Cressey and Steven van den Biot, are in a moment of juxtaposition, with the compass of the horoscope pointing in the same direction. He could touch her or she him. They could fall into either a squalid or a luxurious passion, for they both hear the woods rustling hopefully behind them, the owls calling with a kind of invitation; they see the water with the trout in it catching and bending their faces, willing to carry them with it over stones and hills to the wide salty sea.

'I shall not make love to you, Matilda Cressey,' he says then, as a squirrel moves in a treehole, and a few metres from where they stand a vixen comes home to its mate. 'I shall not make love to you, because I do not make love to women.'

She puts a hand on his arm. 'How can you know now what you'll do with me, Steven? This isn't the NHS. Innovations happen, remember?'

With the windows wide open to the answering night, Steven van den Biot sleeps without moving in the paisley bed. The air breathes cold on his chest, which rises and falls with contractions of his heart and lungs as involuntary as those of labouring women's uteruses, but in a deeper and slower rhythm now, as his brain waves move him into a different and older consciousness.

Half a century ago in Whitechapel Road. The street market: vegetables, clocks, cotton aprons, cheap tin pans. Bustle and smell on a bright morning. The young Steven with his older sister, Lisa, put resentfully in charge of him, pulling him along by the hand, her other hand tightly holding a fistful of pennies. Lisa is seven, Steven three. There are four others: two between, two after. Steven's father has a stall in the market selling jewellery exchanged for other favours in a pub in Limehouse. Steven's mother cleans houses when she isn't having babies, and even when she is. 'Come on, Stevie, can't yer walk faster'n that?' Lisa's impatience drags him on so that he falls, cutting both legs on a pile of broken glass – regularly to be found outside the Three Horses public house. He bawls, Lisa chides: 'Shut yer mouth, Stevie, it don't hurt that much.' But it does. His knees hurt, he hurts, he hates being dragged around by Lisa, he wants his mum. And then an angel from heaven descends, a perfumed lady in a fox fur who, coming along on her way back from a charitable meeting at the London Hospital, with its big clock across the street, is thinking of stories of the street market to tell her city husband, and notices the little boy with the clump of dark hair and the dirty clothes and bleeding knees and picks him up, and carries him off to the hospital, where they tend to him. The lady buys him sweets and gives Lisa

75

money – she gave Lisa sweets at first, but Lisa, true child of her mother, asked if she could have money instead.

The lady seems to have come from another planet. Steven has never seen one like her before. He's struck especially by the skin on her hands, which are soft as cotton wool when she touches him: his own mother's resemble sandpaper. And the scent of the lady's hair and her cheeks in the fruity draught of the street market: the smell of other, better places he's never been, and can scarcely imagine.

A light wind blows from the trees, and Steven, forty-seven years later, stirs, his body reacting to the memory of such consoling femaleness: sight, sound, texture, touch. He aches for the lady. Even now he aches.

The first memories are the easy ones.

Early in March Matilda Cressey pulls her *Guardian* through the narrow slit in her front door, opens it, and sees the face of Steven van den Biot looking at her.

She reads with growing alarm:

> The development outside the NHS which Mrs Thatcher most approves of is private maternity care. A number of 'Alternative Birth Centres' have sprung up across the country in recent years. One of these, Roman Hall in Oxfordshire, is run by Dr Steven van den Biot, the prophet of the alternative birth movement. According to information made available to the *Guardian* recently, Dr van den Biot's clinic is currently under investigation by the Council for Consumer Affairs, now under the direction of a new President, ex-journalist Matilda Cressey. There have been complaints about the standard of care provided in Dr van den Biot's clinic. Dr van den Biot was not available for comment last night. (See leading article, page 16.)

Matilda turns to this. The column is headed: 'The Politics of Health Care: what does money buy?' Most of it is an attack on private medicine, arguing that the control exercised by the state and the lay public over medical standards is inevitably laxer in the private sphere. The last few paragraphs launch into 'faddism' in the alternative birth movement, bemoaning the fact that birth underwater might be throwing the baby out with it, as the gains in safety of the past half-century are likely to be jeopardized by the demands of women (and, by implication, the pockets of people like Dr van den Biot) that a good experience is better than a healthy outcome. 'Women must understand', preaches the *Guardian*, following the rampant rediscovered sexism of the early nineties, 'that NHS obstetricians are acting in, not against, their interests. The charisma of men like van den Biot should not mislead them into thinking an aesthetic birth is to be preferred to a scientific one.'

Matilda chews her toast and marmalade thoughtfully. She definitely does not like seeing, in black and white, herself and Steven van den Biot placed on opposite sides of the fence. The news item is written by someone she knows – Susan Harris, a medical journalist. Matilda presumes she's gathered her information from Ralph Scull.

At the office she's met by Mrs Trancer, who says, companionably, 'Your mum phoned.'

'Oh.' Matilda's surprised. 'I didn't know you answered the phone.'

'Oh yes, duckie. Well, someone's got to take them early calls! Better phone her back, duckie.'

Matilda's mother wants to know who 'that dreadful woman' was, and to invite Matilda to dinner. Matilda calls Steven next: 'What are you going to do about it, Steven? The *Guardian* piece, I mean?'

'Nothing. It'll blow over.' He laughs. 'Depending on what *you* do next, Matilda, of course!'

'Can we meet?' she asks suddenly.

'Yes, but I wouldn't tell the *Guardian*!'

Margaret Watteau, measuring out the coffee, hears this conversation. Her sister Lesley, plotting in the long afternoons in Acton, has already decided that Matilda Cressey and Steven van den Biot will fall in love. This will kill a number of birds with one stone. First, Miss Cressey will be able to have a baby (Les doesn't like to think of any woman escaping her own fate). Second, Dr van den Biot will be put on the straight and narrow – no thwarted passions there any more (assuming there are some now). Third, Margaret will be invited to the wedding, and she, Les, will get to hear all about it. As his mother plans Matilda Cressey and Steven van den Biot's futures, baby Damian is rocked enthusiastically, eventually throwing up in quiet desperation on her shoulder as the only way he has of drawing attention to his own needs.

After his brief conversation with Matilda, Steven van den Biot leaves Roman Hall. He gets in his car and drives very quickly to London, to the East End, parking in a small street lined with wholesale dress shops. Rails of polyester and Crimplene wave in the thin March wind; vans load and unload on double yellow lines between the marches of traffic wardens. Steven's target is a door of bright blue flaking paint between two dress shops. He inserts a key, first ringing the doorbell lightly twice.

She's waiting for him in the front room on the first floor. There's a divan bed in the corner. He takes his clothes off, folding them neatly. She pulls back the cover, takes one look at him, and leaves the room for a few minutes. She comes back in a peach silk slip with guipure lace at the yoke. Its rich folds provide an odd contrast with the doughlike white of her body, which hasn't seen the sun for years.

'Janey,' he says with closed eyes, lying on the divan. 'Janey.' It's an old refrain.

'Yes, my love, I'm here.' She leans over him. He puts out his hand. She knows what he wants.

With shut eyes still, he lets his fingers slide over the silk cups of her breasts, saying nothing. Janey watches him with fondness, with a familiar wisdom. After a while she pulls the slip over her head and leans over him again, and Steven's mouth closes round the pink nipple as she reaches down and takes his erection, already streaming at the tip, in her hand.

She knows he's been waiting for her, only her, amid his frustrated dreams of fox fur and perfume and soft, soft hands. She knows she's the only one he can have. Mother, madonna, whore . . . he moans gently, and puts his hand between her thighs. 'Cunt,' she says, 'cunt,' and falls on top of him, her white flesh fitting over his like the lid of a pie, between them his hard hot penis which she rolls against her stomach until he says, 'Janey, please!' and then she moves and slips it inside her and moves a couple of times more and then stops and he cries out, 'No, go on!' 'I will,' she says. 'But Janey must have her pleasure first, you know that, don't you? Janey has to come first!' Riding high, she clenches the muscles of her vagina and climaxes, and he, underneath her, is forced to contain himself. 'That's good,' she says, 'and now I think we ought to let you come.' Knowing him well after all these years, twenty-five years of fucking in the room between the dress shops in Whitechapel, she watches his clever, confused, intelligent face, and moves slowly and then faster until he cries and lets go of her breast and shoots himself into her manfully, the way he did long ago.

★ ★ ★

78

In the hothouse at Kew Gardens the orchids are in bloom. It's so hot that no one stays long. Matilda and Steven take their coats off.

'You realize you can stop it, don't you?' he points out.

She thinks he means whatever hasn't yet started between them. In the humid air she feels incapable, weak. 'Can I?'

He sees her mistake. 'The media attention,' he explains, 'the publicity. Write your report, clear Roman Hall. Say whatever you like, make whatever left-wing points you want to make about private maternity care, but let me off the hook. I'm not worth punishing,' he ends with feeling.

'What has been started must be continued,' she says sharply, reacting against his perception of her mistake.

'Naturally. But think, Matilda, what good will it do?'

Love or persecution, she wonders, which does he mean? Putting things right: am I a designer of justice, or is this only an illusion? Matilda the Great – William's name for her. Her fingers scrabble around a little in the soil of the orchid plants, burying William. Love, everyone's salvation. Except those who don't allow themselves to have it. The lemon and ochre flowers wave their stamens at her. 'If I do what you say, what then?'

'Then we are free,' he says.

'We are never free.'

'Free of the past,' he replies. 'That's the main thing.'

'But I care about the future,' she says in return, 'don't you?'

'Not much. I've never had a future because I've always had too much of a past. I want to tell you about my past, Matilda: it's time for the past now.'

10
Revenge

'When I got to work about 9.15 – it was raining, the buses are always late then – he was just sitting there,' says Margaret Watteau to her sister, Lesley. 'This man, with hair sort of standing on end, there he was at Miss Cressey's desk. I can tell you, Les, I didn't know what to do. I don't even know', she muses, 'how he got in. I mean we all have keys, but . . .'

'Well, who was he, Maggie?' Lesley is tired; Damian's got a cold, his snuffling kept her up all night.

'Her bloke, Miss Cressey's bloke. I think they've had another row, he hasn't been ringing lately. And then I went downstairs to get Sunny's Whiskas and I heard the phone ring in Miss Cressey's room, Mrs T started to go up there to answer it, and I told her no, but it was still switched through you see, this new system we have . . .'

'Yes, yes, Maggie, get on with it,' says Lesley impatiently.

'Well, *he* answered it. Her bloke, I mean. And I think it was that Dr Buy-it.'

'How do you know?'

'When Miss Cressey came in about half-past nine, he was still there and they had a shouting match.'

'That's better. And?'

'I shouldn't really be telling you all this, Les.'

'It's a bit late for that, isn't it, Maggie!'

'I couldn't hear all of it, of course,' attempts Margaret.

'Tell us what you *did* hear, not what you didn't.'

'Miss Cressey called him some names. You should've heard her language, Les! He said something about talking to her fancy man. She was really riled at that. Told him he'd no business to be interfering in her professional life. He didn't . . . well . . . agree with that. He called *her* names then. I didn't know what to do, Les, whether I should take them in coffee, or what. And then Matthew came up, he said I need to see Miss Cressey urgently, but you could hear their voices all over the building. He didn't approve, Matthew didn't. Not of mixing work and private life. Well, I didn't, either. I suppose it's not her fault, but . . .'

'And then what happened?'

'He threw the laptop at her.'

'The what?'

'The laptop. Oh, you know, Les, the new computer. Miss Cressey ordered one for each of us. They're called laptops because they sit on your lap, though they don't actually, they sit on the desk . . .'

'You should go and have your eyes tested, Maggie,' instructs Lesley, remembering the effects of her own close encounters with an Amstrad in Acton. 'I told you that before, didn't I?'

'Yes, Les, I will, I promise.'

'And then what happened?'

'He came out, Miss Cressey's bloke came out, looking like thunder, and banged right past me and poor Sunny eating his Whiskas and she, Miss Cressey, was chasing him with the laptop, she'd picked it up, it looked a bit mangled, she was screaming, really worked up, she said, "Go on, William" – I suppose that must be his name – "go and stuff reconstituted chicken up your arse, all you're good for is screwing cars."' Margaret pronounces these words with extreme care and the kind of intonation one would give a Beatrix Potter book. 'She was like a wild animal, Les. And then after she realized he'd gone she sort of kicked out, she was that angry, she got Sunny's tail and he leapt at her, you know he can be quite a vicious character, it comes of having been . . . well . . . *altered*, and then the phone rings and it's the *Guardian* and then all morning it's one newspaper after the other. They want to speak to Miss Cressey, and I keep saying she's not available at the moment, she's in a meeting, she's out at lunch, and Miss Cressey's locked herself in her office and won't speak to anyone, and Matthew – I'm not sure he likes Miss Cressey anyway – he said we should phone Mr Newfield, in the Home Office, he's the man that gives us our money, you know, Les, and Rita Ploughman, she phones in and says she's ill, that doesn't help . . . I feel quite knackered, Les,' she ends breathlessly.

'You know what, Maggie, you should ask for a rise.'

'What for?'

'Extra responsibility. With all this shemozzle. Well, you do have it, don't you?'

'I suppose I do,' says Margaret, shifting with more than usual boldness in her seat.

Matilda telephones Willow Cornford. Baby Eve is wailing at the other end of the phone; Matilda shouts above it: 'Willow! I need to ask you a favour!'

'Hold on, Tilly, I'll go and put crybaby in the other room. That's better. Now, what did you say?'

'A favour, Willow.' Matilda's voice is strained.

'Are you all right, Tilly?'

'Not really, no. But listen, here's the favour: could I come and stay with you for a few days? I need to get some work done and I can't do it here.'

'Of course you can. You can have crybaby's room. She's still sleeping with us, unfortunately. What's the matter, Tilly?'

'Oh, I've had another row with William. Rather a bad one. And I've got to write this report on ABCs. I've got a deadline and I'm panicking about it rather.'

Matilda packs the Renault 5 with files and memos, Steven van den Biot's books, her walkperson, a bottle of Cognac (covered with an old blanket). Following Steven's revelations in the orchid house, the two of them have agreed not to meet for a while. Matilda must write her report, come to her own conclusions without being influenced by him. But after she's finished her report, and whatever she decides to say in it, will she come away with him somewhere? She'll think about it. No she won't, she'll say yes or no now! She says yes.

The day is spring-like, holes in the ozone layer encouraging holes in the earth to exude hardy lime-green shoots angled towards a palely luminescent sky. The land is wrapped in mist like clingfilm.

Willow is welcoming. 'It'll be great to have someone to talk to!'

'I've come to *work*, Willow.'

'Yes, yes, I know. Here's your room. I've moved some of Eve's stuff out, but I'm afraid you'll have to live with the rest.'

A citron cave under the eaves. Matilda installs her files and papers next to the gripe water and the castor oil cream. 'Is there somewhere locally I could get this fixed?' She holds up the Zenith X-1200. 'William threw it at me.'

'Come downstairs and have a cup of tea, Tilly, and tell me all about it.'

The tea and the company settle Matilda down. Anthony, who

knows about computers, will look at hers this evening. Why don't Matilda and Willow go for a walk, Matilda can use the time to think things over, work out what to put in her report? Willow needs some air, she hardly gets out of the house these days.

'The problem is this, Willow.' Matilda strides fast across the muddy footpath ahead of her friend, who is encumbered with baby Eve strapped to her chest in a pink canvas parcel. 'Well, leaving William aside, there are two problems really. One is what exactly *is* Roman Hall? What kind of place is it? The second problem is, what should I say about it?'

'I don't understand why there are *two* problems. If you know the truth, you tell it. You're not suggesting there's a case for doing a cover-up job, I hope?'

'I don't know. I can convince myself either way. Steven – Dr van den Biot – says his work can't be evaluated in the normal way. That it's such a different way of doing things, it's not fair to apply the usual rules to it. I can see what he means. Take death, for instance: whatever we do, whatever doctors do, death will always happen. Perhaps some babies aren't meant to live. What do you think, Willow?'

'Is that what he told you when you went to dinner with him?' Willow looks at Matilda curiously from behind her stream of bright hair, now divided by the wind. 'What else did he say? What else happened?'

Matilda wants to tell Willow about her private conversations with Steven, but something holds her back.

Willow feels baby Eve crushed between her breasts, warm, breathing, finally loved. 'Primary maternal preoccupation,' she says suddenly.

'What?'

'That's the technical name for the state I'm in. I love this baby, Tilly. I can't really think about anything else. You can't ask me questions about death now. I don't know how to answer. It wouldn't be me answering, it'd be this mother person.'

'Okay. But you understand what I'm saying? I do see what he means. On the other hand, I feel I *ought* to be suspicious; people are telling me I should be, it's my job. Did you read that piece in the *Guardian*? There was a piece about Roman Hall, and a leader as well. I know the journalist who wrote it. I rang her up. She's quite sure there's something fishy going on there. Well, perhaps not fishy, but she told me that a lot of people have told her – people who ought to know – that what they do at Roman Hall isn't good medicine. They take risks when they shouldn't. I don't want to make a mistake, Willow. But how am I to decide what the mistake would be?'

The two women reach a clearing on the top of a small hill. Below them lie patchwork squares of fields. The countryside seems to be waiting for something. Baby Eve snores gently, her button nose pushed against her mother's coat. A dog barks across the fields, birds fly over still-wintry trees. Matilda breathes deeply, feels more relaxed. This state of nature washes over her, soaks her up into its hypnotic lassitude, impressing her with a sense of moral duty to the primeval world. 'A woman must do what a woman must do, Willow,' she says resolutely. 'Come on, let's go back. I want to get down to work.'

Over the next few days the report is written, and Matilda isn't displeased with it. She asks Rita Ploughman to come down from London to go through it with her. Rita, glad of the trip, takes the opportunity to have a look at Roman Hall on the way; hers is another car Steven van den Biot sees making an approach that never culminates in an arrival.

Steven is distracted these days. He walks a lot, listens to music, tries to keep away from the clinic. He uses as an excuse the fact that he's correcting the proofs of his latest book, *Mother Nature*. It's not even that he feels especially anxious about the text of Matilda's report. No, the real watershed is within himself. Can he afford to let go of the past? Does he want to? By comparison, the dilemmas Matilda Cressey might be experiencing don't seem tortuous to him at all. She comes down one side of the fence, or the other; or maybe decides to sit there, one leg dangling each side. Whichever way it turns out, her soul is not involved.

Two events interrupt Steven's private agitations. One: he receives a letter from Ralph Scull's solicitor warning him that Mr Scull intends to take action against him for unprofessional conduct; the charges are living off immoral earnings and practising incompetent obstetrics. It's not clear whether these two charges are the same or not. Steven crumples the letter up and drops it into the wastepaper basket. Mr Scull is a nuisance, but enraged hysterics are unlikely to carry through their threats.

Two: Claudia Foxman turns up wild-eyed one night, without John Dominic. Steven is at first quite unable to make sense of what she's saying. When he's turned off the music and given her a box of tissues and a brandy, it transpires that she thinks Lord Foxman has given her AIDS – which, moreover, he got from Nanny Pilkington. Has

Nanny Pilkington given it to John Dominic? Despite Steven's protestations that all these things are most unlikely, Claudia is beside
herself: 'Help me, Steven, you must help me!'

It's not the first time, nor will it be the last, that he's heard these
words. 'What do you want me to do?'

She weeps noisily on to the rich blue carpet.

'If you like we can do blood tests in the morning for you and the
baby. We'll need to repeat them in a couple of months, but I really
don't think you need to worry.'

'I'm so *tired*,' she wails, 'I'm so *tired*, Steven, so *tired* of it all – the
pain, the having to cope alone. Give me another brandy, will you?'
She swallows it fast, leans back, looks at him. 'Oh Steven, everything
is so *simple* for you, isn't it?'

'Appearances deceive,' he responds gravely.

A new thought occurs to her. 'What about breastmilk?'

'What about it?'

'The AIDS virus. Is it in breastmilk?'

'I don't know,' he says.

'But you're a doctor!'

'So?'

'Tell me the truth!'

'I have. Actually, no one knows. You shouldn't expect doctors to
know everything, Claudia.'

This infuriates her. She reaches for the brandy bottle, fills her glass
again. He realizes she was probably half-saturated before she got
here. 'You're not much help,' she says angrily.

'I'm sorry, Claudia. I'm not very good at situations like this.'

'No,' she says bitterly. 'You probably have to stage them yourself,
don't you? Despite all those things you say in your books about
letting nature take its course. Well, this is nature taking its course,
Steven, can't you do anything to help it? I tell you what . . .' (she's
seen from his face that he is about to make some further unhelpful
remark) '. . . I tell you what, why don't you try it? Try it, and see if
it's contaminated or not!' Shrieking, she unfastens her cream silk
blouse – a button falls on to the navy carpet and winks like a pearl at
the bottom of the deep blue sea – and pulls out a breast, taking the
area round the nipple in her hand and squeezing it till a fountain of
milk squirts out, falling to join the pearl on the carpet. Then she gets
hold of Steven's hair, pulls his face towards her so he gets milk up his
nose and in his eyes, and forces his mouth on to her nipple. He gives
it a perfunctory lick, like an ice cream, and tries to recover both their

dignities by pulling away from her, standing up and saying things like 'Now, Claudia, that won't help,' and 'How about some coffee?' or 'You'll feel better in the morning.'

In the morning, when Claudia Foxman wakes on the sofa in Steven van den Biot's sitting room, with its view of light over the trout stream, she doesn't feel better at all. Through the fog of her headache, her breasts, crammed with milk, bring to mind the forsaken John Dominic, and though she can't remember exactly what happened last night between herself and Steven van den Biot, she knows the most important thing, which is that it constituted a rejection of some kind. She wanted him to take her in his arms and to his bed and comfort her, instead of which he dosed her with brandy and left her alone to sleep it off on the sofa.

Claudia goes home, feeds John Dominic, showers and puts on a red Jaeger suit. Then she telephones Paul Monkton at Roman Hall and, leaving John Dominic with a girl from the village, sets off to seek her revenge.

'Lady Foxman is here,' announces Karin. Paul is in the common room with a salesperson from the Happy Birthday Company. The salesperson's briefcase is full of illustrated colour leaflets depicting their latest birthing chair, made of a new kind of glowing dark-yellow plastic intended to resemble pine. 'But much more hygienic,' says the salesperson, as instructed. 'And very reasonable cost-wise, Dr Monkton. I don't think you'll find any similar equipment on the market in this price range at all.'

'I suppose your company knows about the latest evidence on birth chairs?'

'What would that be, Doctor?'

'They're associated with a definite prolongation of labour time, and no decrease in perineal damage, contrary to what this leaflet of yours claims.'

The Happy Birthday salesperson hasn't been warned of this, and is at a loss to know how to respond. He only took this job because he couldn't get one selling elevators.

'But thank you for coming in today. We'll have to think about your plastic pine chair. Now, if you'll excuse me, I have another appointment.'

Dismissed by Paul Monkton's crisp tones, the salesperson creeps down the stairs, crossing Claudia Foxman on her way up.

She looks like an angry tigress. 'Dr Monkton, I want to talk to you confidentially.' Claudia looks round the room for signs of unconfidentiality – microphones, cameras, doors that might open and admit Steven van den Biot.

'Go ahead.'

'Dr van den Biot told you that I'd thought of giving Roman Hall some money for a programme of research into the development of the babies delivered here?'

Paul says Steven had told him something rather different.

'Why didn't he tell you the truth?'

'I can think of a few reasons.'

'Tell me!'

'I'm not sure I should.'

'In that case,' says Claudia, 'let *me* tell *you* that I wanted to ask *your* advice about what *you* think the money would best be spent on. On the assumption that I do decide to give it, of course.'

Paul Monkton leans back in his chair, extends his brown corduroy legs beneath the handsome oak table, flips a lock of errant hair back so that his blue eyes, cloudless as a baby's, can look straight into those of Claudia Foxman. 'You want my opinion, Lady Foxman?'

'I do.'

'My opinion is that it's time to carry out a scientific evaluation of the work we are doing here.' He pauses.

'Exactly.'

'You will know, I expect, that we have come in for a certain amount of criticism in the press recently. Those rumours can be scotched only by systematic, careful work – the presentation of statistics as well as, perhaps, a longitudinal study of the babies born here.'

'Do you think Dr van den Biot's practices are unsafe?'

'That's a loaded question. Let's just say I'm sceptical of everything until I have reason not to be.'

They smile at each other, feeling they've reached a certain agreement. 'But what about the herbs?'

'What about them? I expect we can fit them in somewhere,' he says.

'Dr Monkton, I'd like to phone my lawyer and my accountant now. Would you have the time later today for a meeting?'

'I expect I can fit it in, Lady Foxman,' he says.

* * *

Claudia Foxman makes her telephone calls, and Matilda Cressey telephones Steven van den Biot. 'I've done it, Steven, the report's finished. Do you want to see it? I thought . . .'

'No, Matilda, I don't want to see it.'

'Are you all right, Steven?'

'Yes.'

'"Yes." Is that all?'

'Yes,' he says, and puts the phone down.

'What do I do, Willow?' asks Matilda, standing in the kitchen making noises for baby Eve to sleep through. 'What have I done?'

'I don't know, Tilly. What have you done?'

'I've written a report on ABCs.'

'And what have you said?'

'Not a great deal. That is, I've said there's no evidence their practices are unsafe. Mostly because the evidence hasn't been collected. That commercial interests ought, ideally, to be kept out of health care altogether. I know you don't agree with that, Willow, and neither does the government, but I do feel strongly that health is too important to be managed in financial terms.'

'You haven't seen the paper this morning, have you?' says Willow from the stove, where she's concocting a courgette and lentil soup, small pieces of which will be liquidized and fed to baby Eve later in the day, whether she likes it or not. The Cornfords take the *Independent*, which today carries a brief news item about a lawsuit against Dr Steven van den Biot.

'Oh Christ! I didn't think he'd go that far. Poor Steven!'

'Why so poor?' asks Willow, tasting the soup energetically. 'And why Steven? Perhaps Ralph Scull is right. Why are you taking the doctor's side, Tilly? Don't you think it might be a mistake?'

'Maybe I know more about Steven van den Biot than you do.'

'That's what worries me. What *do* you know? Are you getting involved with him?' Willow slams the spoon down on the surface, comes over and looks closely at Matilda's face. 'People can be blinded by all sorts of things.'

'He was, in a way. Oh Willow, don't you see, this is all *our* fault, we've brought this on him! You say Ralph Scull may be right, and I suppose he may, but it wouldn't have got to a lawsuit if we hadn't intervened.' She drops her head in her hands and huddles in anguish over the kitchen table.

'You've got some thinking to do, my girl. Where are your priorities? Go back to the office. Remember you're President of the CCA, not a woman who loses her heart to a man just because he makes out he's full of mystery!'

'I haven't.'

'Haven't you?'

Matilda drives back to London. It's raining, she needs her windscreen wipers on at full speed. Oxfordshire and then Buckinghamshire and then Slough, Hounslow and Uxbridge resemble a slushy grey lake in which rows of grey pink-topped houses float like debris.

She turns on the radio: 'Woman's Hour'. A short story by Patricia Highsmith read in a supine, milky voice. An interview with a designer of hand-knitted silk jumpers; then an item about crisis counselling. There's an agency dealing in this, next to a Provençal herb shop in NW2. That's what I need, thinks Matilda suddenly, crisis counselling. I need someone who knows about these things to help me out of this dilemma.

Moonie Barber lives in a flat above a garage in Golders Green. At £50 an hour (a minimum of six sessions) she almost guarantees to give people a better – or at least a different – understanding of themselves from the one they had before.

Moonie listens while Matilda outlines her view of the crisis. Rain continues to fall, and Moonie's copper bracelets (worn for arthritis of the thumb) jangle in the damp atmosphere between the spray-polished yucca plants. Moonie has spectacular white hair, curled tightly round an apple-like face. She studies Matilda carefully. What she sees is a tense wire, a head full of conflicting ideas and feet that are planted quite firmly on the ground but shift restlessly on it, as though the ground itself is a quicksand capable of eating people.

When Matilda has finished her story, Moonie says in a professionally slow voice, against which the bracelets interpolate a different rhythm, 'Okay, Matilda, now I'm going to ask you three very important questions. I want you to take your time to answer. Try to say what you feel and feel what you say. The first question is: What do you *want* to do?'

Matilda stops herself delivering an instant answer, but try as she might the time-lag doesn't change the answer she gives: 'I want to marry Steven van den Biot.'

'Hang on a minute, you didn't say that was on the cards at all.'

'It isn't – well, nothing's been said. But you did ask me what I want to do. Aren't I allowed to say what comes into my head? Can I only say what I've been given permission to because somebody else has said it first?'

'Hell, no,' says Moonie, 'it's just that you surprised me.'

'Okay. Well, that's what I want. I want him.'

'So. Do you often want people like – like this?'

'Well, I think I probably have something of a reputation as a man-eater. But it's a matter of opinion as to who gets devoured in the act. To get back to your question, the way in which I want Steven van den Biot is different from before. You see, I feel quite sure he's the man for me. *The* man, you understand.'

'I understand,' says Moonie, feeling a flutter of quite unprofessional jealousy. 'Now it's time for question number two. Question number two is: What kind of person are you?'

'Confused, that's why I'm here.'

'They all say that. Think again. Say what you really feel.'

'Confused, as I said, but probably on the verge of something else. Like a butterfly. I've never really flown before, now I'm going to. I've done a lot of successful things, but I think I've been trying to convince myself that I'm a clever person. I'm not clever enough to know what I think, though. How's that for an analysis?'

'It'll do for a start.'

'And question number three?'

'Is one about what would you do with the rest of your life if you knew it was finite?'

'What do you mean?'

'You've got a year left. That's all. After that nothing. What will you do with it?'

'Same answer,' says Matilda. 'Marry Steven van den Biot.' She watches the raindrops on the windows, remembering an A. A. Milne poem about raindrops her mother used to read her long ago. 'But I also think – I see – I have a professional duty here as well. It's important for me to do the best I can professionally to help him. I am the one with the power in this situation. That's odd, isn't it? I don't have the power to make him love me, marry me. But I do, by virtue of my professional position, have the power to clear his name. So what that suggests is . . .'

Matilda leaps up, eyes alight. 'Thanks, Moonie, thanks a lot. I've got to go now. I can't afford to waste any more time, particularly if life is as short as you've made me think it might be.'

11
A Picture
of Health

On Friday April the 2nd, Ralph Scull opens his mail to find a letter from his erstwhile partner Clare Paynter enclosing something called a Declaration of Paternity, which she wants him to fill in for their daughter.

Ralph did go back once after the birth to see Clare at Roman Hall, but it was clear she didn't want to have anything more to do with him. He was relieved, and accordingly moved his things out of her flat with no great feeling of remorse. He's moved in with his old friend Malcolm, an unrepentant celibate, and is finding it much easier to get on with his novel than he had been. The fact that Clare wants him to Declare Paternity comes as a surprise, as he'd rather supposed this was something she'd like to forget.

'Might as well fill it in, Scullery,' says Malcolm in the casual way he has of referring to things of great importance. 'Wouldn't look too good if you don't acknowledge the infant's yours when you're trying to sue the doctor for spoiling it, not to mention your liaison with her mum.'

Ralph notes that Clare's called the baby Clemency Victoria Rose instead of Beatrice, as she'd threatened. Well, it's no concern of his. He's just signing his name on the piece of paper when the doorbell rings. A woman he's never met before stands there in a tightly belted beige raincoat.

'Mr Scull? Please forgive me for calling unexpectedly like this. My name is Matilda Cressey.'

She's not bad-looking, a bit pale and intellectual perhaps – reminds him of Clare. He realizes he's wearing only a tattered robe and underneath it he hasn't washed for days. 'You're the dame I spoke to on the phone, aren't you?'

'Yes. I've come about Roman Hall. May I come in?'

'Well, I . . .'

'I'll wait while you dress, Mr Scull.'

He showers quickly, puts on trousers and a shirt and cardigan of Malcolm's. She's sitting in the kitchen, trying not to look at the Declaration of Paternity on the table. He makes some coffee.

'I expect you're wondering why I've come.'

'Wouldn't you like to take your coat off?'

'Thanks.'

Her dress is, he thinks, rather deliberately high-necked and virginal. A long pearl rope seeks out the crevice between her breasts.

He sits down. 'Okay, fire away.'

'As I may have told you on the phone, I'm the President of an organization called the Council for Consumer Affairs,' she begins.

'That must be nice for you. I hope they pay you well. I expect they do.'

'I wasn't being facetious.'

'No, I was. Sorry, go on.'

'I told you on the phone that for various reasons we've been doing a survey of Alternative Birth Centres. You may have read some reports in the newspapers.'

'Never read newspapers,' says Ralph, 'full of lies. What's worse, it's the same lies, day after day.'

'One of the newspaper reports says you're suing Roman Hall,' Matilda persists.

He scratches his head as though in an effort to remember. 'That was it, was it? Well I never. Yes, that's true. True enough, anyway.'

'What are your grounds for suing, Mr Scull?'

'I'm not sure I should tell you. I won't tell you, there's no reason why I should. So there's an end to it!' He laughs, pleased with himself.

I must be patient, Matilda advises herself. This man is really irritating me, but if I alienate him I won't get what I want.

'Why do you think I've come here today, Mr Scull?' The direct technique, learnt from Moonie Barber.

'Can't think. I could make a few suggestions but I won't, it's too early in the morning.'

'I would appreciate it if you could be serious for a minute,' she says.

'Seriousness isn't part of my nature. It's not a bloody job interview, anyway. You've no right to interrogate me.'

Her fingers go tensely to the dip of her pearl necklace; he watches her playing with it. 'Well, the most likely thing is that you've come here to dig up some filth about that den Pee-ot character for your report. As if you haven't got quite enough already. The man's a charlatan, anyone can see that. The place is a whorehouse. Anyone can see that too. I bet he screws everything in sight, that den Pee-on-it. Screwed you, has he? Is that why you're seeking revenge?'

'I am not seeking revenge, Mr Scull. You are. But I don't know what for.'

'So what are you asking me to do? I think you should come clean, put your cards on the table.'

'I'm asking you to consider dropping your charges against Dr van den Biot. In the public interest, you understand.'

'What would that be?' he asks.

'Malpractice suits waste a lot of money, Mr Scull.'

'Why should I care about that?'

'Taxpayers' money.'

'That's the taxpayer's problem, not mine.' Ralph guffaws slightly, thinking of how he constantly avoids being one.

'They also lead to defensive medicine.'

'And what's that, when it's at home?'

'Doctors interfering when they don't need to, out of concern that someone like you, Mr Scull, will sue them if something goes wrong and they haven't done everything possible.'

'But I thought that was what I was suing old den Pee-it for. For interfering when he shouldn't. Why are you trying to persuade me not to sue in order to stop that sort of behaviour when it's exactly what I'm suing for?' He screws up his eyes at her crossly.

Matilda is becoming confused. 'I still feel it's not in the public interest for Dr van den Biot to be attacked in this way.'

Ralph thinks, looks Matilda up and down. Then he whistles: 'Well I never.' He tips his chair right back, runs his fingers through his hair, engages in a range of gestures indicating how disturbed he is to have Matilda pleading on Steven's behalf. 'Listen, lady, that den Bee-it's a criminal. Nothing on earth could persuade me otherwise. So don't you try, it'll be a waste of time. A waste of your time and of mine. I've got a novel waiting up there to be written, a good novel that I'm anxious to get on with, and you, I suppose, have got some outfit to run, so I suggest you get off your arse and go and run it!'

After Matilda has gone, Ralph finds it surprisingly difficult to settle down to work. The novel has reached a critical point, and although he's adopted his usual technique of leaving it each day with a sentence uncompleted, the more he stares at the space following the words, the less he can envisage what might be put there. He stalks the room like a neurotic tiger, puffing his way through a whole box of Marlboro. He fiddles with the television, rejecting one after the other a programme about anorexia, a rerun of *Limelight*, and a documentary about life on a multi-ethnic housing estate. He shakes his head to clear it, and hears a bell ringing instead. The telephone is under a heap of unread Sunday newspapers. 'Mr Scull, this is Lady Foxman speaking. You don't know me, but . . .'

Another dame on the rampage! This one wants him to meet her in a West End restaurant for lunch. He accepts with alacrity at the thought of a free three-course meal, but in despair for his hero, Algernon Dupont, doomed to stasis by this series of second-order events. Never mind, perhaps he can use today's encounter somehow – for a writer there's always the theoretical saving grace of turning life's more fractious moments into the stuff of Booker prizes.

On his way to L'Escargot in Greek Street, Ralph nips into a pharmacist and buys some deodorizing dental gum. He left his toothbrush at Clare's. Not that the foxy dame's likely to get near enough to him to smell anything, but he thinks he can smell himself and the thought, once had, won't leave his head.

In the restaurant he asks for Lady Foxman's table and is led upstairs to where a black-haired matron in a poinsettia-red suit sits sipping iced mineral water, one white hand folded becomingly over the menu.

'I'm late,' he says, chewing the gum, 'still, that's nothing unusual.'

'Would you like a drink, Mr Scull?'

'Brandy and ginger,' he says curtly. 'You're on the hard stuff yourself, are you?'

Her face looks as though it means business, there's something unremittingly stiff about it. He swallows his drink. 'Let's order first, shall we,' he suggests cunningly, 'and then you can tell me what you want me to do. No doubt there is something?'

'I'll have *risotto aux truffes*.' She closes the menu crisply.

'And I'll have the lamb. You having a pudding?' he snaps at her inappropriately. 'Because if you're not I'll have a starter. No, I'll have a starter anyway, since you're paying. Whitebait, please.' He swings childishly in his chair. 'I love eating the little buggers' eyes.' He takes his dental gum out and hands it to the waiter. 'Dispose of this, will you? If I don't give it to you I'll only stick it under the table, and we wouldn't want that, would we?'

Ralph Scull intends Claudia Foxman to look at him with loathing, which she does. He isn't, as he's making clear, the kind of company she normally keeps. 'You're right,' she says. 'I have come to ask you something. Or rather, to make a suggestion.'

Ralph watches the kitchen door in case his whitebait come steaming towards him. 'Let me guess.' His eyes, filled with a momentary intelligence, remove themselves to Claudia Foxman's face. 'You want me to drop the charges against old den Bore-it.'

'On the contrary, I'd like to suggest we join forces against him.'

Ralph thinks he's beginning to get the picture now. This one's den Bore-it's old flame, while Cressey's the new one. 'You're not bad-looking,' he says, 'quite attractive in fact. In a moneyed sort of way. Tell me, why did the old fart drop you?'

'Mr Scull, I'm not here to discuss my personal life.'

His whitebait arrive. He looks down on them, all jumbled up together, eyes juxtaposed with tails. 'What a tangled web we weave!' He sticks a fork into the largest one, exposing its backbone.

Claudia watches, pitying Ralph his need to attack dead creatures.

'I'll go on, if I may. We have some information about the standard of care in the birth clinic which might help you in your legal case against Dr van den Biot. We're willing to give it to you.'

'We?'

'I'm sorry. Myself and Dr Monkton, Dr van den Biot's assistant.'

So he's got it in for the good doctor too, muses Ralph. Must be quite a bloke to have all these enemies. I wonder what he's done to deserve it?

Claudia Foxman wonders too, but the ignominy of waking up on Steven's sofa flashes before her again, being somehow bound up with Lord Foxman's liaison with Nanny Pilkington and with the awfulness, now, of having to watch Ralph Şcull eat.

'What else?'

'I take it you're not a rich man, Mr Scull.'

'You take it correctly.'

'So how are you going to pay the costs of the case?'

'That's my business.'

'I'd like to offer you a loan. Interest-free, of course.'

'Would you now? Golly golly gumdrops.' Ralph pushes his plate of debris against the yellow carnation in the centre of the table.

'We're anxious to discredit the Cressey Report, so we'd like you to do us a favour in return. You're a writer, aren't you, Mr Scull?'

'On and off. What's the Cressey Report?'

'Matilda Cressey from the Council for Consumer Affairs. She's writing a report on Alternative Birth Centres.'

'I know that.'

'I know you know that. So why did you ask? But the point is, Mr Scull, this report, which is about to be published, is an outrageous whitewashing of the whole affair, but it's likely to be regarded as an authoritative statement and to get a lot of publicity. The matter would end there, were it not for your own case and your own interests in seeing that justice is done.'

'How do you know what's in this report?' It's the first intelligent thing he's said.

'I've seen a copy. There are ways of finding out most things.'

'Okay, lady.' Ralph's lamb arrives, pale pink, just as he likes it. 'Anything you say.'

'Are you serious, Mr Scull?'

'As I ever am.' He eats with revolting rapidity. 'Although, Lady Fox . . .'

'Man, Foxman.'

'You have more faith in the written word than I do. Despite being a writer. It's carnage, absolute carnage.' He waves his fork, speared with the pink meat, around the room.

Matilda's report is published on 1 May. Jeffrey Rowley, his chest hair veritably bursting out of today's lilac shirt, tells her that advance orders total an unprecedented 550. Matthew Ansden's reaction to this is to inform her that on the proceeds they could have the whole of No. 88 Juliana Crescent recarpeted in industrial Wilton (a pale silver shade, chosen by Jason).

On publication day, Matilda goes out early to buy all the newspapers and take them back to bed with her. Her father is the first to telephone with congratulations, then Willow Cornford rings in a less than mollified state to say she doesn't know why Matilda has written such a pack of lies about Roman Hall, but she hopes she and Steven van den Biot will be very happy together. When Matilda explains that she's had no communication recently with Steven, Willow just laughs and says she has to take Eve to the clinic for her first immunization.

Matilda has a bath, peers at the weather (bright and hopeful) and puts on a flowered dress and hat. She is, perhaps, entering a new season. On the way to the office, she buys some primroses. Margaret Watteau puts them in the office vase and tells her there've been ten phone calls already, mostly from media people. 'And that Dr van den Biot telephoned,' she adds pointedly.

Matilda returns the other calls first, so that Margaret's excuse for listening while filing lapses into the lunch hour. When Margaret takes her purse to buy sandwiches, Matilda calls Roman Hall. Steven comes to the phone almost immediately. 'The time has come,' he says, when he learns who it is, 'for cabbages and kings.' At first Matilda thinks he's talking about lunch, but he isn't. 'You've obviously done a good job, Matilda. Now we can get on with our lives. What about this weekend? My plans are well laid. Meet me at Victoria Station on Friday at ten o'clock. Bring your passport. Don't be late.'

She isn't. Actually, she's early, touring the station in a delightful, vexed anticipation. She buys *Cosmopolitan* and then, regretting its weight, jettisons it in a litter bin. Thinking they might be going somewhere it could come in useful, she purchases a silver shower cap. She goes to the Ladies – 50p these days – and stands for a long while in front of a mirror, trying to work out how she looks. To herself? No, not to herself, as women, on the whole, lack that perspective. Instead, she tries to see herself as *he* would see her. Beginning on the ground, with her plain dark-brown court shoes, travelling up her chiselled legs, the skirt of her blue and brown check suit, hips in evidence but not too much so, the sapphire blouse, and the butterfly pin, the determined shoulders, the high curves of her cheeks, her laughing, slightly Chinese eyes – a quirk of heredity more than the memory of Shanghai.

Standing under the clock, she sees him come in a taxi, its black and silver matching those of his raincoat and hair and the small black suitcase he carries, everything groomed and gleaming. When he stands in front of her, she feels she's somehow *earned* him. 'Where are we going?' she asks.

'Into the future,' he says. Steering her through the tail end of the rush-hour crowds, he expands his statement. 'It's not about geography, is it, Matilda? East or west. Train or plane – the mode of transport doesn't count either. I can't even promise to transport you to heaven.' She sways a little, as she did once in Roman Hall, feeling pale next to his encapsulated darkness. 'Oh, by the way, we'll be away a week. Do you need to phone the office? Or anyone else?'

'No,' she says, not being able to think about the office or anyone. Else. 'But where *are* we going?'

'North,' he replies. 'Well, to be more precise, east, then north. Up.

Towards the North Pole. To meet Father Christmas, you know. Haven't you always wanted to do that, Matilda? Find out the truth behind the myth. Is Santa really an old man with a beard? How many reindeer does it take to pull a sleigh?'

12
To the
Finland Station

They fly to Helsinki, where snow edges the airport runways and the sky is a promissory blue. Matilda wonders why Steven has chosen Finland. Paris she might have expected, or Venice, or Amsterdam. But Finland? A country marked by eras of imperialist desecration and, before that, by lines of low ridges left by the retreat of the ice age? She would have liked to explore Helsinki, but Steven tells her they must change planes directly and head for Rovaniemi, the capital of Lapland, designed by the Finnish architect Alvar Aalto, and rising like a phoenix from the flames of the German burning of the old city in 1944.

The flight to Rovaniemi takes one hour and five minutes. The pilot informs them that it's minus 57 outside the plane and minus 4 in Rovaniemi. The Finnair stewardess, with her stylishly knotted silk scarf, passes with drinks and a smoothly landscaped face, bland like the snow and set with a lakelike smile. 'I'm not equipped, Steven,' says Matilda suddenly. 'I mean I'm going to freeze.'

'They have shops in Lapland, Matilda. As soon as we get there we'll take you to one and have you kitted out like a snowman. Or woman. I forgot to ask you, do you ski?'

'I can. My father's keen on it; as a child I went to Austria every winter. My mother sat in the hotel reading and writing postcards to her friends while my father and I disappeared into the Alps.'

They land in a row of Christmas trees and walk to the airport building, which is fronted by one of these strung with lights and guarding a sign declaring this to be the official airport of Santa Claus.

'What do you want to do first?' asks Steven. 'Buy clothes? Check in at the hotel? Have lunch?'

'Sounds fine to me,' she says.

In Rovaniemi town centre Matilda is appalled at the Finnish prices. Steven tries to pay for the purple ski trousers and jacket and the white moon boots she picks out, but she forces him to compromise by paying only half. They buy a bright pink hat and gloves to complete the outfit and take a taxi to the hotel, which is on a hill outside the town. 'I've booked two adjoining rooms,' he says. 'I take it you'd like to preserve your independence?'

Each room has its own private sauna in a cupboard. The whole of the opposite wall is a double-glazed window, unopenable except for a grille at the bottom. The curtains have a dark lining – this is the land of the midnight sun. Matilda's window is a picture postcard of snow-hung fir trees marching in lines up the hill and interrupting a pale grey horizon.

She changes quickly into a pair of white trousers and a sweater. Steven tells her she looks like a fir tree herself. After a lunch of grilled herrings and cold beer, they rent skis and go outside to inspect the environment more closely. A map near the hotel shows alternative cross-country routes. They pick the shortest, about five kilometres. Matilda slides her feet into the skis and snaps the metal clips in place, remembering the old slightly exciting feeling of being trapped she had as a child accompanying her father. As the steely air whips her face and globules of snow immerse themselves in the fibres of her pink hat, she feels even more as though she's going back into the past.

On the slower portions of the track, Matilda studies the landscape. Although every colour is either grey or white, there are far more shades of each than could ever be imagined. As her eyes become more used to the scene, they grow also more discerning: what began as a series of uniform hues break and reassemble as a veritable jeweller's of different colours: green-grey, yellow-grey, pink-grey, brown-grey, lemon-white, blue-white, diamond-white; and against all these the deep burnt sienna of tracks etched by the sharp blades of many different skiers all passing through the forest at a similar angle, knees bent to divert the force of the wind, arms outsplayed to prevent descent, like psychotic fir trees that have suddenly picked up their roots and decided to seek transplantation elsewhere.

Matilda's so busy studying everything that she almost forgets Steven. When she turns round to look for him, he's no longer there. She goes back, using the track on the other side. Steven comes round the corner, somewhat lugubriously. 'I'm obviously not as good at this as you are.' He falls over with a flourish and she goes to pick him up – expertly, so as not to join him on the ground, though she might have liked to.

'I'm sorry, Steven, I didn't realize. I'll go more slowly.'

'Not at all. You go at your own pace.'

But she doesn't, mindful of his possible need for her. In any case, the steadier pace allows her continued study of the forest. She even sees a reindeer streaking past in the middle distance, but decides not to call out to Steven to draw his attention to it, for fear of disturbing his balance again.

When Matilda and Steven make love that night, in Matilda's room, with the curtains open to admit the natural light of the sky, the earth doesn't move and the fir trees don't even give up any of their snow. Matilda thinks fleetingly, fondly but despairingly, of William. Steven believes each time isn't only new but a cosmic as well as an individual event: life forces joined, the centre of the earth's gravity changing, creativity bursting forth in germinal sparks. On the other hand, they are both aware that their union represents an end as well as a beginning.

Afterwards he leaves her and she dreams of a white liquid world. She's watching the green edge of water lapping the shore, advancing and retreating with loud sucking noises as though someone has taken the plug out of the bottom of the sea. It grips her, the pull and push of the tide, but it's worrying too, as the sea becomes a gigantic smooth-bottomed swimming bath, and then what starts to cover its emptiness down there isn't the water coming back, but a sea of frozen snow formed in the shape of a hearth rug with the flattened face and claws of a polar bear. It edges its way over, filling the whole vacant space, and Matilda knows she's doomed: everything is frozen over, solid, it's the end of breathing for ever. The sound of voices breaks her panic and figures trip down the stairs to her left (stairs on the seashore?) with rouged faces, ringlets and long red and white dresses. Coppelia dolls carrying others. And though the voices speak a language she doesn't understand, not unlike Finnish, Matilda considers there's hope still: life will establish its own circadian rhythms above the surface of the ice, a new world might be built on the skating rink of the old.

The next day they hire a car and drive to Santa Claus's office, which is located on the line of the Arctic Circle about six kilometres from Rovaniemi. A low series of log-like brown buildings lying in the snow advertises Santa's home, and he duly emerges on the hour, every hour, striding in his boots across the shiny pine floor. Off-season there are few children to greet him, so Steven introduces himself and Matilda, and they shake hands. Matilda notices that Santa's hands are hardly those of an old man, and he has a baby's face behind his spectacles. He speaks excellent English, and offers to show them his office. They go with him to a little room crowded with painted chairs and rugs and chests full of letters from children asking for things they will never get, and sometimes telling him stories of things they have too much of: sorrow, pain, anger, fear, confusion, algebra, baby sisters, snakes, ghosts, blisters, vegetables, war, death. 'We answer them all,' says Santa proudly, showing them the glossy leaflet about himself enclosed with each reply.

For 10 finnmarks Steven buys Matilda a certificate proving she's crossed the Arctic Circle. They go outside to see the reindeer asleep under the trees, having just been fed, and not looking at all capable of pulling anything. And then they drive 150 kilometres north, right into Lapland, through snow-covered marshes where cloudberries grow in summer, past many pastel houses with their wood stores and ladders strung up to the roofs to dry reindeer skins, and between many ordinary Lappish forests where the snow falls with a persistent reclining gentleness.

Though it's warm in the car, Steven wears a heavy dark-blue jumper. The light-brown contours of his face are dark against the snow.

'Where are we going?' she asks again.

'I thought we might try some downhill skiing. We're getting into fell country now. There's one place in particular I want to take you to. After that there's a hotel where we can have a meal. And a sauna, if you like.'

'How come you know this all so well?'

'I've been here three or four times.'

'Who with?'

He smiles. 'Myself.' He takes his hands off the wheel in a gesture as concealing as it's dangerous, here, where not even the heavy snow tyres are a guarantee against skidding directly into the lorries that pass, one every fifteen minutes or so, carrying wood and other natural materials from the north. 'I like this country. I feel at home here. I feel it suits my personality. Better than England, better than central or southern Europe. Certainly better than France.' His left eye flickers with a nervous tension she's noticed at other times. 'I first came here about twenty years ago. I went to do a six-month research job in Stockholm and someone invited me to their summer house near here. You should see it in the summer, Matilda. We'll come again then.' His eyes light up, the steering wheel is almost illuminated.

She finds his affinity for the landscape curious.

'Don't you understand what I like about it?' She shakes her head. 'It's so brooding, so endlessly brooding. Finland frowns, it thinks, while other countries grin inanely, or are mindless. This landscape has emotion in it, is made out of it, but in other places emotion is poorly contained, runs riot, plagues and ruins any sense of harmony or order. This has a structure, a marvellous emotional structure. Don't you feel it? See – that's the fell we're making for.' It's hard for Matilda to make out the shape of the hill, its division from the snow-bearing sky. 'Round the other side there's a ski lift and a place where we can rent downhill equipment.'

She goes with him, becoming part of his own enthusiasm for making tracks over the marshmallow hill. At the top, a loudspeaker emits a Finnish radio station. Matilda dislikes the idea of radio waves polluting the snowy purity. They ski down, fast; Steven is better at this than the cross-country variety. But she prefers the chance to look at the country offered by a more horizontal passage through it. Up they go again and, poised at the top, catch their breath, looking and watching. A group of three skiless figures below string themselves out in a zigzag pattern, two women and a child climbing the hill. The child, who is wearing pink like Matilda, falls shrieking with delight deep into the snow and, holding a bright yellow plastic bag beneath her, slides down rapidly on her bottom, coming to rest in a shallow incline further down. She lies flat in the snow and moves her arms and legs sideways and back several times. 'Look!' she calls, surprisingly in English – Matilda and Steven can hear her voice quite clearly in the lunar stillness – 'Look, I'm making an angel!'

Steven makes a slight noise in his throat that could be a laugh. Matilda looks at him sharply and at the same time the phrase 'making an angel' etches itself on her brain. 'I want to make an angel too,' she says quietly to herself.

'What did you say?'

'Nothing, Steven.'

'Come on, let's go.' He takes her hand, turning her so she faces the steepest part of the hill, and takes off, carving a series of S's across it.

* * *

Back in England, Channel Four does a hastily put together documentary on the alternative birth movement. Roman Hall beams out of one million television sets, along with other clones and various pundits, including Steven van den Biot himself, in an old clip the director found. A picture is shown of the cover of the Cressey Report, superimposed on a shot of 88 Juliana Crescent in the sunlight. A voice-over remarks that neither Matilda Cressey nor Steven van den Biot is currently available for comment, as both are out of the country. Karin Druin expounds on her midwifery philosophy; many people watching are impressed by the artistic movements of her hands. Ralph Scull and Clare Paynter are interviewed (separately). Ralph, knowing how to present himself on television, gives a rousing performance. Clare is nervous, but the baby wails throughout, convincingly demonstrating the unhappy outcome which is the subject of the criticism of Roman Hall she's being interviewed about. In Steven's absence, Paul talks about the need for scientific evaluation of alternative health care, giving an impression of a most level-headed young man.

Margaret Watteau, watching the programme in Speedwell Avenue, Acton, with her sister Lesley, moans about the number of telephone calls to be expected the next day.

'Come on, Maggie, you're in the thick of it! Why don't you sell your story to the *Sun*?'

'No, Les, I couldn't do that. I'd lose my job.'

'Plenty of other jobs, Maggie, especially now you can do spreadsheets and Wordperfect.'

'I know, Les, but . . .'

'Where are they anyway, Maggie?'

'Finland.' Margaret thinks of the odd call she had from Miss Cressey, the line really distant, all crackly, and she just gave a phone number, made Margaret write it down and repeat it to her and said she'd be away a week, she was taking a week's leave. Of course Margaret didn't *know* that was where Dr van den Biot was, but she'd heard Rita Ploughman phone the clinic and leave a message for him about a small printing error in the report and be told he too was away for the same week, and coming back to England the same day.

'It's not very romantic,' observes Lesley. Damian, wrapped in his Garfield duvet, asleep on the sofa between the two sisters, snores softly with the remnants of his cold. 'Why didn't he take her somewhere more normal? Where is Finland anyway?'

They turn over to Channel Three to watch a science fiction film about a young man with liver cancer who is put in a freezer by his mother for ten years.

As Margaret and Lesley watch television in Acton, a woman is admitted to Roman Hall in heavy labour with her seventh child. Priscilla Mayhew is aiming for eight. She likes to claim that childbirth is akin to shelling peas, though privately she feels a better metaphor is firing a cannon. She and her husband breed Siamese cats as well as children, being deeply into heredity. But for all that, Priscilla Mayhew is a perfectly nice and ordinary woman. Her children – Timmy (two), Imogen (three), Lily (four), Sammy (six), Cassandra (seven) and Victoria (nine) – see her as children should see their mothers: as a reasonably stable repository of cuddles, reprimands and understanding. In short, Priscilla Mayhew in no way deserves to die, and her children do not deserve to lose her.

Priscilla's widower, Christopher, finds himself face to face with the cannon that backfired and killed the maternal apparatus – number seven, a robust eight-pound boy with the normal blond curly Mayhew hair. Priscilla died from a massive haemorrhage. The blood flowed suddenly and unpredictably out of her. Mary Elliott and the other midwife in attendance weren't able to marshal help fast enough. There had been no doctor in the clinic at the time; Steven was in Rovaniemi and Paul was in London defending his thesis on labour positions.

The case was going to achieve notoriety, they all knew that. Mary had already resigned, feeling herself incapable of defending the inadequate medical back-up which had been indirectly responsible for Priscilla's death.

The newspaper headline, 'Mother of Eight [a little exaggeration never did most people much harm] Dies in Private Birth Clinic', doesn't reach Steven and Matilda in Finland. At 88 Juliana Crescent there's much discussion about whether to interrupt Miss Cressey with the news on her holiday. Matthew Ansden says definitely yes, Rita Ploughman and Jeffrey Rowley say she should be left in peace. Margaret refers privately to her sister Lesley's opinion. 'Give them a chance, Maggie, I thought you wanted to go to the wedding?'

As the journalists write their columns, Matilda and Steven sit in the hotel Levitunturi at Kittila in west central Lapland discussing what to do next. To be more exact, they half-sit, half-lie in the jacuzzi pool, their feet resting on the central tower of bubbles that rises with considerable force over a cascade of underwater lights.

'We could go and hunt for gold,' suggests Steven, 'but the rivers are probably all frozen even further south. We could go and search for the reindeer herds – the Lapps put them in corrals this time of year. Or we could go back to Helsinki. What do you think, Matilda?'

'I think we should have a serious discussion, Steven.'

'About what?'

'About us.'

'Here?'

'Not here. Later.'

'All right, Matilda, but let's have a sauna first.'

Matilda showers and studies the signs. On the wall by the sauna, there's a picture of a swimming costume with two circles on it and a line across. Accordingly, she takes her costume off and hangs it on a hook. When she opens the door, the steam hits her like a hot wet wall. She fumbles for the tiled seat, almost choking on the atmosphere, and sits as low as she can, remembering that heat is supposed to rise. There do seem to be a lot of bodies in here, but she can't really make them out. A large woman passes her, waddling like a duck and holding a bucket. She heaves herself up into the steam and Matilda hears rather than sees the water hitting the coals: a fierce hissing announces an abrupt rise in the temperature. She folds her arms self-consciously around her English body. A door opens on the other side of the room and another body enters, breastless, but adult: a man. Matilda hadn't noticed the mixed-sex sign. It is possible that this is Steven. But Matilda can't tell if it's Steven or not. She peers hard through the steamy darkness trying to cut a hole in it with her eyes, but very little more is revealed to her. The heat, moreover, is overwhelming. Something, someone, touches her from behind, but she feels too hot and panicky to work out what's going on. She gets up abruptly and half-slithers out.

Matilda and Steven have their discussion in the hotel bar, over a bottle of Finnish champagne, to the sound of Lara's theme from *Dr Zhivago* and the deterring presence of a large green bird illuminated by means of a laser device on a screen suspended outside the window. As the violins sweep and fall, so the green bird alters the angle of its wings against the darkening landscape. In the middle of the floor, Finnish couples dance with old-fashioned courtesy, the men holding the women stiffly like frozen fir trees with a space between almost sufficiently large to admit a ski instructor. Matilda envies them their glacial familiarity with one another. They've been together twenty, thirty, forty years. Copulated a thousand times, incubated little fir trees and set them on their own pathways down the fellside; they've watched and eaten reindeer together, taken on board the glowing sunsets and lack of them as routine events, munched many lingon-berry pies, seen rivers freeze and liquefy, grown used to each other's ways and habits, accepting of the need to preserve through time what must also change with it.

'So what's the discussion you want us to have, Matilda?'

'I want to know what we're doing here together, Steven.'

'I would have thought it was obvious,' he says.

'I don't want to have just another relationship.'

'Do you love me, Matilda?'

'Oh yes. Do you love *me*, Steven?' She studies his face gravely, hoping to derive his answer from it.

'In so far as I'm capable of love, yes, I love you, Matilda.'

'Why don't you just say yes? It's much simpler.'

'The truth isn't simple. But I do mean what I say, at least that!'

'I don't think you understand what I mean,' she says dubiously.

'Oh, I do. You want me to stop the world and get off. You want to marry me.'

'Yes.' It takes courage for her to say this little word, and then to look at him in the smoky atmosphere and await his response.

'I think that's an excellent idea.'

'You do?'

In Helsinki, to prove his point, Steven takes Matilda to Lindroos on Aleksanterinkatu and buys her a silver Lapponia ring. The design is pleasingly angular, like an Alvar Aalto library. Matilda enjoys twisting it round on her finger, and likes to watch it steaming up in the sauna in the Hotel Intercontinental, where they stay for three days before returning to face the music in England.

Meanwhile, they hear some: Sibelius in the visionary Finlandia Hall overlooking gardens and water, still coated in a faint sheen of white, but now set off against a porcelain blue sky, deepening in the evenings to the colour of an SAS aeroplane interior.

13
A Polonaise
for Polar Bears

They're waiting to pounce at the airport, microphones held out like stethoscopes. A young man from the *Daily Mirror* has the loudest voice, and so gets in first: 'Dr van den Biot, how do you explain the fact that a woman has died in childbirth at *your* clinic?'

Steven's mouth drops open, he lets go in alarm of Matilda's newly ringed hand. Next to Loud-voice is Susan Harris, who wrote the *Guardian* piece. She observes not only the expression of panic on Steven's face, but also the presence of Matilda Cressey, whom she knows, behind him. 'You are *aware* of the death, aren't you, Dr van den Biot?'

'I've been on leave,' he says.

'Of your senses?' interrupts Loud-voice.

Steven sets his flight bag on the floor, puts his hands in his pockets to give himself a more confident aura, takes a deep breath and delivers a series of staccato sentences: 'I've been on leave, as I said. I have not been in touch with events at my clinic. I therefore have nothing to say to you. I'm on my way to the clinic now. Please get out of my way so I can get there as quickly as possible.' Matilda, from the side, notes the customary curling of his lips into their downward quoting position.

Matilda and Susan exchange looks. In Matilda's eyes there is pleading – for Susan not to reveal her identity. The gaggle of journalists is clearly here to meet Steven. Someone at Roman Hall must have alerted them. It's him they want. Cameras whirr, Matilda's identity won't be a secret for long, but Susan lets her pass.

'I must go straight to Roman Hall.' In the car park, Steven looks hunted, anxious.

'I want to come with you.' She does.

He puts his hands on her shoulders. 'No, Matilda. You must let me find out what's happened and handle it my way.'

'But . . .' she raises the hand with the ring on it so it catches the only stream of light that reaches in among the cars from the leadlike sky outside. 'But Steven, we're going to be part of each other's lives, why should we pretend to be separate any more?'

'Public and private,' he says. 'And never the twain shall meet. In any case, the world has no right to know how we feel about each other. Besides which your report, which may be my only ally in all this, will be discredited if people know about us.'

'But my feelings for you have nothing to do with my professional opinion about your work!' Matilda stamps her foot like a frustrated bull.

'Well, I know that, you know that, but journalists are evil people.'

'I used to be one,' she recalls.

'In that case, be thankful you've redeemed yourself.' He unlocks the car sharply. 'I'll drive you to a station and call you later.'

Alone in her flat, Matilda puts the kettle on, then starts to unpack, then paces up and down, then goes back to her unpacking. She finds the unread programme for the Sibelius concert, wherein the finale of the Violin Concerto is described as 'a polonaise for polar bears'. She folds the programme up and pushes it under the pile of clothes. Finland is in the past. She listens to her answering machine. Her mother: 'How are you, darling? I wanted to ask your advice about the new curtains for the study.' The pang of guilt that Matilda feels – she hadn't told her mother she was going away – is quickly erased by the next message: 'This is Chicken Kiev stroke placenta stew speaking, I just wanted to tell you how entirely dumb you are. That's all. Oh, and by the way, I looked your new friend up in the Medical Directory. There's something very fishy about him. But I don't care a tit what it is.' A message from Susan Harris asking for Matilda to ring her back; and several others, culminating in Margaret Watteau's nervous voice: 'Miss Cressey, it's me. Could you ring the office as soon as you get back?'

I don't know whether I can face it, thinks Matilda. She makes a cup of tea and takes it into the bedroom. The bed's white cotton spread is rumpled with the suitcase and the half-spilled-out clothes. For a moment she hears William's voice in her head – on the answering machine warning her, in bed warming her. Perhaps she'd been wrong to jettison William. The essentially untroubled nature of her relationship with him sweeps over her like a tide of Fenjal-laced water, settling in gentle swirls round her feet. Looking down, she feels quite rooted by it, but at the same time disloyal to Steven, with whom she's become so suddenly involved. Strangely frightened, Matilda tips the suitcase and the clothes off the bed and gets into it, holding her tea like a comforting transitional object. The room's familiarity in the fading afternoon light wraps her up, and the daffodils in the window boxes wave their heads knowingly, like old women whispering secrets through the glass at her. She puts her tea down on the table by the bed and closes her eyes.

The press, or some of them, are waiting for Steven van den Biot as his car streaks down the drive to Roman Hall, the crowd of journalists resembling an ink blot on the clinic's peppermint façade.

'Nothing to say.' He pushes his way past them. Mary Elliott opens the door and helps him to close it firmly in their faces. She's wearing a sombre grey dress, not her normal working clothes. 'What's the matter, Mary? What's going on?'

She looks up at him wide-eyed. 'You don't know, do you? I was afraid of that. Can we go into your office for a moment?'

The curtains are drawn, though it's still light. He goes to pull them back, but Mary stops him. 'Don't do that. You'll find yourself being watched if you do. It's been like Buckingham Palace here.'

Steven takes off his jacket and sits down at his desk. 'Tell me, then, Mary. Enlighten me, for God's sake.'

'I will. But first I have to tell you I've resigned.'

'Why?'

'That's part of it. But although I've resigned, I decided I should stay until you got back. You need to know from someone at first hand what happened, you deserve a clear account; that's the right word – deserve. I don't think anyone else will give you one.'

Mary tells Steven of the events leading up to Priscilla Mayhew's death. 'I think it's possible', she concludes, 'that she would have died wherever she was. I've never seen a haemorrhage like that in the whole of my professional life. But the fact was, there was no doctor here when it happened. That doesn't look good. It's indefensible, in fact. And against the Department of Health guidelines.'

'Where was Paul? He was supposed to be here.'

'Paul was in London having his thesis examined.'

'Why the hell didn't *I* know that? I wouldn't have gone on leave if I'd known.'

'The date was changed at the last minute. One of the examiners had to go abroad, so the date of the examination was brought forward.'

'Paul should have got a locum in.'

'Yes,' says Mary quietly, 'I think he probably should.' She feels hopelessly trapped in this battle for power between Paul and Steven. Though Steven says it's a dispute between paradigms, she feels it much more simply as a contest for authority between two ambitious men. It's a cause of particular distress to her that they should have made a battle out of childbirth, when the whole *raison d'être* of Roman Hall is to remove from childbirth the ordinary spoiling motives of control and power. That was why she'd come to work here.

'Where's Paul now?' Steven's voice slices through her interior monologue.

'He's here. There's a woman delivering in labour room two. Since the Mayhew case he's been present at every delivery.'

'Can you do something for me, Mary?'

'I'll try. What is it?'

'Get me all the figures. You know, the ones Paul cherishes and I don't.' His left eye starts to blink uncontrollably. 'Find them and bring them here. I'm going home to have a shower and change, I'll be back in half an hour.'

'I'll do what you ask, Steven, but I don't advise you to leave the building. They'll follow you.'

'Damn.' He's forgotten the journalists. 'Okay, I'll have a shower and change here.'

'I'll get you the statistics and a Thermos of coffee. Have you had anything to eat?'

'On the plane.' For a moment, Steven remembers Matilda, the structured silence of the snowy Finnish forests, the confident stride of Santa Claus in his office on the thin imaginary line that encircles the world. 'Thanks, Mary. I appreciate the fact that you stayed to fill me in.'

About to exit, Mary comes back at this expression of gratitude and closes the door. 'There are some other things you ought to know, Steven. Paul and Karin are having an affair' – she speaks quickly, as though this will sanitize her disclosures – 'Mr Scull saw them together. It's one of the things that upset him. And Lady Foxman has been talking to Paul. With her lawyer. I don't know what about. But Paul certainly hasn't been anxious for me to know.'

'Anything else?'

'Mr Scull's lawyers have been down, too. The same day as Lady

Foxman's, actually.' There'd been so many lawyers in Roman Hall, they hadn't known what to do with them.

'Yes?'

'The Cornfords haven't paid their bill yet. And Mrs Lemon's resigned.'

'Fine.' Steven's face is tight with curtailed emotion, like the portcullis gates at Tower Hill when a queen is about to be beheaded. He lifts up the corner of the curtain; there's a clump of journalists on the back lawn, where Claude Semerie's helicopter once stood. 'How am I *ever* going to get home?'

'If you issue a press statement, they might go away,' suggests Mary helpfully.

He's in the shower when the man from the Department of Health rings. 'Dr Biot?' (pronounced Bear-it). 'Good afternoon. My name's Oates. Bernard Oates, Department of Health. You seem to have hit the headlines recently, Dr van den Bear-it. I'd like to come down in the morning if I may and have a word with you. I'd appreciate it if you could have all your staff present.'

Steven starts to explain that this might be difficult, then stops. When Oates has clinched the deal, Steven presses the intercom and asks Mary if Jung is around. He feels far too tense to make sense of any of this.

Under the calming influence of Jung's Eastern hands and some strawberry-scented oil in labour room three, Steven's head begins to clear; he begins to understand what he has to do.

'Are you resigning as well, Jung?' he demands.

'No, Steven. Unless you want me to?'

'Of course not. I want you to stay. But there'll have to be some changes round here. You need to understand that.'

'Will you still go ahead with the moxibustion project? My sister has a friend in Japan who's interested in joining us to develop it.'

'Of course. Yes.' The idea of a new project floods Steven with the memory of the energy he usually has for work. 'Once we've got all this sorted out . . .' He leaves the sentence unfinished.

She strokes his calves expertly with long fingers. 'I wish you luck, Steven.'

'Thanks.'

The statistics spell out a very clear message to him. In 1035 deliveries at Roman Hall, they've had ten perinatal deaths, including two pairs of twins. That gives a perinatal mortality rate of 9·6, which compares with – Steven checks against the latest OPCS Monitor in

112

the file – a rate of 11·2 in England and Wales the previous year. Since 1989 the national rate has crept up, as the health effects of Thatcherism have manifested themselves. Many people had warned that this would be so, particularly in the North, where the privatization of health services added insult to pre-existing injury in the form of gross poverty and nutritional deprivation. If there were few greengrocers' shops on working-class housing estates before, there's now not a single carrot to be seen for miles.

Priscilla Mayhew's death is the first maternal death at Roman Hall. In the country as a whole there's roughly one maternal death for every 10,000 live births. This means that they shouldn't expect another at Roman Hall until their deliveries exceed the 10,000 mark. Time will tell, as time usually does. But how to convince the journalists or the Department of Health? Steven sighs with his old impatience at this game of science and statistics. The problem is that no one agrees on what science is, or on how to interpret statistics. And in that disagreement lies the problem: that the scientific mode, being not one but many, cannot help but be unscientific – that is, a matter of opinion.

This is one of the points he's tried to explain to Paul in the past. Paul seemed to agree, but Steven doesn't imagine it's a conversation that's worth continuing now. He leaves a message asking Paul to come and see him when he's free. The two men confront each other across Steven's desk. 'Sit down, Paul.'

'I'd rather stand.'

Steven stands as well. 'Can you answer one question first? Why did you ever come and work here?' His voice holds as much anger in it as the sky before a thunderstorm.

'I respected what you were trying to do. I wanted to work somewhere where I wasn't bound by petty NHS rules. But you know that.'

'And it's in the past tense? Tell me why, Paul.'

'Why try to understand? Why not just accept I've changed my mind? I suppose that's too much for you. Everyone has to agree with you, don't they? There's only one right way of doing things – your way.'

'Not at all. But you're right about one thing. Karin's a very personable young woman. I don't know why you had to keep it a secret.'

'Who told you?'

113

'That's *my* secret. Let's just say you aren't as clever as you think you are.'

'Neither are you.'

They glare at each other like two schoolboys over a single plate of baked beans.

'You're fired, Paul.'

'If I go, Karin goes.'

'I would have thought that's up to her.'

'Mary's going, isn't she? You won't have anyone left. It won't look good, will it?'

'You should have thought about that before you started on this' – he has difficulty finding the word – '*betrayal*.'

'Like Jesus,' says Paul. 'Only you aren't.'

'I beg your pardon?'

'Like Judas betraying Jesus in the Garden of Gethsemane. You do think you're God, don't you, Steven? And all this' – Paul's gesture takes in the clinic, Steven's own jewel of a house, its sparkle now reduced due to Mrs Lemon's absence, the grounds, every trout swimming in the brown water, even the sheets of figured paper spread out on Steven's desk and recording lives to be lived and deaths inevitable or avoidable, even the Eurocheque slip in Steven's jacket pocket recording the purchase of Matilda Cressey's Lapponia ring – 'All this, Steven, all this territory, all these facts, are your kingdom, and you expect *us* to worship you, to help you to preserve it as you want it, as *you* say it ought to be.

'I'll tell you something else, Steven, you should have been straight with me about your past. We all make mistakes, but lying about the past's a particularly good way to lose friends.'

Steven ignores this last allegation. 'You've been wanting to say that for a long time, haven't you?'

'Yes, I have.'

'Why didn't you tell me how you felt?'

'I did. I told you we ought to keep statistics. I told you we should keep a record of what we do, we should be prepared to open our books for everyone to see. I told you we should have not only the courage but the *wisdom* of our convictions.'

'You want to be the Director of Roman Hall, don't you? You want to take my place! That's why you didn't want to discuss with me how you felt. But you're wrong about me, Paul. I don't want to be God, I only want to be human. But that's much more difficult.'

As Paul Monkton leaves, Mary Elliott comes in. 'I'm going home now, is there anything I can do for you before I go? Are you all right, Steven?' She senses the argument hung in the close air of the room, sees the evidence of Steven's flushed face.

'Yes.' He looks at her above the mound of papers. 'I'm fine. But I need the latest report on *Confidential Inquiries into Maternal Deaths*. Do we have it?'

'No. I've already looked. You want to know how common haemorrhage is as a cause of death?'

'That's right.'

'I'll get a copy in the morning. I've got a friend who's doing midwifery at the John Radcliffe in Oxford. I'm sure she can sneak one out of the library for me for a few hours.'

'We need it tonight.'

'Why? You look so tired, Steven . . .'

'A man from the Department of Health is coming down in the morning. Can you be here?'

'Yes.' She stands up.

'Surely the journalists have gone home now?'

'Not all of them.'

'We'll have to risk it. Can you ring your friend and get her to meet us somewhere with the report?'

Mary looks doubtful. 'I'll try.'

'I do appreciate this, Mary,' he says again.

Matilda is woken by the phone. It rings in the bedroom, but the answering machine is still on, so when she picks it up she hears her own voice twice, syncopating against itself.

'This is Claudia Foxman speaking.'

'Hold on a minute, please.' Matilda gets out of bed, goes into the sitting room, turns the answering machine off, gets back into bed.

'You've been away, Miss Cressey. I hope you had a pleasant time.'

'Sorry?'

'So am I. We have met, in the Chelsea Physic Garden. I was with Dr van den Biot at the time.' There is a suggestive lilt to the phrase 'at the time'.

'Oh yes.'

'I read your report with interest, Miss Cressey.'

Matilda's head is heavy with sleep. 'Why are you calling me?'

'I'd like to talk to you about your report. Amongst other things. Could I come to your office in the morning? At, say, ten?'

What does Claudia Foxman want? Why, moreover, isn't Steven, who might just possibly know the answer to this question, ringing her as he promised? Matilda looks at her bedside clock – 10 p.m. She's slept for more than six hours.

Whoever answers the phone at Roman Hall is adamant that Steven isn't there.

'But I'm not a journalist,' wails Matilda. 'Are you sure he isn't there?'

'Quite sure.'

She leaves a message which they promise to give him on his return.

In a transport café on the A40 under bright yellow lights, Steven van den Biot and Mary Elliott meet Mary's friend Jackie Salter, who has a copy of the latest *Confidential Inquiries into Maternal Deaths* in her handbag. 'We'd better have a cup of tea,' hisses Mary, 'or it'll look odd.'

Steven opens the report, starts taking notes on it. The women talk inconsequentially of this and that. Mary orders him some toast. 'You haven't eaten, you need to keep your strength up.' He takes his eyes off 'main causes of death' for a moment, and sees the thick steam rising off the plates of cabbage and sausages, smells the oil and smoke-laden air, observes the men coming noisily and familiarly through the door with tabloids rolled up under their arms. At the next table one gets up, leaving his paper behind. Steven's eyes flicker over it: 'Bogus Doctor Lets Mother of Nine Die'. He picks the paper up. Some journalist has been doing some elementary detective work and has discovered that the name under which Steven practises isn't his by birth, or rather, wasn't his when he qualified. Mary and Jackie read it too. 'Is this true?' asks Mary.

'Sure it's true. I changed my name for personal reasons. But it doesn't mean I'm not properly qualified.'

'You should sue them,' says Jackie, an open, honest young woman with a fringe and round blue eyes, matching her uniform. Her unselfish indignation seems to Steven, like Mary's concern for him, an oasis of decency in a world of conspiracy and corruption. 'Maybe. Come on, let's go. I think I've got what I need from this report now.'

Mary drives him to the back entrance of Roman Hall, where he climbs over the wall separating his garden from the field at the back of the estate and lets himself silently, like an intruder, into his own house. It's a black, cold night – black and cold enough to have sent the journalists on their way at last. Steven gets himself a whisky and sits for a while looking out across the lawn in the dark. There's enough light to see the trees wave against the sky. He remembers then that he promised to call Matilda.

'Where have you been?' He tells her of the need to present a good case to the Department of Health in the morning, which necessitated the getting of a particular report from the library, but doesn't mention Mary and Jackie or the transport café.

'Your friend Claudia Foxman called me,' Matilda tells him.

'Did she? What did she want?'

'She wasn't very friendly.'

'Matilda,' says Steven suddenly, 'Claudia Foxman is not my friend, either. And this will all be over one day. It won't last. We mustn't drown in it. But we mustn't see each other till it's over.'

'Are you trying to get out of the relationship?'

'Of course not. I'm trying to be sensible. I love you, Matilda.'

When Matilda goes to the office in the morning, Claudia Foxman is already waiting, trim and pristine in a pale-blue suit with a mahogany briefcase the same shade as her hair, which she's recently had treated with henna in Bond Street. Margaret Watteau raises her eyes clumsily to the ceiling, attempting to convey the fact that she's sorry Lady Foxman's already there, waiting to pounce.

'It's all right, Margaret. Are there any calls?' Margaret gives her a list. 'Would you like to come in, Lady Foxman?' Matilda's voice is as frosty as Claudia's suit.

'Miss Cressey,' mouths Margaret urgently, 'I forgot to tell you the coffee machine's broken.'

'You'd better get someone to mend it, then, hadn't you?' Margaret sits humped over her Zenith feeling tears come into her eyes. She's not sure she can cope with all this. Maybe she's premenstrual. Les says she ought to take hormones for it, but Margaret read in *Woman's Own* that the treatment comes in suppositories you have to put up your bottom, which is quite the worst idea she's come across for a long time.

At the same time as Claudia Foxman and Matilda Cressey come face to face at 88 Juliana Crescent, Steven van den Biot walks over to Roman Hall and is surprised to hear a considerable commotion wafting across the landscape towards him. People – women? – shouting. The horns of cars. He stops in his tracks to take a few deep breaths; above his head a hawk circles, dips towards him, and then is gone into the clouds.

'*Choice* in childbirth, *choice* in childbirth!' The chant floats hawk-like into the sky followed by another: 'We want the doctor, we want the doctor!' Steven peers round the side of the building. A hundred or so colourful campaigning women have arranged themselves there with banners and babies, and in the midst of it all is an official-looking car containing (presumably) Bernard Oates. Steven strides ahead with more confidence than he feels. The women, spying him, cluster around, and one tall redhead takes him firmly by the hand. 'Dr van den Beer-it, we're very pleased to see you. Elizabeth Martin, I had a baby at Roman Hall last year.' He notices then a parcel tied round her waist. 'That's Katie. Isn't she beautiful? They're all such beautiful babies. That's why we wanted to come and show you our support. I'm from the Natural Childbirth Society myself. My friends here are from a variety of organizations, including the Upright Birth Movement, Water Babies, Women Against Handicap . . .'

Elizabeth's welcome is interrupted by a man in a suit who is trying to ensure Bernard Oates' safe delivery out of the car and into the building. 'Excuse me a minute, will you?' Steven goes over to the car and helps Bernard Oates out. 'I'm really sorry about this, Dr Oates. I had no idea it was going on, it's nothing to do with me, I assure you.'

Bernard Oates isn't pleased. The women start chanting again: 'Stop the persecution, stop the persecution!'

'It really is very embarrassing,' says Steven again in his office.

'What is, Dr Bear-it?'

'This' – Steven indicates the crowd on the gravel – 'support.'

'Quite a mess you've got yourself in, haven't you, old chap?'

'It's not of my making. I've merely been doing my work. The work Roman Hall was set up to do.'

'That's what I'm here to discuss.' Bernard Oates sits down and takes a sheaf of papers out of his briefcase. 'I'm only concerned with one matter, you understand, and that's whether you've been breach-ing the terms of your licence. I'm not interested in the kind of medicine you practise, I'm not even particularly interested in whether it's dangerous or not. That's up to the client these days. It's one of the benefits of private medicine, isn't it, the client's right to make his own mistakes!' Bernard Oates guffaws like Eeyore. Steven has no idea whether he's serious or not.

'Can I say something?'

'Anything you like, old chap. Please, go ahead.'

'I take the point about the terms of the licence. Unfortunately we are somewhat in error there. I was on leave the week the incident happened.'

'You mean the Maternal Death?'

'I do. I was on leave. My assistant, Dr Monkton, had assumed directorial responsibility, but he was unexpectedly called to London for a meeting. He should have arranged locum cover. That is our normal practice under such circumstances. Unfortunately he omitted to do so.' Steven's lips gesture downwards, indicating that this is the end of the matter.

'So it was Dr Monkton's fault?'

'I didn't say that.'

'Look, Dr Bear-it, I think we need to establish the rules of plain speaking here. No beating about the bush. Say what you mean. Clearly. And I'll do the same.'

'Fair enough. To continue: the clinic is in error with respect to medical cover for a short period, some six hours, last week. But to get to the actual circumstances of the death, I'm afraid it's likely that Priscilla Mayhew would have died wherever she'd been. I don't know if you ever did much obstetrics, Dr Oates?'

Bernard Oates had been a dermatologist in Corby for a while, but doesn't like to admit this too often. 'My experience in the field is limited, Dr van den Bear-it.'

'Well, it was a torrential haemorrhage. One gets that sometimes in a grand multipara. Quite without warning, you know. I have the greatest respect for the midwife who was in attendance. She's been with us ever since the clinic started.' Bernard Oates is writing some of this down. 'And I spent last night reviewing our mortality statistics.' Bernard Oates looks up sharply from his notebook. 'I've put the essential information down for you.' Steven passes Bernard Oates a sheet of paper from his desk. 'I think you can see from it that we're not at all out of line. In fact, when you consider some of the high-risk cases we get here, we've really done rather well.'

The Man from the Ministry looks at the paper and scratches his head. After a while he folds it up and puts it in his briefcase. 'Yes. Well, of course I shall have to take this back to my colleagues. There are one or two other matters, however. I take it you've seen the newspapers this morning?'

'No.'

'The allegation about your lack of qualifications?'

'Oh, that. Quite unfounded.'

'You can prove that, I take it?'

Steven passes Bernard Oates two more sheets of paper: one, his medical certificate; and two, the statutory declaration of change of name.

'Hmmm.'

'Those are the originals, if you'd like copies I'll arrange to have them made.'

'Now what about the Cressey Report?' Bernard Oates extracts that from the file, waves it around like a flag.

'What about it?'

'I suppose you realize it's one of the strongest pieces of counter-evidence you have? It was produced before all this, er, hoo-ha.'

Steven is relieved to hear Bernard Oates describing it as a hoo-ha. 'Yes. Though, to be honest, Miss Cressey's report, the survey on which it's based, was undertaken as the result of a complaint made by one of our clients. I expect you know that.'

'Dr den Bear-it,' Bernard Oates is feeling irritated again now. 'Why do people keep complaining about you? I mean you seem to me a perfectly ordinary chap; what is it you're doing that gets people's backs up so? And if you know what it is, don't you think you ought to stop doing it? After all, the bottom line in all this is that you could lose your licence. I'm not suggesting', Bernard Oates adds hastily, 'that you *will*. The Minister's not keen to withdraw licences from thriving private health clinics of this type. You make a healthy profit, don't you? Eight hundred k wasn't it, last year?'

'Was it?'

'Forty per cent of your clients come from overseas.'

'Do they?'

'That's particularly healthy.'

'Is it?'

'You don't seem very *au fait* with the figures, Dr van Bear-it.'

'I'm interested in the work, Dr Oates, I like helping women to have babies. I don't enjoy these hassles.'

'Neither do I, neither do I. But it's my job to sort them out. Now I'd like to see the rest of your staff, if you don't mind.'

Steven, curious to know what Claudia Foxman wants with Matilda Cressey, phones Matilda while Bernard Oates is seeing Paul, Mary and Karin. He gets through to Margaret and calls her by her first name, which quite revives her. 'I'll put you straight through, Doctor,' she says in a singing tone of voice.

'Claudia Foxman's just gone,' says Matilda. 'It was quite extraordinary, do you know what she wanted? She came to ask me to go on a Board she's setting up to oversee a programme of research she's funding into the physical and emotional development of babies delivered at Roman Hall.'

'Is that all?' Steven doesn't quite know what he imagined Claudia's business with Matilda would have been, but he's been vaguely worrying about the scorn of rejected women for some time.

'Why, Steven? Why does she want me to do that?'

'Co-opting the enemy, obviously. Did she say anything else? Anything more personal?'

'Hints only.'

'Hints only. What do you think she knows?'

'Only that we were both away at the same time. And that I didn't find anything wrong with Roman Hall in my report. When can we meet, Steven?'

'Matilda, didn't you hear what I said last night?'

'I can't live without you.'

'Nonsense. You lived without me for the first however many years of your life, you can perfectly well live without me for a short while now.' Steven remembers the Steven of another age believing in the impossibility of survival without love. Matilda recalls panic in Shanghai.

'We carry our history with us,' she says.

'Yes, but we live in the present, Matilda,' he replies. 'Or we try to.' As he says it he understands how rarely he achieves this. The struggle to emancipate himself from his own past is not nearly over. There is a bridge that needs to be built from then to now, something strong and sensible that will take him to unarguably new terrain. Matilda Cressey will be that bridge. But it's probably as well she doesn't know this; she has enough roles to play as it is.

Ralph Scull sits on the Circle Line reading a large pile of newspapers. He's been right round once, more by accident than by choice, as he was right in the middle of Matilda's defence of Steven van den Biot when the doors opened and closed very quickly at Edgware Road. He's taking the Declaration of Paternity to Clare Paynter and their daughter Clemency in Paddington. He could have posted it, but he feels a strange interest in seeing the baby again.

Clemency is in her baby chair in front of the television watching a programme about chemical fertilizers. Clare is reading a large book about how to look after babies by Hugh Jolly. She isn't pleased to see him. 'I brought you this.' He hands her the completed Declaration.

'Thanks.'

'Can I just say hallo?'

'It doesn't give you any rights, you know,' she says defensively.

'Don't turn it into a drama, Clare, I just want to see my daughter for a minute.'

He kneels down between Clemency and the television and looks into her little blue eyes. She looks at him very seriously for a minute, then opens her toothless mouth and smiles dribblingly at him. Ralph's heart quite melts.

Clare pretends not to have noticed. She's in the middle of a chapter on early potty training, the disadvantages of. 'I didn't know they smiled at this age,' says Ralph. 'She must be very advanced. Is she very advanced, Clare? Can I pick her up?'

'No.'

'Why not?'

'One, you're not supposed to be here, and two because she'll throw up all over you. She's just been fed and she always throws up afterwards if you jiggle her around.'

Ralph undoes the strap in the chair and lifts Clemency up. He takes her in his arms to the window to have a look at her. 'Hasn't she got lovely skin, Clare? It's like silk.' He strokes it gently with his hairy fingers. 'Does she always have pink cheeks?' He touches them, as though they were as fragile as apple blossom. Then he cradles her head with his hand and notices the spot on the top where the bones haven't yet joined. 'She's got a hole in her head, Clare!' he says with alarm. 'You can feel her little heart beating through it. You must take her to the doctor!'

'Don't be silly, Ralph. That's her fontanelle.'

She looks it up in the index. 'Where, show me!' He reads the bit about the fontanelle and Clemency exudes some sour milk down the front of Malcolm's cardigan.

'That's enough, Ralph.' Clare takes the baby firmly from him. 'It was very nice of you to bring the form. Thank you for coming. Clemency's going to bed now.'

He kisses the baby's throbbing fontanelle and beats an ignorant retreat, feeling wounded. Halfway down the street, he remembers what he wanted to say to Clare and goes back.

'What is it now?'

'Let me in a minute. I want to talk to you.'

'I've put Clemency down and I'm not getting her up again. Dr Jolly says . . .'

'Bully for Dr Jolly. Listen, Clare, about this van den Beet chap, I've been thinking that perhaps I was . . . well . . . rather hasty. I mean, what do you think?'

Clare's eyes look surprisingly liquid. 'You do what you want, Ralph. As far as I'm concerned, the whole thing was an awful mistake.'

'What whole thing?'

'You. The baby. Roman Hall.'

'But don't you love her?'

'Of course I love her. But I've made a mess of my life. An awful mess.'

Ralph pokes around in Malcolm's trousers looking for a hanky. 'Come on, silly, it's not as bad as all that.'

'Get out,' she says behind her tears, 'get out. I don't ever want to see you again!'

Later in the day, when Ralph tells Malcolm about his encounter with Clare and Clemency, Malcolm tells him Clare's got postnatal depression. 'You have to be careful with that, Scullery. She might need treatment. About twenty per cent of ladies do.'

'What do you know about it, Malcolm?'

'Not a lot. But I've just been to the dentist and I read an article about it in *Woman*. Or was it *Homes and Gardens*? About hormone treatment for various disorders actually. Did you know there's been an eighty per cent increase in prescriptions for progesterone supplements over the last five years?'

'Maybe it would do me some good too,' says Ralph gloomily.

Elizabeth Martin holds a press conference outside Roman Hall. Steven, Matilda and all the other protagonists and participants in what has become known as the Roman Hall affair watch the results on the six o'clock news.

'We believe,' says Elizabeth in her clear, strong, schoolmistressy voice, swinging her curtain of copper hair back away from the microphone, 'we believe that obstetricians have taken birth away from nature and away from women, and Dr van den Biot is one of the few doctors in the world who understands this. Few people realize', Elizabeth's voice rises, 'that in some places four out of five women now have their babies by Caesarean section. All babies are electronically monitored during pregnancy and birth, despite the fact that no research has been done on the possible long-term hazards of this. Many women become extremely depressed after childbirth because of this medical intervention. That is one reason why they come to Roman Hall. That is one reason why Dr van den Biot is a good doctor. He understands that childbirth is a natural process and women have a right to choose how they have their babies.'

Through this monologue one can see the reporter trying to interrupt Elizabeth, but Elizabeth, being a practised campaigner, has developed the habit of tying the beginning of every sentence on to the end of the previous one. She is simply uninterruptable. 'The death of Mrs Mayhew is, of course, tragic, but we don't believe it was due to negligence. There's no evidence that the standard of care practised in Dr van den Biot's clinic is in any way deficient.'

The reporter sums up with difficulty against the background of cheering women and wailing babies. The camera, panning away from the scene, shows Roman Hall serenely guarding its secrets.

'Well I never, Maggie!' says Lesley on the sofa in Speedwell Avenue. 'What does Miss Cressey think of all this?'

'She hasn't said, Les. But she did shout at me this morning.'

'What for?'

'Because the coffee machine's broken.'

'Phooey. Is she a caffeine addict or what?'

'The water just falls out the bottom. As fast as you pour it in . . .'

'Get one of the men to mend it. That's what men are for, isn't it, Maggie, mending things!' Damian in his highchair, chewing a soggy finger of toast and Marmite, spits a large piece of it out at them.

'I don't think he really likes that Marmite, Les.'

'Babies like Marmite, Maggie,' says Lesley firmly. 'Has she said anything about her holiday? Has Miss Cressey said anything?'

'No. But I did notice something, Les.'

'What?'

'A ring. Miss Cressey's come back from Finland with A Ring.'

'Is it on the right finger, Maggie?'

'Yes!'

Lesley thinks. 'This could be difficult for you, Maggie.'

'How?'

'It's privileged information. About The Ring I mean. I mean, we don't *know* the doctor gave it to her, do we?'

'No.'

'But it does seem likely. What sort of ring is it, Maggie?'

'I haven't had a good look, Les, but it's kind of silver and modern, if you know what I mean.'

In the light from the television, Lesley looks a little sadly at her own engagement ring, a High Street diamond, then gets up and lifts Damian out of his chair, feeling in need of a cuddle.

Matilda watches the same news in the Cornfords' house. Anthony is away doing his annual vineyard trip. Willow, apart from regaling Matilda with baby Eve's latest antics, is keen to hear her side of the story.

'I know you disapprove of me, Willow, for writing the report the way I did.'

'Disapprove's not the right word.' Willow gets up and fetches a bottle of nonalcoholic wine from the kitchen. She opens it, pours two glasses and hands one to Matilda. 'Try it. It's good stuff.' She sips her own. 'No, it's not that I disapprove, Tilly. I feel you allowed your personal feelings to colour the report. I still think there's something odd about Dr van den Biot. I don't know what, but I feel it. I think you had the opportunity to evaluate his work in such a way that a question mark would hang over it and then maybe this death wouldn't have happened.'

'Steven and I are going to get married,' says Matilda abruptly.

'Gee! You are a dark horse, Tilly. And when did this happen?'

'We went away together. After the report was published.'

'I rather gathered that. Where did you go?'

'To Finland for a week. It was wonderful, Willow, absolutely wonderful. Quite out of this world.'

'Yes, that's what worries me,' says her friend. 'It ought to be *in* this world, then I'd believe you. When are you going to get married?'

'Oh, we haven't decided.'

'What's he like in bed, Tilly? I've always wanted to know about the private life of gynaecologists.'

So have I, thinks Matilda. Finland flashes before her, or rather through her. The synonymy of Steven's sexual stance towards her and the frozen, sentinel-like scheme of the landscape had seemed unsurprising at the time. Like everything else about Steven, it had the air of being scrupulously planned. It wasn't that he'd done anything wrong: far from it. Being a gynaecologist, he'd certainly known *what* to do – how to tell what pleased and what didn't, what was working and what was unlikely to. He'd told her she had a fine sensual body, but that wasn't news either – though perhaps had he not said it, she would have required him to. And he, for his part, had seemed aroused in the right way at the right time and suitably in control of his sexual crescendos and explosions. She hadn't been able to detect any problems – except one, that maybe his heart wasn't quite in it. She sensed that beneath the carefully sculpted movements and the considered texture of their conjugations there lurked a man quite thoroughly out of sorts with himself. But it serves to encourage her, this prospect of the subterranean Steven to be discovered. He becomes even more alluring and mysterious, and it is, she knows, in bed that she hopes to wear him down.

So in answer to Willow's question, Matilda surprises them both by blushing. 'He's fine.'

'Okay, don't tell me then.'

'Listen, Willow, I'm confused about something, can I talk to you about it?'

'Well, if you won't talk about your sex life, I guess we're going to have to find some other topic of conversation, aren't we?'

'He wants to keep it a secret. I mean, Steven doesn't want anyone to know about our – our engagement.'

'And that makes you kind of uncomfortable?'

Matilda nods.

'It would me, too. Why does he want to keep quiet about it?'

'It's all these accusations being made about his work. He says I'm – the report I wrote – is about the only thing on his side, and he needs all the friends he can get. But don't you think, Willow, don't you think that love conquers everything? "Passion makes perfect what the world neglects."'

Willow raises an eyebrow.

'Browning.'

'If you say so. No, I don't, as a matter of fact. But you always were a headstrong character, weren't you? Have you told Steven how you feel?'

'I've tried to. But he won't see me at the moment, while all this is going on. That's what I meant by keeping it secret.'

'I think you *must* see him once and he must agree a date when, whatever happens, it won't be a secret any more.' Willow feels quite clear about this.

'That's a good idea. Can I use your phone?'

'Go right ahead.'

Steven's vacuuming the sitting room when Matilda rings. He hadn't realized quite how much detritus is trapped by navy-blue carpets – Mrs Lemon's departure has ruffled him nearly as much as all the other events put together.

'Steven, we have to meet. Not for long. You can make it as secret as you like, but I need to talk to you.'

'It'll be difficult. I think I'm being followed.'

'Shake them off, I'm sure you can do that.'

'It's really important, is it, Matilda?'

'Yes, it is.'

He names the transport café where he examined the *Confidential Inquiries* report. 'Eleven o'clock tonight. It's easier in the dark.'

'I think you enjoy all this subterfuge,' she accuses him when they meet in the café.

'Not so.'

He's wearing a casual jacket she hasn't seen before. 'It doesn't work.'

'What doesn't?'

'No one would mistake you for a lorry driver.'

'Ah, but it has another purpose.' He unzips it and brings out from an inside pocket a single, perfect, silvery-lilac rose. 'This is for you. An early Blue Moon. Hybrid tea rose, you know. I've never picked a rose in the dark before.' He shows her three strips of Elastoplast on his fingers. The combination of Elastoplast and rose effectively dissipates her anger.

'It's good to see you, Matilda, I've missed you.'

'Oh, Steven!'

'Don't cry, darling. Not here.'

'Why not here?'

'I don't know, it doesn't seem right.'

She laughs weakly.

'What was it you wanted to say?'

'That I hate being hidden.'

'I know that. But it's not for ever.'

'Can we set a date for the wedding, Steven?'

'July the twenty-third,' he says. 'I've already booked the registry office.'

'Oh, Steven!' she says again, quickly followed by: 'But don't you think I should have been consulted about the date?'

'I was going to,' he says, 'but I thought I'd book it just in case. I'm not going to let you go, Matilda.' He reaches through the forest of sauce and condiment bottles for her hand, the one with the Finnish ring on it. 'Now I've found you, I'm not going to let you go. I know it's a difficult time for you, you're finding it difficult to trust me, you need a sign of my commitment. That's why I thought it would be a good idea to fix the date. It is a good idea, isn't it?' He searches her eyes with a touching apparent insecurity.

'Oh yes.'

'We can talk about the details later. Drink your tea. We can go for a walk round the lay-by provided ITN aren't skulking behind one of the vans.'

Behind a Danish bacon van Steven kisses Matilda, pushing her head roughly against its scraped metallic surface. He locates a breast beneath her black jersey and tweaks the nipple momentarily. She feels his penis against her, like the metal of the lorry behind. The unsolicited, unexpected, almost unkind nature of the interaction is intended to bind Matilda more firmly to Steven, and succeeds in doing so.

14
Good
Fathers

Ralph Scull is working hard at his novel, interrupted by frequent stray thoughts of baby Clemency's blue eyes. Whenever he bursts out of the house on one of his cigarette or chewing gum or beer-buying expeditions, he always seems to pass toy shops whose windows are cluttered with cerise pandas and tawny baby giraffes with bent necks trying to tell him something. He's still having trouble with his hero, who refuses to go on the Outward Bound course which will enable him to discover the computer code needed for access to police files, which in turn is needed for the discovery of what really happened on the building site in Wapping.

One evening in the pub, Malcolm, who is taking a vicarious interest in Ralph's doings ('You're wearing my clothes, Scullery, that *entitles* me to be interested'), asks him about the husband of the woman who died at Roman Hall.

'I don't know. How should *I* know?' Ralph blows a smoke ring and hides behind it.

'Alone with all those kids,' reflects Malcolm.

Ralph sees a row of Clemencies lined up in identical baby chairs. 'She's really getting to me, Malcolm,' he says suddenly.

'Who is?'

'Clemency. My daughter. I don't understand it, it's not in character. I *hate* babies. Clare wanted one, she swore blind she'd look after it. I didn't imagine I'd have much to do with it. And now look what's happened.' He stares morosely at Malcolm.

'Well, what's happened is that you *don't* have much to do with her; what's wrong with that?'

'I *want* to. Oh, I don't mean I want to change nappies or get up in the night, but I *do* want to *see* her. She is *mine*, after all.'

Malcolm finds the development of possessive feelings odd in one so disinterested in property that most of the time he uses other people's.

He pursues the original topic of conversation. 'This other father, Scullery, perhaps he's suing as well? Don't the two of you have something in common? Shouldn't you at least express your sympathy?'

The next day, when Algernon Dupont still won't budge, Ralph takes Malcolm's green Citroën and drives to the Mayhew home. It's not difficult to get the address – the name, the area and the business were all well publicized in the press.

Ralph's not at all sure what he's going to say to Christopher Mayhew. He decides to leave the car at the gate to the drive, and walks up towards a neo-Gothic semi with peeling woodwork and outbuildings sitting at ludicrous angles. A large number of cats skirmish among dead daffodils in the garden.

The door is opened by a female child, about seven or eight, with bare feet, unbrushed hair and wearing a dirty T-shirt with a red elephant on it. 'Who are you?' she demands.

'I'm Ralph Scull.'

'I don't know you,' she says firmly, closing the door in his face. Nonplussed by this, Ralph walks round the side of the house into the garden. A small boy is sitting on a pot singing to himself while another, slightly larger, is trying to cram a fluffy grey kitten into an old handbag. As he watches this scene with mounting panic, another little girl, not the one who answered the door, comes out wearing shoes that are much too big for her. 'You shouldn't do that, Sammy,' she says bossily, 'I'll tell Dad when he comes home.'

'It doesn't matter, Lily, this one went wrong. I heard Mum say that. It shouldn't have been fluffy. The big tom down the lane got into its mum's bottom one night when no one was looking.'

The children notice Ralph standing there and at the same time a car grinds to a halt round the front of the house. 'Daddy!' shrieks the child attached to the pot. The others run round the side of the house and come back a minute later with an agitated wild-haired man encumbered by several Tesco carrier bags. 'Who are you?' he demands as well.

'I'm Ralph Scull.'

'Am I supposed to know you?'

'No, I . . .'

'Why are you here, then?'

'Could I come in a minute, Mr Mayhew?'

Without saying anything Christopher Mayhew strides into the house, followed by his brood. 'Take those shoes off, Lily. Where's

Cassie? Go and find her and tell her to wipe Timmy's bottom.' He dumps the bags on the already cluttered kitchen surfaces and puts the kettle on, all in one gesture. Fishing a small black cat out of the sink, he washes his hands and turns round to face Ralph. 'I won't offer you a cup of tea, we haven't got enough clean cups. What did you say you'd come about?'

Ralph opens and closes his mouth inarticulately, then offers Christopher Mayhew a cigarette.

'Good God, no. Can't smoke with this lot around.'

The female child who opened the door comes into the kitchen. 'Be a good girl, Cassie, go and prise Timmy off the pot.'

Cassie looks hard at Ralph. 'I found this man outside, Daddy, but I didn't know him so I wouldn't let him come in.'

'That's right, Cassie. I don't know him either.'

'So why did *you* let him in?'

'Mr Mayhew . . .' begins Ralph insecurely.

'You're not a journalist, are you?'

'No. No. I *have* come about Roman Hall, though.'

'She shouldn't have gone there, of course. Priscilla. My wife. She should have gone into hospital. Everyone told her that, but she wouldn't listen. She liked breeding, you see. But she liked to be left alone to get on with it like the cats, and she said they don't do that any more in hospital. They interfere all the time. It cleaned us out of money, too.'

'Well, I don't know about that. My wife' – Ralph pauses on the lie – 'had a baby there too recently.'

'Oh God!' says Christopher Mayhew suddenly. 'I left it in the car.' He flies out and comes back with a basket which he places on top of the boiler.

Ralph peers in. 'Is that . . . ?'

'Yes, that's number seven. Cassie!'

'I wiped his bottom but I'm not emptying the pot,' says Cassie. 'He's done a big one.' She disappears with a flourish.

'Well, yes,' Ralph tries to continue, 'as I said, my baby was born there too.'

'And you've come all the way here to tell me that?'

'No, no. What I wanted to say is that I'm taking legal proceedings against the place. For medical incompetence. And other things. I thought perhaps you . . .'

'Am I going to sue as well? Not bloody likely. How am I going to find the time to do that? Couldn't even get to see a solicitor with seven children in tow.' The basket on the boiler begins to fuss. An elegant blue Siamese springs from somewhere into the basket and stands on top of the baby, mewing.

'All right, Petrol, I *will* feed him. Thinks she's his mother, you see.' Christopher Mayhew opens the fridge and takes out a bottle of milk with one hand while lifting the cat off the baby with the other. Then he pours some water from the kettle into a saucepan and tries to stand the cat in it.

When Christopher Mayhew picks the baby up, Ralph notices how large his hands are in relation to the size of the baby. 'Couldn't you get some help?'

'How? There aren't any relatives. Priscilla's mum's been in a mental home for years. Her only sister's in Australia. I've got a sister but she's an opera singer. There's no home help service any more. It *was* part of the welfare state, you know, that utopia we once had. I can't afford to pay anyone. Not on a part-time teaching salary. Been a bad year for cats as well. One of them got out at Christmas and we wasted a litter.'

'Yes, I know,' says Ralph abstractedly. 'I don't suppose there's anything I can do, is there?'

'You can hold the baby while I get the lid off this bottle.'

Ralph looks into the face of the hungry infant and remembers Clemency. Christopher Mayhew unscrews the bottle, puts the teat on, tests the temperature in a most professional-looking way, offering his milky hand to Petrol, who's waiting on the draining board. Ralph hands the baby back. 'Well, in that case I'd better be going,' he says offhandedly.

'I wouldn't try going out of the front if I were you, the hall's all cluttered up with some game of the children's.'

Ralph opens the kitchen door and goes out. He comes back in again. 'Mr Mayhew, I meant to say I'm really sorry. You know, about . . .'

'Thanks,' says Christopher Mayhew.

'I need some advice, Daddy,' says Matilda.

John Cressey, surprised to be visited by his daughter at his surgery rather than at home, closes up Mrs Leadbetter's notes, in which he's been writing about her referral to BUPA for a haemorrhoidectomy.

'What's the matter, darling?'

'I don't know how to begin, Daddy. You remember Steven van den Biot?'

'How could I forget? Always seems to be in the news these days.'

'Well, I . . . I'm going to marry him, Daddy.'

John Cressey's glasses descend down his nose. 'Is that wise?'

'What do you mean, wise? I love him, Daddy.'

'Well, I hope so. I mean presumably you do, or you wouldn't want to marry him. But how old is he?'

'Fifty.'

'That's a big age gap, fourteen years. I take it you've thought about the implications?'

'It doesn't seem very important.'

'Isn't he married already?'

'No.'

'Divorced? Widowed?'

'No.'

'Why not? I mean, why didn't he marry? What are you doing wanting to marry a doctor anyway? He *is* a doctor, is he? I mean a proper one, one of us?'

'Listen, Daddy, don't interrogate me about Steven, please. I'm old enough to know my own mind. That's not what I need advice on.'

'No, I expect you want to know what to think about all these allegations that are being made about him. I always feel sorry for doctors who lay themselves on the line – as this chap undoubtedly has with this natural childbirth business – and then get pilloried for it. But it said on the news the other night he's getting a lot of support from the ladies' organizations. That must be a good thing, mustn't it? Means something, surely?'

Matilda nods.

'I should think the Department will close the place down while they sort it out, that's what usually happens. He'll get a break then. Do you think he's been doing something wrong then, darling?'

'No, of course not.'

'You do, don't you? What is it? There's a chap who's suing, isn't there, for incompetence and something else – some story about immoral goings-on, sounds like a trumped-up case to me. I don't think my little girl would fall for a man mixed up in anything like that. But there was a Maternal Death, too, wasn't there?' She nods again. 'Could have been an accident, we all have them. Nature's a savage beast. She's always sacrificed some women on the altar of motherhood. I wouldn't worry about it, darling, it'll all blow over.'

Matilda finds her father's sage platitudes as comforting as she did on the dark nights when she couldn't sleep as a child, when the wind rattled the windows and drainpipes danced thoughtlessly against buildings. She blows her nose. 'But I am in a very difficult personal position, Daddy. Because of this report which I wrote *before* I got involved with Steven, but nobody will believe that, will they? And because Steven feels we should keep our relationship secret at the moment. I don't like being a skeleton in somebody's cupboard, Daddy.'

'I think Steven's right,' says John Cressey, perceiving his daughter's need for patriarchal firmness in this confusing situation. 'It would only damage both of you if the truth came out now. By the way, what should I tell your mother?'

'Nothing. For the time being. I don't want to worry her.'

'Come on, I'll take you out to lunch. I've got a meeting at the College this afternoon, it's a nice day, let's go to the new open-air restaurant in Regent's Park. You look as though you could do with a square meal.'

Lord Foxman comes back from Africa with a new wife.

'You look rather tired, Lady Foxman,' says Paul Monkton to Claudia at a meeting of the newly set up Claudia Foxman Trust. They've just concluded the technical legal business required to establish the research programme under Paul Monkton's directorship, with a proviso that if Paul's appointment at Roman Hall is terminated, he'll be able to take the endowment with him. The trouble Steven is in doesn't seem to have deterred Claudia from her desire to institute a scientific evaluation of the clinic's work; it has, if anything, caused her to redouble her efforts, though she has been adamant about setting it up so that Steven himself has no control over it.

'Personal problems,' she indicates, in answer to Paul's concerned observation. She stands up and packs her briefcase, now the meeting's been successfully concluded.

'Oh?'

'There's no secret about it. My ex-husband has returned from abroad and is asking for custody of John Dominic. He's found himself a new wife. I am quite distraught, Dr Monkton.' She turns a severely sad expression on him. Paul Monkton notes the beauty of her face, highlighted by suffering. 'He won't get it, of course. Who would take a ten-month-old baby away from his mother? But the bastard' – Paul

134

is thrown but engaged by her language – 'is arguing that he can provide John Dominic with a proper family, whereas I, who am only his mother, cannot.'

Paul tentatively invites Lady Foxman to dine with him. With alacrity, she accepts. At the end of the evening, spent in a French restaurant in North Oxford, Paul's made up his mind to provide John Dominic with an alternative nuclear family.

Algernon Dupont finally goes on his Outward Bound course. Ralph Scull, Algernon's creator, is so relieved that he gets definitively drunk with Malcolm and a group of mutual friends. The following morning he's woken by a phone call from Clare Paynter's social worker, a well-meaning young woman who's thinking of changing careers and applying for a job as manager of a bird sanctuary. (If social work was a struggle in the old days, it's unmitigated disaster now.)

'I didn't know she had one,' says Ralph Scull, summoned from his alcoholic bed by a voice that says it belongs to his daughter's mother's social worker. Apparently Clare has developed something called postpartum psychosis. The health visitor called and found her tearing pages out of Hugh Jolly and using them as nappies. So Clare has gone into hospital to be cured of this thing. Clemency can't go too – there isn't any space for her.

'But she doesn't take up much,' wails Ralph, remembering Christopher Mayhew lifting his own tiny child off the boiler. His protestations are to no avail, and Amanda Lychwood, the social worker, is asking him to take Clemency. More than that, she is proposing to deliver her at eleven o'clock. Ralph can't think of anything appropriate to say – except, of course, that he doesn't know how to look after babies, which Amanda Lychwood in no way regards as a problem as she will teach him how to.

'Malcolm, wake up, Clemency's coming!'

'That's nice for her,' says Malcolm, turning over and putting the pillow over his head.

'No, you don't understand. My baby. I've got to look after my baby. She's coming here at eleven o'clock.'

Malcolm sits up. 'What, on her own?'

'No, you ass. Miss Lychwood's bringing her.' Malcolm shakes his head to clear it and lies down again, but Ralph's got the duvet off him.

By the time Amanda Lychwood brings Clemency up the front

135

path, Malcolm has done a week's washing-up and Ralph has been out and bought six of the small cerise pandas. He's draped them in a welcoming way round the television set.

Clemency, in her smart carrycot, is said to have been fed an hour ago. 'Of course we've had to wean her,' says Amanda efficiently.

'Have we?'

'Mr Scull, Clemency was BREASTFED.'

'Oh yes, of course she was.'

'I'd like to show you how to make the feed up.' Amanda takes some tins and other equipment out of her capacious social work handbag. While she's measuring out the SMA in the kitchen, Malcolm comes in with the newspaper and some cornflakes. Ralph introduces him to Amanda Lychwood, who frowns. 'I didn't know . . .' she begins.

'We're not,' says Ralph quickly. 'Nothing like that. Just old friends.'

Half an hour later Amanda Lychwood has gone, leaving not only Clemency in her carrycot but a large amount of baby stuff, a list and a phone number. Malcolm offers to go out and get some fish and chips for lunch.

'I don't think she eats fish and chips yet,' says Ralph dubiously. 'What am I going to do, Malcolm?'

Clemency wakes up crying. 'It's not time for her feed,' says Ralph, looking at his watch, which has stopped.

'Listen, Scullery, remember that 1980s film about three men who get landed with a baby? Well, it's not going to be like that here. This one's yours. I'm offering you lunch, then I'm off to the office.'

Ralph pushes a £5 note into Malcolm's hand. 'Okay, I get the message. But get me some nappies, will you? And some of the other things on this list.' He picks it up from under one of the cerise pandas, and reads: 'Tins SMA silver top. Six feeding bottles, packet of teats. Sterilizing tablets and container. (Boots are best.) Disposable nappies size two. Large packet cotton wool. Baby lotion (unperfumed). Jars of apple, vegetables. Packet of baby cereal. Dummies?'

Malcolm looks at the list. 'Didn't Clare have any of this stuff? What's Dummies, question mark?' He has to shout now above Clemency's crying, but fortunately Miss Lychwood has left one bottle already made up. Malcolm departs with the list and Ralph fetches the bottle from the kitchen. He stands in the sitting room looking from it to Clemency to the pandas, then, inspired, tips a few drops of milk on to his wrist. He has no idea what it ought to feel like, and in the absence of a cat to clean his hand is quite at a loss as to what to do next.

But they manage somehow. Over the next few days, Ralph Scull and his daughter Clemency Paynter develop a partial knowledge of one another's habits and limits. Ralph learns it's one of Clemency's habits to wake up regularly twice in the night and to have a bowel movement at 5 a.m. By the third night he's got this sussed, and goes to bed with a bucket of water waiting. But he doesn't find the lack of sleep quite so easy to remedy, and Algernon Dupont stays on his Outward Bound course for an indefinite period. By the time Ralph's bathed Clemency in the morning and made her bottles and gone out and done the shopping, he collapses in front of afternoon television with a cheese sandwich and a pint of beer. He falls into a light and uneasy sleep during the repeat of what Malcolm calls 'Dienasty' at 2.30. Clemency wakes him at 3.30 and off they go again.

On the fifth day Amanda Lychwood calls by and tells him he ought to be taking Clemency for a walk every day as well. 'But there isn't any time!' he complains. 'It takes an hour to feed her every time. That's six hours out of the twenty-four for a start. And then I need my sleep. So does she, except that she doesn't. Babies aren't machines, you know. She requires to be amused sometimes as well. And the washing . . .' Hearing his own voice complaining thus, he wonders where he's heard it all before. An assorted company of women's voices chatter at the back of his head. 'Don't forget I'm the breadwinner too,' he reminisces, recalling his erstwhile struggles with Algernon Dupont. 'You do realize Algernon's still up a mountain?'

'Algernon?'

'My hero,' he says wistfully.

Amanda Lychwood doesn't seem very pleased with his accomplishments. She tells him Clare is 'responding to treatment', but will be in hospital several weeks at least. 'You'll be able to visit her soon,' she says reassuringly.

'But I don't want to visit Clare,' he says. 'We're separated.'

'Oh yes, so you are.'

'Have you ever looked after a baby, Miss Lychwood? I mean on your own, all the time?'

'Well, no.'

'Where do you get all this – this *knowledge* from, then?'

'My training. Books.'

'I see.'

She leaves soon after that.

He's feeding Clemency and watching a programme for small children about flower gardens, when his solicitor rings about the instructions he's giving a barrister for Ralph's case against Steven van den Biot. There's work to be done: research to be carried out, information to be gathered, decisions to be made. In the middle of the conversation, Clemency on his knee burps loudly.

'What was that?'

'What?'

'I thought I heard a noise like a car exhaust. I didn't? Oh well, anyway, Ralph, as I was saying, I think you'd better come into the office tomorrow morning for a couple of hours so we can chat through some of these things.'

'I can't,' says Ralph.

'Would the afternoon be better? I've got a client at three, but I can probably change that.'

'I can't do that, either. I can't do any morning or any afternoon for the foreseeable future, I am unfortunately completely indisposed.' Ralph slams the phone down. Clemency, startled, cries. Ralph holds her close, croons into her ear: 'Daisy, Daisy, give me your answer do . . .' Abruptly she stops crying and something which will transpire to be her very first laugh on this earth develops low down in her tiny abdomen and rises, with a delightful tremulous gutturality, to break into Ralph's left ear.

'You see, Clemency,' he says later, when she's finished laughing, her bottle and a jar of carrots and potatoes, and is looking at him with the adoration of utter saturation, 'you see, Clemency, I don't think I've got time for any of that now. How about we let old Beer-it off the hook? To stew in his own juice? Or whatever the appropriate phrase is. He's had a good shock, after all. Perhaps that's enough. We chaps have got enough to do looking after you lot, haven't we?'

15
When Did You Last See Your Daughter?

As John Cressey had predicted, the Department of Health withdraws Roman Hall's licence 'pending the results of investigation'. 'Sorry, old chap,' says Bernard Oates to Steven, for whom he's developed some respect. 'Protocol, bureaucracy, you know. I shouldn't worry too much. Why don't you go and have a holiday? I expect you could do with one.'

Paul Monkton appears to have left Roman Hall. This is what Karin tells Steven when she brings the latest large pile of mail to his office on the morning of May the 31st. He has noticed, as he jogged around the grounds this morning, that spring is visibly maturing into summer. The yellow foxglove already carries new little flowers on its tapering stems, and on the fig by the back gate expansive creamy white effluences mark the change of season. The dawn chorus has been getting louder and earlier too; Steven knows about that because he's often awake at odd times in the night these days.

'So you're going, too?' he asks Karin.

'No.'

The question had been almost a statement; thus her reply commands his attention. 'But I thought you and Paul . . .'

'Not any more,' she says crisply. 'You may as well know, Steven, Paul and Claudia Foxman have got together.'

'Got together? Got what together?'

'I don't know exactly.' She puts her hands in the pocket of her white cotton trousers and looks down at her clogs. 'I think they're planning to set up a clinic of their own together.'

'That's interesting.'

'I don't find it particularly so, myself,' she remarks.

'Has he hurt you, Karin?'

She shrugs her shoulders. 'I've got my children,' she says.

'The Department is withdrawing our licence.'

'I know that. I read it in the paper.'

'So we'll have to close down for a while. I'm thinking of going away for a bit.'

'Would you like me to look after the place for you? I'd be happy to move in with Lena and Ransen if that would help.'

'It would, Karin. Thanks.'

Steven packs a small bag: a couple of changes of clothing, some novels, his CD player. He empties the rubbish (still no replacement for Mrs Lemon), then finds the half-eaten carcass of a chicken in the fridge and moves it into the freezer to save himself another trip to the bin. He calls Matilda to tell her he's going away for a few days. He needs to think. She shouldn't mind, or worry.

'Where are you going?'

'France,' he says, and it's the first he's heard of it.

He takes the boat to Boulogne. It seems to be some sort of school holiday; the noise of crisp packets is quite appalling. The Channel has pockets of action in it, as though baby whales are playing beneath the surface. Steven has lunch in Boulogne, a simple steak and half a bottle of claret. Then, over coffee, he looks at his map. The weather here is dull, not conducive to anything. It seems obvious he should drive south. He changes some money at a Banque Populaire, buys a bar of chocolate and a bottle of Evian water, and sets off for Nice.

He wakes the next day in the Hôtel Suisse to bright sunshine and the selfsame blue spread of the Bay of Angels as he remembers from twenty-five years ago. His room has a little balcony with a table and two chairs. He takes his breakfast out there and sits facing the Bay. A light heat haze hangs over the sea, the palms round the Promenade des Anglais are almost, but not quite, still. He can even see the Negresco in the distance, set like a child's pink cake against the rolling green coastal hills. Slowly he drinks the good French coffee, slowly he allows himself to remember what it really was like; but this requires, first of all, the discarding of the memories themselves – like the thickened skin of old apples, they must be peeled away, thrown away, leaving the apple itself to be held like a juicy orb, though possibly full of maggots, in the palm of one hand.

The village of Biot is twenty-one kilometres from Nice, and the same from Cannes and from Grasse also. It has a village square and a fifteenth-century church, which shares the cramped end of the square with the town hall: church and state rub shoulders with one another, the priest lives on the other side of the church. There are pink arcades in Biot, cobbled streets, orange and persimmon trees. The village sits on the top of a hill like a tipsy stone crown, and the bright blue of the Mediterranean glows in almost every season a short distance away.

In the summer of 1967, Steven was in Biot celebrating the end of his medical training. Most of that summer he spent with a young woman called Béatrice Billandot. Béatrice was the daughter of a local duc, who owned much of the land around the Brague valley, which Biot overlooks. The family went back to medieval times. Béatrice was the only daughter out of four children and was spoilt, in addition to being rich. She was eighteen when Steven knew her, just out of school in Switzerland. They met in a nightclub in Cannes. She had the vivacity of a young cat springing its way over the rooftops at night-time. Her eyes were like a cat's; but her hair, black as the Biot night, had stars in it. Steven was very much in love with Béatrice. But Béatrice liked male attention, and she had a lot of suitors, though Steven didn't know that at the time.

The Billandot house in Biot was on the main street, the rue de Sebastien, opposite a café. The Duc and Madame Billandot never spent the summers in Biot, which was too hot for them; they always went north to their home in Alsace. So Béatrice and Steven were alone there, except for her brothers and the housekeeper, a fierce old lady who disapproved of all Béatrice's young men.

Every morning that summer Steven woke up in fine white linen sheets, opened the dark-green shutters on to the unbelievable Mediterranean skyline, and crept down the corridor to Béatrice's room. She was like a bad-tempered cat in the mornings, but he could make her purr.

When they weren't dancing in the nightclubs in the evenings, they ate in the Biot restaurants and walked around the Biot streets and gardens and terraces and Roman remains. Dizzy with the scent of anemones and mimosa, Steven asked Béatrice to be his wife and come to England to live with him in Birmingham, where he had a job waiting at the children's hospital. But Béatrice laughed at him, and told him she'd only think about it. Steven was desperate for her to say yes. He knew he had a chance, she didn't find him a bad lover. On the other hand, she was only eighteen and this was her first real taste of freedom.

At the end of the summer, Béatrice had to go away to visit her parents. Steven took a room in Nice to wait for her, and earned his board washing dishes in the hotel restaurant. His room was an attic cupboard where the maids kept their cleaning things. But the sordid nature of his daily life merely added to his love for Béatrice, made their shining future together more promising and more likely. Out of the small window in his room, to which he climbed every night after washing the dishes, he could see the whole sweep of the Bay of Angels, the full glass bowl of the sea; he sat and stared out at the thin horizon, marked only at the darkest times by the airport lights to one side, and dreamed about the future into which Béatrice and he would pass together. In his state of suspended animation Steven despised ordinary social relations, speaking to almost no one. But after a month, in which he wrote to Béatrice every day (sending the letters poste restante to avoid the Duc's censorship) he had an unexpected visit from Béatrice's eldest brother, Terence. It was about nine in the evening, Steven's day off. He was in his room reading Stendhal's *Le Rouge et le Noir*. Terence said: 'How are you, Steven?' And then he said: 'I've got some bad news, I'm afraid. Béatrice is dead.'

Steven couldn't take in the words at first. What could they mean? Béatrice *dead*? He repeated the words; they echoed round the little room, round its cobwebs and vacuum cleaners, and then scurried out through the badly fitting window glass – out and into the sea, joining hands with the angels. Later, when Terence and he had drunk some wine together, and the bottle was emptied, Steven asked a lot of questions. Though he still didn't believe she was dead, he wanted to know everything. He became very obsessed with her last moments, her conversations, her encounters – all the things he knew the Billandot family would keep from him if they could. But Terence said very little. He did, eventually, admit that Béatrice had been pregnant, and that she died because she tried to abort the child without anyone knowing. He said she'd gone to Cannes for the abortion. There was a thriving abortion trade there then. She'd stayed with a friend a day or two afterwards and become ill, and the friend, alarmed, had driven her back to the house in Biot, but the dirt from whatever instrument had been used was already everywhere inside her and it was too late for anyone to do anything. The family doctor diagnosed septicaemia as the cause of death.

Naturally, Steven blamed himself. It had been his child. Why hadn't Béatrice come to him, he was a doctor, he would have known what to do, he never would have let her go to some untrained abortionist, who did to her what he'd seen women die of in England. Ironically, Steven had just taken part with other medical students in the campaign to get the Abortion Act passed, which put a stop to all that. Béatrice should have gone to Switzerland, it would have been safe there.

After a while, Terence said: 'It might not have been your child, Steven, you know. I don't think you should blame yourself.'

Steven was shocked by that. 'What do you mean? We were to be married!' Béatrice hadn't said yes, but he knew she would in time.

'I only meant what I said. There were others, other men, in Béatrice's life. You must have known that.'

'But she only loved me! Béatrice loved *me*!' Steven started to cry then, and Terence sat with him for a while, then he left.

When he'd gone, Steven watched the dark night clouds over the Bay of Angels scatter into a million separate shapes before he slept. It was the afternoon when he woke. The sun was in the middle of the sky, a brazen clementine of a sun, and it hung there giving off the most useless light; all he wanted was to take his fists to it and bang it out of the sky. His eyes hurt. He rubbed them violently to get rid of the hurt, thinking he could make it all go away, and it would just be a normal day with people going about their business as usual. He'd go down to the restaurant a little late, but never mind, and scrape all the leavings of the rich off their smart plates and bury them in suds and think of Béatrice. She'd been going to join him in a week; he had a piece of paper by his bed on which, like a prisoner, he crossed out the days. But she would never come now. He looked around his little room: she had never even been here, he was deprived even of remembering her bright face in this room, the musty scent of her skin, her words hiding in the atmosphere. He went through his suitcase: what did he have left to remember her by? He found a scarf of hers he'd taken once: red, purple, blue and green, the kind of jumble of colours she adored, and wore as if they were jewels. She'd laughed at him for taking it: '*Tu es fou*, Steven! Are you going to take it to bed with you?'

He went down to the kitchen and told them he wasn't well, he had a fever. The chef, occupied with a dish of squid, looked at him and nodded: Steven did, indeed, look terrible.

He took a table at a café by the *ascenseur* to the hilltop view above the town and ordered a coffee, putting four lumps of sugar in it, trying to sedate himself with sweetness. He was surrounded by elderly yellowing representatives of Nice's resident population, or by tourists, with their stupid preoccupations and mindless twattle. Two women next to him, one with a dog bound to the table with a leather thong, were eating sardines. One had the brightest orange-red lipstick you'd ever seen. Like the sun.

'I love steak, but I can't eat it because of my arthritis. My brother's had five heart attacks.'

'Has he?'

'He's not a well man.'

'Is he married?'

'Sixteen years.' The dog whined. 'No, darling, tonight, not now.'

Geranium-lips dabbed at them with her napkin. Steven looked at her with undisguised disgust. She looked away. 'Does he like salad?'

'Who?'

'Your friend here.'

'Of course.' Geranium-lips fed the dog pieces of lettuce, the dog's jaws dropped saliva on to the table in gratitude.

People have no right to feed their dogs lettuce when other people die. Rich old women, nothing to do but eat and drink. What have they done to deserve any kind of life? Winters of bezique, thick pastes of henna and anti-wrinkle cream, pouches for the eyes, potions for the neck, pills for the heart, every pharmaceutical treasure purchased to postpone the appearance of mortality.

Steven didn't want to think about what Terence had said. His Béatrice – she *was* his Béatrice – had been carrying his child. Steven ordered a Pernod, and then another. Slobby-dog and Geranium-lips pretended disinterest. Steven stared at the sun, trying to outwit it, but all he saw was the hot curled-up ball of a fetus, Béatrice's child, his child. He was angry with her for killing it, for not giving him the choice. They ought to have been better about contraception, but Béatrice didn't like it and neither did he.

Later in the afternoon he left Geranium-lips and friend and walked, parallel with the sun. The air was full of it. Palm trees stood still; seagulls slept. He walked round the curve of the Promenade des Anglais, and then the pink dome of the Negresco came down out of the sky towards him.

'*Un whisky à l'âge.*' If he wasn't of age now, when would he be? The waiter looked at Steven sourly. He slapped a fifty-franc note on the table. So many people who think things they don't want you to see, but they should be more careful, shouldn't they? The whisky rose in his throat; he couldn't help but think of the abortionist who wasn't. Of the man who'd been responsible for Béatrice's death. Or woman? An old woman in black with a bottle of gin and a cache of knitting needles.

A woman in silk brushed past him on her way to a table by the window; her perfume made him choke. The sun, over the bay, was lower. People were streaming back across the Promenade with towels. Steven realized he'd eaten nothing all day and the Pernods and whiskies were destroying his stomach, which in this respect was standing in for his heart.

He left the Negresco, crawled crookedly down a side street and into an Italian restaurant, where he ordered a pizza margherita, without looking at the menu. There were only a few tables in front of him, but the place was mostly full of couples, which he now understood he would have to endure for the rest of his life. Directly in front of him, there was an elderly man eating alone. He wore a white open-necked shirt, navy trousers, white shoes, and seemed perfectly content. He was reading a magazine about cars. He had eaten and paid; his change sat in an orange plastic saucer on the table. But he read on languorously, feasting on leather interiors and real walnut fascias, oblivious of the complexities and sorrows of the human mind. It was all expressed in the attitude of his hand, which was draped, flopping down – it would move like a palm leaf if you touched it – over the neighbouring chair. A gold watch round it said something also. This man was alone and happy, he provided for himself. This man couldn't be touched by death, by cats that can be made to purr in the early morning, by the shade of green shutters in the afternoon, by suns that sit up there like glazed clementines refusing to go away. Steven decided that was how he would have to be: alone, and indestructible.

When night came, he went down to the beach and trod the broad pebbles till his feet hurt. There were men fishing – to get away from their wives, he supposed. He noted that a man with a fishing rod is a man without pain, suffering only the possible indignity of catching inedible things. He sat down on the beach, his back against the wall that bounded the road, crouching into it, hoping to dissolve into it. The fishermen packed up and went home, full of stories about uncaught fish. Steven's eyes were drawn to the sea's edge, to the great enormous blackness of the sea, a soup of ink with candyfloss edges, going on and on to the shores of Africa and back, a soothing, flooding, wrapping darkness, at one with the inverted inkwell of the sky.

He'd struggled to get here. Not just to this beach, a long way from Whitechapel, but through school and to study medicine and then to qualify. He'd done it through cleverness and determination, hard work and on the back of poverty – it was important never to forget that. He'd fought to be allowed to love Béatrice, to wander through the orange and mimosa groves of Biot, even to wash dishes in a Nice hotel. And having fought, what now? To go on fighting. Steven knew he must win the fight. He thought of the fishermen who hadn't caught any fish, but would say the fishes' acuity defeated them. Of Slobby-dog and Geranium-lips and their salacious storytelling. A straight route never brought success. Success is a fabrication, a construction, using whatever materials come to hand. Whatever Terence had said, whatever view of him Béatrice's haughty parents had kept to themselves, whatever Béatrice herself had done, whoever these figurative others might have been, he would do whatever was required to put him in the prize position. But in order to achieve this he would have to become someone else. He must protect himself against the same thing happening again. But how, Béatrice, how? Saying her name, chanting it against the beating waves, gave him the answer: change his own, give himself a culture and a credence no one will be able to see through – unless, of course, he himself chooses to let them.

Thus Steven decided to take the name of Béatrice's village. But to throw people off any scent they might pick up, he'd inserted 'van den' in the middle. Steven van den Biot would be untouchable in a way the old Steven would never have been.

Béatrice's voice protested in his head: to trade off the catastrophe of her death isn't fair. He owes it to himself and to her memory to be a finer person than that. And so he made a second decision: to devote himself professionally to what Béatrice, through God knows what devious and awful motives, and encouraged by the state's literally poisonous and punitive view of women, was never able to do: he would aid and abet nature in turning women into mothers. Let the black Bay of Angels confine itself to tales of the uncaught. He, Steven van den Biot, had his own tale to keep!

And so he does, he keeps it to himself until he tells it to Matilda Cressey in the orchid house at Kew. Who, to be honest, doesn't really know what to make of it.

Does he? Two conflicting sets of feelings struggle for ascendancy in the limited empire that is his soul. One set tells him what an idiot he was to allow that Biot summer to condition everything he's done since. The other set of feelings informs him of the huge hole that continues to occupy his life: he has no family of his own. He's not been able to forgive himself sufficiently to acquire what Béatrice's death took away from him then. Can he do it with Matilda? Nice is full of ghosts and fills him with terror that he can't.

He goes out into the sparkling day to retrace some of his steps and maybe have a word with some of the ghosts. The hotel he washed up for is still there, but smarter. The row of attic windows blinks at him from a great height, reminding his knees of the stairs that had to be climbed before he could fall into his musty sanctuary each night and dream of Béatrice. Down on the beach, tourists' children put their clothes in piles and plunge into the incoming tide. Dogs bark; a plethora of poodles, Steven notices. There's an Indian restaurant behind him where a plain old-fashioned fish establishment once stood. The palm trees have seen it all. With his feet in different pebbles Steven stands, listening: to the cries and the languages and the animals, to the arguments, the bad jokes and the implacable thalassic beat of the tide. He himself, Steven van den Biot, was born on this beach. Born to be ruined all over again? And if so, by what – the onslaught of a world unfriendly to those born first in a Whitechapel slum, or some defect or deceit in his character, way down there where he can't see or repair it?

He walks away from the beach up the steps and on impulse hails a taxi. 'Biot,' he says.

The taxi drops him off on the corner of the rue de Sebastien. At first he walks in the opposite direction from the village centre, past the police station and on to higher ground, where he can look back at the village squashed like a handful of pastel paper chains against the stern cliff. It looks, he imagines, the same as it did twenty-five years or a couple of centuries ago. It has a medieval impermeability, a resistance to temporal corrosions. Then he walks back and down the main street. With careful steps he passes the Billandot house; it's newly painted, with tubs of fresh orange flowers on the steps, bright against the sombre stone. Someone's living there: the shutters and the windows are open, the heavy lace curtains move a fraction in the stirring midday heat.

In an hour he's covered the whole of the village. The Roman amphitheatre, where children are rehearsing a play, down to the glassworks and up the several roads that climb the hill. It's the smell that reminds him most of the past. Mimosa, and orange blossom, and cats and clean washing. He has a *saucisson* sandwich and a coffee in the Café de la Poste and walks back out into the bright afternoon sunlight. Further down the main street a beige Porsche is parked and a woman, with a baby, is getting out of it. It reminds him of the brochure for Roman Hall. The car is the same colour and make, and so is the baby.

The woman swings round so Steven can see her face. She has dark hair and olive eyes. 'Natalie!' she calls, in a clear voice. 'Alice! *Venez!*' The door of the Billandot house opens and a young woman comes out. The woman with the baby goes up the steps and hands the child to her. She runs down the steps and fetches something from the car, takes it up the steps into the house. Another young woman comes out. The car is locked, the baby is put in a pushchair. The three women pushing the baby set off down the street towards Steven.

He's in the shadow of the Café de la Poste watching, and he has the oddest feeling one of these women is his Béatrice – ghosts again! Blinded by the past and the dazzling afternoon light, he steps out into the pathway of the women and the baby.

He looks into her olive eyes. She looks back at him. 'Hallo, Steven,' she says quietly.

'Béatrice?'

'Excuse me.' She turns to the young women next to her and tells them, in French, to walk a while with the baby, she'll catch them up.

He watches them walk away. 'Is it really . . . ? But I thought . . .'

'I was dead. I know.'

'Who are *they*, Béatrice?'

'Natalie and Alice are my daughters and the baby is my grandson, Jean-Pierre, Natalie's child.'

'I don't understand anything.'

'Poor Steven. No, I don't suppose you do.'

'Tell me, for God's sake explain it!'

She looks frightened. 'Not here. Not now. Are you staying in Biot?'

'In Nice.'

'I'll meet you in Nice this evening at seven. On the Promenade, opposite the Indian restaurant.'

She's there before him. He's tight-lipped, restrained but agitated. 'I don't expect you to forgive us, Steven. I know you won't, you can't be expected to. It was my father, you see. He wanted to get rid of you. He was afraid I was going to marry you. So he took the law into his own hands, and sent Terence to tell you something had happened to me.'

'I believed Terence,' says Steven. 'It was the end of my life.'

'I know.' She puts her arms out and holds him tightly in an embrace of silk and perfume of exactly the same quality as he

148

remembers from 1967. 'You must believe me, it was difficult for me too. My father didn't tell me then what he'd done. Terence told me much later. They just said you'd gone. I did love you, Steven. But you weren't the only one, you knew that, didn't you?'

'No, I didn't. You deceived me.'

'Poor Steven.'

'Stop saying that,' he says angrily.

'I'm sorry.'

'That too! And those girls of yours, is one of them mine, then?'

'I don't know. It's possible, yes.'

'You bitch!'

She shrugs her shoulders. 'Yes, I thought you'd say that. That's one reason I didn't tell you. The other one was that I didn't know how to without making things worse. It has, hasn't it?'

'Indeed.'

'I'm going now, Steven. But I'm glad that you do know. I hope you can find a way to accept it in the end. And that you are happy.'

The beige Porsche is waiting for her; she gets into it, and drives off with a slight wave, as though nothing of much consequence has happened.

16
Channel
Crossing

Sunny the cat sits watching in the kitchen of 88 Juliana Crescent. Mrs Trancer, putting her brooms away, talks comfortingly at him: 'If you sit there long enough, me boy, you might see something worth seeing. A wedding mebbe, with the bells of the church clanging oranges and lemons say the bells of St Clement's, or them junkies down the street smashing windows again more likely. People come, people go, but the world stays the same. D'you want your milk, boy? Milk for Sunny, nice thick creamy milk, clogs up your hearteries they say on the telly, but I 'spect yours is clogged up already like mine. We don't care, do we?' The cat turns and looks at her, blinks, wraps his marmalade tail more tightly round his feet. Mrs Trancer straightens herself, goes over to the window and strokes him with her craggy hand. He purrs like a badly muffled pneumatic drill.

Sunny and Mrs Trancer watch Matthew, Jeffrey Rowley and Jason come up the road. Jeffrey's got his arm round Jason. The streak of white hair in Matthew's hedge of curls is the same colour as Sunny's milk. Mrs Trancer tightens her lips disapprovingly. 'What d'you think about that, Sunny?' They bang the front door. 'Noisy little boys, aren't they, playing their games together!'

The phone rings. Mrs Trancer answers it before anyone else has a chance. 'Who's that? Who? From the what? The Home Office? What do you want with us? We're very clean here, very clean. I even does Sunny with the flea powder once a week. No, Miss Cressey ain't here yet. She ain't an early riser, Miss Cressey. Some folks is and some ain't. Well I never . . . !' She replaces the receiver and addresses herself to Sunny once again. 'That's a very rude gentleman, me boy, it's a good thing you didn't hear what he was saying!'

In his office in the Strand, Norman Newfield at the Home Office doesn't feel very well after his conversation with Mrs Trancer. He'd called to speak to Matilda, to warn her that the Minister has decided, in view partly of the recent concatenation of opinions about Alternative Birth Centres in general and Roman Hall in particular, to close down the Council for Consumer Affairs. Norman Newfield doesn't like delivering bad news, and he likes even less delivering it to people he likes – who include Matilda Cressey.

'But why?' she asks when he does get through to her later in the day.

'A variety of reasons, Matilda. The Minister feels the CCA's no longer needed. That your involvement in this Roman Hall business has been a bit of an embarrassment. The Minister's not in favour of anything that curtails private medicine.'

'But my report supports Roman Hall!'

'Well, yes,' he admits, 'but it was rather *political*, wasn't it, if you know what I mean?'

'You mean that the government doesn't want ordinary people to have any say in the kind of health services they have, or anything else that determines their quality of life?'

'Something like that, yes.'

'Power belongs to the experts. Who don't know what they're doing but don't want anyone else to find them out,' she says grimly.

'I expect so,' says Norman, trying to seem affable.

Matilda is very disturbed by this news, but the main reason for her disturbance surprises her: it is that she can't bear the idea of having to tell Matthew Ansden, Margaret Watteau, Rita Ploughman, Jeffrey Rowley, Jason and Mrs Trancer that they've lost their jobs. It even occurs to her to envisage Sunny as a displaced person. Over the months she's been there she's really grown rather fond of them all. Despite their odd, even sometimes loathsome, habits, the crew are loyal, they've shown they can close ranks around her. They haven't been obviously insurgent the way Steven's staff have.

As she sits there thinking, Margaret Watteau brings her coffee in a nice thick French cup and saucer, the dark green of worn rural woodwork with a resurrecting gold line around the top. Margaret is at last trained to make proper coffee, though only Matilda and Matthew Ansden drink it; Margaret sticks to Maxwell House and Jeffrey and Jason are on the herbal teas.

'How are things, Margaret?' asks Matilda unexpectedly.

Margaret frowns. 'How do you mean, Miss Cressey?' She doesn't recall Matilda asking her this sort of question before.

'How are you feeling? How's the family?'

'They're all right, Miss Cressey. Same as always.' She wonders if she should say more, and if so what.

'How's your sister's baby? He must be getting on now.'

Margaret produces the latest snaps of Damian and Lesley and all at Speedwell Avenue. Matilda is struck by Damian's chubbiness, by Lesley's wan and washed-out appearance. By the smart red leather sofa and large teak-cabineted television in the background. By Margaret and Lesley's mother and father, she a birdlike woman in primrose Crimplene, he large and blustery – Damian sixty years on.

'Damian's dad took the photos,' explains Margaret, 'that's why he's not in them.' She doesn't want Miss Cressey to get the wrong idea.

Matilda hands the pictures back. 'Do you like working here, Margaret?'

'Well, yes, Miss Cressey, you know I do. Why, don't I suit?' She's alarmed suddenly.

'Of course you do, Margaret. I was just asking.'

'Les says I'm lucky to have such an interesting job. She didn't, she says, that's why she had Damian. Well, I don't suppose it was the *only* . . .'

'Ah. Don't you want a Damian, Margaret?'

Margaret blushes. 'Not yet, Miss Cressey. Anyway, I haven't got a boyfriend. Plenty of time, Les says.'

'Plenty of time,' Matilda repeats to herself. But there isn't, that's the problem.

Matilda phones Norman at the Home Office. 'I don't want to be abolished,' she tells him. 'I want to be privatized. If you can privatize everything else, why not the CCA? We could become a business just like everything else. Run at a profit, but at the same time profitable in other ways.' She thinks of Matthew Ansden downstairs, a frustrated capitalist if ever there was one. 'What do you think, Norman?'

'Brilliant, Matilda, quite brilliant.'

It takes a lot of arranging. No one seems to think that simply floating the shares on the market would attract any interest; it's not as though the CCA is an oil company. It seems more likely that it'll be bought by someone with some kind of moral concern for perpetuating democracy, the truth, choice, freedom of opinion, that sort of thing.

Matilda talks to a number of her journalist friends, including Susan Harris, who wrote the *Guardian* piece about Roman Hall. She thanks Susan for concealing her identity that day at the airport, and invites her to write a short article about the condemned CCA, the significance of the closure for the future development of health, education and welfare services in Britain. 'A Matter for the Experts?' the pieces is called, and it's no mean feat, but a good half-page on a Saturday.

The following Tuesday, Norman Newfield rings Matilda. 'You know Cracker bars?' he begins. She assents. 'Well, how do you fancy being one?'

Cracker bars – oats, dried oranges, treacle and whole bran – are made by the British subsidiary of a large European confectionery conglomerate, which apparently wants to be seen to be more socially conscious than the numbers of E's in their products might suggest.

'Is there any alternative?' Matilda asks nervously.

'One. A pharmaceutical company. I told you about Cracker bars first because I didn't think you'd fancy the other option. Not that you're supposed to have any say in who takes you over, Matilda. You do understand that, don't you?'

'Of course.'

'The director of Gauche-Mogy is coming to see me later today. Then he'd like to see you.'

'What do they make, Norman?'

'Tropical medicines mostly. Anti-malarial drugs. Mosquito nets – no, I'm serious, they've developed a new way of impregnating them with stuff that keeps the little devils away. Oh, and talking of impregnation, they also do something in the contraception line.' He pauses significantly, thinking of Matilda's connection with Roman Hall, of which he's received wind through an ex-school friend of his, George Foxman, whose ex-wife has just married a doctor who used to work there. Norman doesn't quite have the whole picture, but it seems that George Foxman is angry with his ex, Claudia, because he wants the product of the union and had a good chance of getting it until this doctor married her, but Claudia herself is angry about the other doctor who didn't want to have anything to do with her, because he was having a thing with Matilda Cressey whom he used to meet secretly in orchid houses and in government offices on the Arctic Circle.

'They also make beds and pillows and relaxation tapes and organic breast pumps,' he explains, 'for natural childbirth,' he adds helpfully.

'What's wrong with that, Norman?'

'Nothing, I don't suppose.'

The director of Gauche-Mogy UK, Dr Alan Percy, is tall and adept at wrapping his double-jointed limbs round one another. He has a habit of talking very fast, and a black nylon shoulder bag with lots of compartments instead of the obligatory briefcase. Dr Percy is a Quaker. His interest in drugs and natural childbirth equipment, although commercial, is also humanitarian. It appears he's conceived the idea of running the CCA as a charitable trust, and has much the same ideas of its watchdog function as Matilda herself. She's cautious with him, in her office, as the June sunshine tumbles across the marble pigeons and blank computer screens. But caution is the right note to adopt, and pretty soon Alan Percy is offering Matilda the directorship of the new Gauche-Mogy CCA. 'We'd want it to expand, of course. About four times the size would probably be about right. With different sections for the different areas – health, environmental issues, education, and so on.' His eyes wander briefly round the office. 'And it should move from here. To somewhere larger and more central. What do you think, Miss Cressey?'

'How much control would the company exercise, Dr Percy? Over the work of the CCA, I mean?'

'I didn't imagine you meant anything else,' he responds crisply. He looks at her piercingly, quite seeing through her cool dark suit to the passionate, wilful, selfish Matilda underneath, the one he wants to run the CCA for him. 'Financial control, of course. You'd have a Board of Trustees with some say in policy. But the Director and the staff would have virtually one hundred per cent power to decide on the content, form and dissemination of the work. Though dissemination is an area we'd want to develop. Much more could – and should – be done there. We've got a very good staff in our London office who specialize in in-house printing, artwork, marketing and sales strategies. We'd want to see liaison with them over that.' He stands up. 'I'm afraid I have to get to a meeting the other side of London in half an hour. I'll leave you with those thoughts for now, shall I? I'll have the different documents drawn up. The Board will make a formal offer to you. We'll need to have a meeting with Norman – we were at Christchurch together, you know. I hope you find the idea congenial, Miss Cressey.' He offers her one of his double-jointed hands. 'I think we could work well together.'

'Who was that?' asks Margaret nosily when Dr Percy has gone. 'That was our new boss,' says Matilda grandly. 'Call the staff together, will you? We need to have a meeting.'

* * *

Meetings and meetings. Steven van den Biot is free of them on holiday in France. The day after he sees Béatrice there's a minicyclone and the poodles are more ruffled by it than the palm trees.

Steven watches the wind and the waves in the Bay of Angels from his double-glazed sixth-floor hotel window. There are no planes landing or taking off on the other side of the bay; the airport is closed. The streets are empty, save for litter, cans and newspapers and orange peel and dead flattened baguettes chasing each other across the pavements. Everyone's at home with nothing much to do. No business or sunbathing or sightseeing for the tourists. The couple in the room next to Steven conjugate to pass the time. Hump, hump through the wall; they don't even turn the television off when they do it. Steven sits by the window looking at the whipped cream of the waves. The water pulsing, the primitive energy of the water coming and going, water outside and inside for bathing embryos in – his, even or maybe, that became a fetus and then a neonate and then a busty fertile young woman of her own. Natalie, mother of Jean-Pierre. Béatrice, wife of . . . ? He hadn't asked. There's much he doesn't know, may never, and probably doesn't want to. Most of all – it goes without saying, but he needs to – about himself; it's himself that's the problem, the past isn't one, not on its own. He realizes how much easier it was to think of Béatrice as dead. Better that than to understand she'd abandoned him. Béatrice dead was like his mother dead: the two could live on as *he* chose them to, draped in his own selected mementoes. In life they were – would have been – more awkward, forcing him to look them in the eyes and see a reflection of himself, not of his choosing but of theirs. Just before Steven's mother had died in his first year at medical school, she'd gripped his hand and fixed her weary blue eyes on him – a creased, faded blue with whites coloured by disease and perpetual fatigue – 'Stevie, my Stevie,' she'd croaked at him. 'When I look at you I know it were all worth it, I'd do it again a thousand times for you, I would!' He'd felt so alien from her, yet so bound up – so guilty, he supposed, both for her life and for not staying there, even for not being the same as her; for the impulse to be different, which is so close to the need he has not to solve things but to escape or deny them that he can't tell the difference.

As he stares out of the window, the wind drops suddenly. The palm trees stand to attention, the beer cans rest in the gutters. Out in the Bay of Angels, the whipped cream is absorbed into the vitreous depths from wherever it came. It's still, like a lake. Paused for a moment, taking a breath before resuming the old rhythm, folding away into its memory this temporary local disturbance of early summer that took everyone by surprise.

Steven calls Matilda: 'I'm coming home.' She says she has a lot to tell him. 'And I you.'

The hump, hump starts again behind the wall. 'The time has come,' Steven says.

'To talk of . . . cabbages and kings,' finishes Matilda.

It takes Steven a while to reach Dieppe. He's decided on a longer sailing back. He needs to feel himself travelling at the same time as having the space to allow everything to fall decently into place again. He sits in the tourist lounge at a round plastic table drinking orange juice. The boat is full of families. There are a number of child discipline problems. Next to him a young couple are the desperate owners of an inconsolable baby. They can't be more than eighteen or twenty. The young man is always looking for something in one of the many pale baby bags they carry, head down searching for a dry nappy, a new dummy, a bottle of Ribena. Or else the young woman dispatches him on some errand: for tea, or chips, or once a magazine for her which she can't read because of the baby. She tries everything: milk, water, food, singing, distraction. For a few minutes the baby gets his hands on the inside pages of her *Woman's Realm*, but the newsprint leaves traces on his fingers and Mum is consequently agitated, taking it away from him and creating a new feeling of deprivation in addition to whatever was already causing his distress. That's what life is, thinks Steven, a series of lessons in gratification followed by an exactly matching series in deprivation. One might as well not be gratified in the first place.

The horizon dips and lifts itself through the gauzy portholes. The child's thin scream rises with the smoke in the gritty air of the lounge: people are irritated but won't do or say anything except in undertones to one another.

'Would you like me to take him for a bit?'

She stares at him. Who is he?

'I'm a paediatrician.'

'No thank you,' says the young father, proud as a lion for an instant. 'It's the boat and he's teething.'

'Yes, that's right, he's teething. Aren't you, Joel?' She's shocked by this man offering to relieve her of her baby, for the worst shocks are undoubtedly the ones that touch our fantasies.

Steven sees them again getting off the boat. Joel sleeps now, his father manoeuvres the pushchair through the crowds and his mother is like a camel with her bags in the breakfast-time desert of Newhaven.

Then he's stopped by the Customs officer. 'I've got a case of wine, nothing else. I think you'll find it's within the limit.'

'Are you a doctor of medicine, sir?'

'Don't I look like one?' The Customs officer studies Steven's passport photo and then the real man. 'Yes, come to mention it, sir, you do. I only asked because I thought you might have drugs with you, sir.'

'I left them all in England. This trip was purely pleasure, officer.'

'Okay, sir.'

Pleasure? Steven drives fast, but not to Roman Hall. He goes to Whitechapel, stopping once to make a quick phone call and buy an armful of yellow roses.

'What is this?' says Janey. 'Why, love, you shouldn't!'

'Yes I should, Janey. Think of everything you've done for me all these years.'

'And everything you've done for me, Stevie,' she says quietly.

'Have I? Come Janey, let's lie down together.'

In the narrow bed, they lie naked covered with a thin blue blanket and look at the ceiling. 'Do you remember Miss Moorhead, Janey?'

'And Debbie that day when the Inspector came!' She giggles. 'Miss Moorhead's face when she saw the bubble gum all over his smart overcoat!'

'We didn't learn much at that school, did we, Janey?'

'We learnt about life.'

'It contained us,' he says, 'for a while.'

'My girls went there, you know, Stevie,' she says, not listening to him.

'Are they doing well, Janey?'

'Well enough. What about your sisters and brothers, Stevie? Lisa I hear about, she's a manageress of that clothes shop now, but what about the others?'

'I don't see them,' he says sadly.

'You should, before it's too late.'

'Too late for what? Make love to me, Janey. I don't want to think about things like that.'

She touches his beloved body – beloved to her, now, for more than thirty years, since the first time they had each other in the park on an August Tuesday evening when she was meant to be with her girlfriend listening to Lonnie Donegan, and Steven was on his way home from his paper round. The empty sack on which was written 'J.M. Whitley Newsagnts' lay on the grass nearby. As Steven fought with her clothes and she with her conscience, and then he kissed her wet and broke her with his fingers and sharply put himself into her, she couldn't help but see those letters, 'J.M. Whitley Newsagnts', next to them, and always since in her mind. She sees them now, not a mile away from that spot in the park, as she smooths her hands over Steven's body, chest, arms and legs and flat, flat stomach – so good for a man of his age – and then his penis, full of blood, stretching nearly as far as his navel.

'That's right, Janey. Turn over now.' He opens his eyes; it's a long time since he did that with her. She lies beneath him like a wife – or a bride. She feels like a bride – the one she would have liked to be, not the one she was. Carefully he holds each of her breasts in his hand and then each nipple; moves down and sweeps her thighs apart, with moist fingers strokes her lips and then the inner surface of her vagina, pink and liquid waiting for him. 'You've been good to me, Janey, so good,' he murmurs and then moves inside her in that old way, the way of 'J.M. Whitley Newsagnts' and, slowly like the grass growing that summer when they were both fifteen, he takes her to a place where she is happy, where trouble and work and unpaid bills and roving half-drunk husbands don't exist, a place where Janey has her Stevie and is loved for herself as women ought to be. She knows they will come together this time. Knows him, his movements, his history, so well, and sees and feels his muscles tense, the tip of his penis soften inside her as the moment approaches and then, with a strange sadness, floods over and through her, taking her with it.

Afterwards he stays with her for a while. They talk of the old days again, have a cup of tea. 'Put the roses in water, Janey,' he says then. 'They won't last for ever. I'll send you some more when they die. But I'm not coming to see you again. I'm going to be married next month to a woman called Matilda Cressey.'

The tea chokes her. 'And live happily ever after, Stevie,' she says, though more as a question than as a statement of what will be.

17
Another
Conception

Steven sits in his chair, watching the sun lowering itself over the trout stream. He caught some the other day, some of the new, improved, sexless ones.

He holds in his hand a letter from Claudia Foxman offering to purchase the estate of Roman Hall. Karin's already told him that Claudia married Paul Monkton in Micklesham church two Saturdays ago. So she got her doctor at last, he thinks. And now she wants to take over Roman Hall, to make the transaction complete. Well, he also thinks, perhaps I should let her do just that. She and Paul won't find it easy. He hasn't got my charisma, he's technically inexperienced. Her motives are the wrong ones. But let them make their messy bed; and then lie on it.

In Steven's absence, things have died down a little as regards Roman Hall. The Department is mounting its own investigation. The Natural Childbirth Society and several others have combined and issued a 'Manifesto in Support of Natural Childbirth' which has been leafleted all over the country. Elizabeth Martin has sent him a hundred for his own use, together with a floral note: 'Thinking of you'.

Nothing further has been heard of Mr Scull's allegations. The media are occupied with a new medical scandal concerning the Prime Minister's grandson's tonsillectomy.

Matilda has told him on the phone that the Cressey Report's sold out and the CCA is being privatized. From July the first she'll be earning £50,000 a year and moving to offices in Victoria. Steven and Matilda have agreed to meet in Woodstock tomorrow. Matilda will stay with her friends the Cornfords tonight.

Steven opens a bottle of champagne, the best he has. He takes it up to his bedroom and removes Béatrice's scarf from the wall opposite his bed. Smiling to himself, and half-drunk, he takes it out later when the moon has risen and buries it under the apple tree in the topsoil above a pile of placentas and other human tissue. Taking his glassful of bubbles in the moonlight, he looks at it all: at the sweeping landscape of hills and fields and foxes and squirrels with bushy tails and holes in the earth, and crumbling white walls, and he knows he doesn't want to leave it, but he must. He sees it in all its seasons: dry as a bone one August when it never rained; under snow like one of the babies' lambswool fleeces; in spring with clumps of daffodils the same gold he'd given Janey, blue forget-me-nots and pale crocuses and purple lobelias like pubic hair on tops of walls; grey and musty like a Swan Lake set with jumping figures merged and blurred through an opaque curtain; dark in the nights without stars and a waning moon crushed between thick clouds; bright as now – as bright, in some ways, as a summer's day, with the outlines of everything picked out and shining, straight and silver as the trim on a good old car, not soft with the wavering heat of a sun set at a melting angle to the earth – his place, which he bought and made and owned and gave a new bit of history to – Roman Hall, a line on a thousand certificates of birth and a few of death, but he's not bothered by that, as everyone knows.

Karin Druin, guarding Roman Hall, sees Steven out there but says and does nothing.

Willow Cornford sees Matilda maniacally bright at her dinner table and says, 'It's an ill wind that blows nobody any good. You've sure been blown some, haven't you, Tilly!'

Matilda chatters on about the new offices and how the move will mean the end of Mrs Trancer. 'Oh no, duckie, I wish you well, but I make a rule, I only do within walking distance.' Mrs Trancer's worried about Sunny. Will he be able to make the move? 'I'll keep an eye out for him here in case he comes back, the old devil.'

Margaret Watteau will be promoted to Administrative Assistant now. 'I told you you should ask for promotion, didn't I, Maggie? Well, I knew what I was talking about.'

'You always do, Les.'

'Now about the wedding . . .'

'July the 23rd,' says Margaret.

'How do you know?'

'There's a line through it in the office diary.'

'A line could mean anything,' says Lesley wisely.

'Not when there's a Harrods wedding bureau leaflet tucked in next to it, it couldn't,' says Margaret confidently.

'But has she *said* anything yet?'

'No, not yet.'

'I wonder why?'

'It's obvious, isn't it? She's protecting *him*.'

Lesley looks at her sister with admiration. 'You're coming on, Maggie, aren't you?'

'Willow,' says Matilda, 'and Anthony' – she leans across the table and takes both their hands – 'I want you to know something. I want you to be the first – well, almost the first – to know, because you were in at the beginning, you were responsible for it really . . .'

'We're very happy for you, dear,' says Willow.

'I've already put the champagne in the fridge,' says Anthony. 'Perrier-Jouet Belle Époque 1978, will that suit you?'

'But how did you know?' asked Matilda in amazement.

'It's obvious, isn't it?'

Anthony looks at Willow admiringly for getting so much – in fact, nearly everything – right.

But while everyone in Oxfordshire drinks champagne, some people in London N19 are less than happy with the direction events have taken. Ralph Scull holds Clemency Victoria Rose to his bosom, or rather Malcolm's red shirt, as though the action will prevent the inevitable, which is Clare coming to take Clemency back now she's out of hospital and more or less her old self again. In his desperation to keep Clemency, Ralph has even asked Amanda Lychwood to marry him. He's discovered that Malcolm meant it when he said it wasn't going to be like three men and a baby. It wasn't; it was one man and a baby and then the other one coming home in the evening and rapidly going out again to the pub. But for all that, Ralph has discovered a purpose in life with more longevity than Algernon Dupont's paltry exploits. When, to seal this, he asked Miss Lychwood to marry him, she threw a packet of nappies in his face and passed the case on to someone much worse.

'Come on, Scullery, you'll get your freedom back.'

'I don't want my freedom, I want Clemency.'

'Make it up with Clare, then.'

'I don't want Clare.'

'I want Clemency, yes I know. But don't you see, Scullery, you have to have one to get the other! It's the price you pay. I think it's too high myself, but every man's entitled to his own opinion. And by the way, you're going to have to do some washing soon, I've got no shirts left.'

Ralph throws another packet of nappies at Malcolm as he exits for the pub. 'What do you think, Clemency, shall we buy your mum a box of Black Magic? It might be the only way to get Algernon off that mountain.'

They've been mowing the grass at Blenheim Palace. Not for Steven van den Biot and Matilda Cressey's benefit, but because a film crew is there doing a remake of *Elvira Madigan*. But the scent of the moist green cuttings is like the best perfume, evoking both past pleasures and future escapades wrapped into one olfactory pancake. What was and what might be are the same, and there's no stronger seduction than that.

'Isn't it wonderful, Steven!'

He agrees, not knowing what she means. But the air and the sunshine, the pleasure of seeing Matilda again, and the feeling of having got rid of something rather important and burdensome from his own past make him want to whistle and dance – if he could, but he's too old for that.

'Anthony said last night that "ageing potential" is prized in a wine,' offers Matilda consolingly.

'But not in a man.'

'I love you,' she says. 'Oh how I love you!'

He doesn't tell her about Béatrice or about Janey, he doesn't want to spoil things.

'What did you do in France, Steven?'

'Not much. Toured around, stayed in hotels. Had some good meals. Thought about things. About Roman Hall. About you. What kind of future are we going to have together, my love?'

'We're going to live in Roman Hall. That is, you are and I am most of the time. But I'll need a little flat in town, near the office I thought, there are lots of blocks of flats in Victoria.'

Steven remembers Claudia Foxman's offer. 'I'm going to sell Roman Hall, Matilda.'

'You are not!' She turns on him fiercely. 'That would be giving in. You shouldn't give in, Steven, it's not worthy of you. You don't need to, either. And more than that, you don't want to. Roman Hall is your work. It's what you're known for, it's what you've built your reputation on.'

'Yes, Matilda,' he says gravely.

'Listen to me!'

'I am.'

'What would you do without Roman Hall?'

'I could write, I could go back into the NHS, I suppose, though not to obstetrics. Or I could be something quite different. Do you think Anthony Cornford would take me on as a partner in his wine business?' He laughs.

'Don't be silly!'

'I might like being a wine merchant.'

'Well, I wouldn't like you to be one.'

'Why do I have to do what *you* want, Matilda?' She hears William's voice then. Well, some of that was bound to happen, it always did. Tread softly, Matilda, she says to herself. Behind every successful man there's a good woman. Or something like that.

'I want you to be happy, Steven, and I don't think you'd be happy away from the childbirth business. Now would you?'

'No, you're probably right.'

'There you are, that's settled then,' she says happily.

'Not quite. There are a few little details. Like: will we get our licence back? Will anyone want to come to Roman Hall any more? Maybe the Foxmans, or the Monktons, or whoever they are, will set up a rival business a mile away.'

'Let them. What you do is better. And you've got lots of support from all those banner-waving women. I'm sure you'll get your licence back.'

'How can you be sure, Matilda?'

She smiles. 'I know a few things you don't.'

She doesn't actually, but just saying so is enough to convince both of them.

As he told her in the transport café, Matilda Cressey and Steven van den Biot are married in Oxford Registry Office on July the 23rd. In the Randolph Hotel, where the reception is held, John Cressey feels the same generation as Steven, which bothers him until Steven starts to call him 'Dad'. Matilda's mother, in a satin mayonnaise suit and a hat covered in green roses, thinks Steven looks smashing in his morning suit, and is glad it isn't William standing there. Matilda, in ice-blue silk, slips her Lapponia ring on the same finger as her wedding ring after the ceremony and feels properly married: two rings on the same finger, that's the true sign.

There has been some difficulty over Steven's relatives. At first he wouldn't admit to having any, but Matilda wormed it out of him and made him invite his sister Lisa and her husband and family and the one brother, Gavin, whose whereabouts he knows. 'They won't come,' he told her, 'I haven't been in touch with them for years.' But Lisa does come on her own and gives them a very nice wedding present, an eighteenth-century white lace tablecloth, and she tells Steven not that all is forgiven, but that she'll help him try to repair family relations if that's what he wants, and she hopes he and his new bride will be very happy.

At the reception, Matilda sees her getting on famously with Margaret Watteau. Though Rita Ploughman has tried to advise her against it, Margaret's choice of costume, white organza, is unfortunate. She brings a camera instead of a wand and is continually snapping at people; even as Matilda says 'I do', she hears Margaret clicking away to her left.

'It's for Les, Miss Cressey – whoops! Mrs van den Bore-it,' she explains later. 'Les likes weddings, you know, I promised to take some pictures for her.'

'It's all right, Margaret,' says Matilda, 'and I'm not going to change my name. You can stick with the old one. It's easier anyway.'

'That's right,' says Margaret's sister Lesley that evening. 'I approve of that.'

'You do, Les?'

'Course I do. She's a professional woman, got a career of her own. Doesn't want to be an appendage of his, does she?'

The wedding is reported in the *Oxford Mail* and the *Evening Standard* and there is even a small paragraph in the *Observer*:

> Childbirth expert Steven van den Biot married Consumer Council President Matilda Cressey in a civil ceremony in Oxford yesterday. Dr van den Biot's clinic has had its licence temporarily withdrawn pending an investigation into irregular practices reported to have occurred there. Miss Cressey came out in Dr van den Biot's defence in a report published in May by the CCA. Friends say the marriage is unexpected. The honeymoon will be spent abroad.

In a cloud of white confetti about the same density as the snow that fell on them in Lapland, Steven and Matilda go off to have another look at Finland.

At this time of year, it's almost perpetual light there, and as much of Finnish life as possible is spent out of doors. The sky over Helsinki is pink with conversation even at 11 p.m. One morning early, Steven takes Matilda to the stone church, Temppeliaukio, carved out of a piece of rock in the city centre. They sit down on the wooden seats: someone is playing the organ gently, singing some kind of modern hymn; strange cadences float up to the windows perched where the rock meets ground level, through which a sparkling light falls down all over the natural surfaces and green plants and on to Steven and Matilda's faces. After a while he says to her, 'I would have liked to have married you in a consecrated place, but the trouble is that I don't believe in it.'

'This *is* sacred,' she says, taking his hand and holding it tightly.

'You remember the first time we came, when we were in Lapland and we saw that English child making an angel in the snow?'

'Yes.'

'What were you really thinking, Matilda?'

'That I wanted to make a little angel, too.'

'I thought so,' he says.

At the beginning of August, a lorry load of Matilda Cressey's material possessions arrives at Roman Hall. Matilda follows in her car. Aided by Karin Druin and her two daughters and Mrs Lemon's replacement, Steven has tried to clear some space in his bachelor establishment.

A week later Steven is in London for a meeting with Department of Health officials, and Matilda is putting her books on the shelves in the sitting room. It's a fine day, the French windows are open, butterflies flirt round them and in the lavender bushes either side. A clear wave of air comes up from the meadows the other side of the trout stream.

'May I come in?' The voice isn't at first recognizable, but the person who follows it is. 'Claudia Foxman.'

Matilda turns guilelessly, duster in hand.

'The new bride,' says Claudia, 'very touching.' Her eyes briefly survey the room, including the sofa and the carpet a little to the side of it.

'What have you come here for?' asks Matilda, nervously. 'Steven's not here. He's in London today.'

'I know that. That's why I came. I wanted to bring you this.' She lays a bulky manila envelope down on the desk under the window.

'What is it?'

'Information. About your new husband. What's the motto of that organization you run – I forget the Latin, but I recall the meaning: to know is to be able to choose? Well, it's a bit late for that, since you seem already to have chosen. Still, better late than never. You will find in that envelope details of your new husband's exploits. You may find some of them interesting. For example, he seems to have women everywhere, but particularly in France and Whitechapel, and also somewhere off the A40.' Claudia fancies the colour has gone from Matilda's cheeks. 'Still, I suppose that's his business. I always thought it odd that he'd never married. Perhaps you need to ask yourself what you're being used for. He wants to be respectable again, doesn't he? But then there's quite a streak of that in you, too, isn't there? Perhaps you're using each other.'

Matilda is silent.

'But as I said, Steven van den Biot's private life is up to him. Though I do think you should know about it. Because I don't imagine he's told you about it, has he? No, of course he hasn't. But the more serious information in that envelope concerns Steven van den Biot's practice of medicine. He went to Australia once. He hasn't told you that, either, has he? Mind you, he used another name then. Not the one he was born with, or the one he uses now. There was a lot in the papers about that name. He had a clinic there too, there was some funny business to do with aborted fetuses. They never quite got to the bottom of it. And then on the way back he had a spell in Singapore. Same sort of thing as happened here. Someone died when they shouldn't have. Makes you think he doesn't know what he's doing, doesn't it? That's where he found out about herbs, incidentally, in Singapore. Met an old Chinese doctor there who gave him a book he'd written, not to mention a whole index he'd built up over a lifetime. I think I've said enough, but I did want to say something, otherwise you might not have opened the envelope. Regard it as a wedding present from me if you like.' Claudia holds out a hand encased in a glove the tawny colour of her hat and dress. 'Goodbye, Matilda, I won't wish you every happiness. Nobody can expect that.'

She turns sharply and vanishes, taking the butterflies with her.

In bed that night, Matilda asks Steven about Claudia Foxman.

'She came here once quite drunk, expecting me to take her to bed, and I didn't, I don't think she's used to being rejected. Lord Foxman's sins were bad enough.' Steven goes on for a bit and then asks Matilda why she wants to know.

'Oh, Karin was talking about her,' says Matilda carefully.

'Well, understandably Claudia's not Karin's favourite person.'

'No.'

'I'm tired, Matilda, can we turn out the light?'

They lie side by side in silence for a while. A nightingale regales them from a tree. Matilda thinks of the unopened manila envelope, now in a suitcase at the back of the wardrobe.

'Steven?'

'Yes.'

'Are there things you haven't told me about your past?'

'Of course not. I mean yes, obviously, but nothing important. Why?'

'I just wondered.'

They listen to the nightingale. 'Why did you marry me, Steven?'

'Oh, love,' he turns to embrace her, 'because I love you. Because it was the right thing to do, the only thing, why else! Why so troubled tonight, my love?'

'I'm not, not really, Steven.'

'It's the middle of the month, Matilda.'

'Is it? You're the doctor, not me.'

'I always was good at maths.'

'Amongst other things.'

Steven begins to touch Matilda. As the nightingale begins its song again, she opens her legs. It's over quickly but is only a beginning, as ovum and sperm conjoin in the darkness of Matilda's left fallopian tube.